**Raves for the p̶̶̶̶̶̶̶̶̶̶̶̶̶̶̶̶̶̶̶̶̶̶̶̶̶̶ ̶̶̶̶̶̶̶̶̶̶̶̶̶̶̶̶̶̶̶̶̶̶̶̶̶̶e Demon:**

### And for the earlier Kara Gillian novels:

# SINS OF THE
# DEMON

## DIANA ROWLAND

# DAW BOOKS, INC.
## DONALD A. WOLLHEIM, FOUNDER
375 Hudson Street, New York, NY 10014

### ELIZABETH R. WOLLHEIM
### SHEILA E. GILBERT
### PUBLISHERS
www.dawbooks.com

First Printing, January 2012
1  2  3  4  5  6  7  8  9

*For Jennifer, Shawn, Katie, Ellie, and Ashley.*

# ACKNOWLEDGMENTS

Every time I start a book I tell myself I'm going to create a file to keep track of all the people who help me during the book with research or support. And I forget to do so Every. Single. Time. So, once again, I'm doing the mad scramble at the end of the process where I desperately try to remember everyone who held my hand. Eep!

Many thanks go to:

My awesome husband for being my biggest fan.

My beautiful daughter for snuggling me when I needed snuggles.

Dr. Mike DeFatta for continuing to answer my bizarre questions.

Cpl. Judy Kovacevich for refreshing my memory regarding crime scene procedures.

Daniel Abraham for the advice, encouragement, and support.

Carrie Vaughn for helping me work my way through the mid-series hump.

Ty Franck for being irreverent.

Walter Jon Williams for inviting me to the mountain.

Roman White for letting me bounce numerous ridiculous ideas off him.

Nicole Peeler for being the best critique partner EVER.

Nina Lourie for being who she is.

Matt Bialer for being a wonderful agent and friend.

Lindsay Ribar for EVERYTHING.

Betsy Wollheim for even more EVERYTHING.

# Chapter 1

Someone had recently taken a leak in the alley behind the Beaulac Police Department. Splash marks were still visible against the bricks, and the beam from my flashlight reflected off the rivulets that led to a broader puddle in the center of the alley. Some other sort of noxious liquid dripped from the corner of a dumpster in viscous plops to mingle with the piss, and the dregs in a broken beer bottle added one more pungent ingredient to the resulting aroma.

I carefully picked my way around the various pools of who-knew-what as I made my way out of the alley. Along the ground behind me ran a faint track of arcane sigils, appearing in my *othersight* as silvery-blue shimmers, and completely invisible in normal vision. In front of me, Eilahn patiently traced more patterns along the back end of the building, using nothing but the movement of her fingers and her will.

This side was easy. The Beaulac Police Department and its parking lots took up most of a block in downtown Beaulac. We'd started with the back-alley end and the south side that held the detective's parking lot and the

entrance to the Investigations Division. Those were un-
occupied at this time of night. The main entrance with its
broad glass doors faced the street, which would only be
tricky if anyone driving by happened to see us and wonder what we were doing. But the north end of the
building—the one that held the entrance to the Patrol
Division—would be the most difficult, since officers
came and went through there at all hours.

For decades, the station had been a brick and chrome
example of seventies' era architecture, but thankfully it
had been renovated in the past year to remove the majority of the chrome and restyle the structure to better
fit the "elegant southern town" feel that the rest of the
buildings along the street were striving for. Across from
the station was the city administration building, built
well over a hundred years ago and looking more like a
plantation building than a government facility, complete with massive columns and a broad balcony. The
rest of the street was taken up with smaller city offices
and about half a dozen small shops and restaurants. The
city had done its best to make the downtown area picturesque by replacing the big sodium vapor streetlights
with smaller ones that were meant to look like Victo-
rian gas lamps. Wrought-iron benches had been painstakingly bolted down along the sidewalk, and large
planters interspersed between them. But right now, any
elegance was overshadowed by the cheap and tacky
Christmas decorations that the city workers put up a
few days prior. Maybe next year they'd have enough in
the budget to buy decorations that didn't look quite so
sickly.

*Probably only if they cut salaries*, I thought sourly. As

long as they didn't cut mine, I could put up with a Santa Claus who looked vaguely leprous.

I shifted out of othersight and peered at my watch using my flashlight. Four a.m. We'd been at this for nearly an hour and were barely halfway around the Beaulac PD building. But Eilahn had been adamant that the places I spent the most time should be protected—at least as much as was reasonable. She was a *syraza*, an eleventh-level demon, assigned—gifted? loaned?—to me by the demonic lord Rhyzkahl after it had become clear that someone or something in the demon realm wasn't thrilled about my association with him. And Eilahn took her job damn seriously.

The wards on my house had been beefed up into intense and powerful protections, with an outer layer of aversions that would hopefully make intruders lose their desire to continue into my home. Needless to say it wasn't practical or desirable to have that sort of thing on the Police Department building. Instead, these protections were the sort that would make it highly difficult for me to be summoned while I was inside them—necessary since someone in the demon realm seemed to be intent on doing just that.

The wards were undetectable by anyone without arcane abilities. At least I sure hoped so. But even though they couldn't be seen by the naked eye, the process of laying them down looked pretty damn weird. Hence the reason we were out at oh-fuck o'clock in the morning— after the bars closed and before the sun came up.

I sighed and cast a longing glance across the street at the dark and closed coffee shop that had recently opened up next to the city administration building. *Grounds For*

*Arrest.* The painting of a steaming coffee cup on the window seemed to taunt me.

Eilahn softly cleared her throat, and I dragged my attention back to the matter at hand. Slipping back into othersight, I let the sensations wash over me as I checked for gaps or weak spots in the chain of sigils. Even incomplete, the patterns buzzed against my senses pleasantly, like a flow of warm water over my skin. If any part of the sequence had been wrong or poorly scribed, I'd feel it like a vibration in the back of my teeth. But no, it was clear that this demon knew what she was doing.

"You there!"

I straightened and turned at the male shout from behind me, squinting in the sudden light shone into my eyes. Beyond the glare of the flashlight I could see it was someone in a Beaulac PD uniform. Crap.

"What's going on here?" the officer demanded.

I lifted a hand to shield my eyes. "Could you lower the light please? I'm Detective Gillian. Who're you?"

The officer obligingly lowered the flashlight. I tried to blink away the spots that now swam in my vision. "Oh, hey, Kara. It's me, Tim Daniels. Sorry. Y'all looked like you were doing some serious skulking." He gave a small chuckle.

I returned the chuckle. Luckily we'd already come up with a hopefully believable fiction for why we were tromping around the PD in the middle of the night. "Nope, nothing nefarious. I was bringing my cat to the vet earlier and it got away from me, so my roommate" —I gave a vague gesture toward Eilahn— "and I are trying to see if we can find it now that there aren't a lot of people and cars around to scare it."

His gaze shifted to Eilahn and lingered there. I couldn't really blame him. The form she'd taken after I summoned her was female. Or, to be more specific, *smokin' hot chick*. Tall and athletic, with violet eyes and sleek dark hair that flowed past her shoulders, she somehow managed to look Asian, Jewish, Indian, Swedish, and black all at once. Right now she was dressed in jeans, low-heeled boots, and a snug-fitting long-sleeved black shirt. Yeah, I'd have stared too if it was my first time meeting her. I tried not to think about the contrast between us. I was about three inches shorter, with boring gray eyes, poker-straight mud-brown hair that was more fly-away than sleek, and, while I wasn't pudgy, I sure as hell didn't have anything resembling an athletic build.

"I just got off shift," he said, gaze not leaving Eilahn. "I'd be glad to help you look. What's your cat's name?"

Eilahn shot me a glance, and I masked a grimace. Crap. We hadn't counted on anyone actually wanting to help us look for a cat in the middle of the night. "Erm, its name is Fuzzykins."

The demon's expression didn't change a whit, but I could feel the withering *Fuzzykins? That's the best you can do?* as clearly as if we'd shared a telepathic bond. Damn good thing we didn't. I really wasn't sure I wanted to know what she was thinking most of the time.

"Fuzzykins," the officer repeated, grinning. "I love it. I'm Tim, by the way," he said to the demon. "I don't think we've met."

"Eilahn," she replied with an easy smile.

"Nice to meet you, Ellen," he said. I bit back a smile as her eyes narrowed at his mispronunciation. "So, what's this cat look like?"

Her eyes flicked back to me. Damn it. I was on the hook again. "It's, um, a calico." Those were sort of rare, weren't they? "Without a tail."

"A calico Manx. Well, that shouldn't be hard to miss," he replied with a laugh.

Ah, hell. He really did intend to help us look for this nonexistent feline. So much for getting the warding finished tonight.

"Tim," Eilahn said with a tilt of her head. "Perhaps you could run to the store for us and purchase some food for Fuzzykins to help lure her out." She gave him a smile that even dazzled me. I quickly dug in my pocket and came up with a battered twenty-dollar bill that I passed to her. In turn she pressed it into his hand without ever breaking eye contact, letting her fingers linger on his.

The poor boy never had a chance. Half a minute later he screamed off in his cruiser.

I cocked my head and regarded the demon. "How the hell did you learn how to do that?"

Her brow furrowed in puzzlement. "Do what?"

"That smile-seducey, make-men-drool thing."

She tossed off a shrug. "I read a lot."

Damn. I needed to hit the bookstore.

I moved to the corner and peered down the street. A damp and chilly breeze ruffled the wrinkled tinsel wrapped around the lamp posts. One of the eyes of an illuminated reindeer flickered on and off, making it look like it had a twitch. A dog barked somewhere several streets away, but otherwise the smooth silence remained unbroken. No cars. No one to see us.

Eilahn turned back to the chain of arcane symbols, then paused, eyes narrowing. A whisper of arcane brushed over me even as a scuff of sound from the roof drew my attention upwards. I barely had time to note a black shape swooping down before Eilahn leaped at me in a flying tackle.

I remembered to tuck my limbs in, and somehow she managed to roll with me so that I didn't hit the ground in a painful sprawl. The attacking demon was fast though. In the next instant it was on us, one clawed hand seizing my left bicep, and its other three on Eilahn. I tried to bite back the yelp of pain as one of its claws pierced skin. This was a *graa*—easy enough to recognize with its multiple arms. Hopefully this one only had the four. I'd seen some that had as many as eight—multi-jointed and ending in strange hands consisting of a thumb and two fingers, each tipped with curved claws. They looked almost spider-like—if spiders had wings like roaches and heads like crabs and hindquarters like a lizard.

Twisting, I tried to wrench my arm out of its grip, but I might as well have been a kitten trying to escape a lion's mouth. Eilahn seized something on its head that looked like a spicule or antenna and yanked harshly, wringing a hiss like a teakettle from it. The three of us rolled in a weird tangle of arms and legs and claws—a strangely quiet fight, punctuated only by my breathless cursing and the *graa's* hissing and snarling. They didn't have vocal cords, and one of the reasons I rarely summoned this species of demon was because I had such a fucking hard time understanding them.

Eilahn had broken two of the demon's arms, but now it was doing its best to slash a claw across her throat while she struggled against it, her own face set in a fierce rictus. I wasn't wearing my duty weapon, but I had my backup piece in an ankle holster. It took a few more seconds of Twister-worthy contortions, but I finally managed to yank the little Kel-Tec .32 out of the holster, shove it against the demon's midsection, and fire.

The demon let out a whistling shriek and released us both. I rolled aside, gasping raggedly, but Eilahn apparently had no desire to let it recover to attack another day. Her face twisted into a silent snarl as she pinioned three of the arms together. The fourth arm flailed uselessly against the pavement as the *graa* whistled and thrashed.

"Again, Kara," Eilahn said calmly. "The side of the head should be sufficient."

I staggered to my feet and shoved the gun against the creature's head. It went still, oddly human eyes blinking at me, then it shuddered and looked away.

"Forgive me," I murmured. This demon wasn't attacking me for personal reasons. It had been summoned, and a bargain had been set for it to perform this service. My true vendetta was against whoever had sent it. But I had to do this, and there was no way it wouldn't hurt the demon.

I fired once. The demon jerked, breath going out of it like a pierced balloon. Eilahn released it and straightened, standing over it as its limbs twitched and then went still. I stepped back as white light began to stream from the holes in its torso and head. Cracks appeared in its skin and the light flared to blinding levels. A heartbeat later a ripping crack split the air, and the demon was gone, leaving behind only the sour smell of ozone and a rancid perfume of rotted flowers.

With a shaking hand I hurriedly shoved the gun back into my holster and scooped up the two casings, stuffing them deep into a pocket. I knew I hadn't actually killed the demon. Since it wasn't of this plane I'd simply sent it back to the demon realm. It wasn't a threat anymore—at least for now. That was the important thing.

"Are you injured?" Eilahn asked, gaze sweeping over me. I shook my head, then winced at the sound of running footsteps. I'd been hoping that the pop of my little gun wouldn't be enough to draw attention, but apparently even a .32 was significant.

"Look annoyed," I warned her as two uniformed officers came cautiously around the corner with their guns drawn.

"It was firecrackers," I called to them, fixing a scowl to my face as I held up my badge. "Some assholes thought it would be funny to throw firecrackers out of their car at us."

Both officers relaxed at the sight of my badge and holstered their weapons. "They're lucky you didn't pop them back," one said, matching my scowl.

"No shit," I agreed, adding a fervent snort for emphasis. "If my gun wasn't in my car, I might have."

Fortunately they seemed satisfied with our explanation, and didn't look around for any detritus that firecrackers would have left behind. Probably helped that I'd had my badge ready to flash, and there was no reason to doubt my story. After the pair walked back toward the squad room entrance Eilahn turned to me.

"You are bleeding," she said, a small frown pulling at her mouth.

I glanced down at my arm. My jacket was black so the blood was almost impossible to see, but there was definitely a rip, surrounded by a darker spot. When I touched it my fingers came away sticky. Scowling, I shrugged out of the jacket. "Damn. I liked this jacket." I had on a long-sleeved grey shirt underneath, but I didn't have any sentimental attachment to it. Hooking my fingers into the small tear, I ripped it wider.

The *syraza* peered at the wound. "It does not appear to be very deep."

"The bruise will probably hurt worse," I replied. "It just needs a Band-Aid or something."

She retrieved the first aid kit from my car and bandaged the puncture. The worry on Eilahn's face didn't abate, and I knew it matched the queasy unease in my own gut.

"This is the first time I've been attacked by a demon when there's been no doubt it was meant for me," I said. Earlier this year I'd had an unpleasant encounter with a creature called a *kzak*—a non-sentient denizen of the demon realm. But Special Agent Ryan Kristoff had also been there, and I had plenty of reason to suspect that he'd been the true target of that attack.

"Yes," she said. "There is no mistaking that you were the target." Her frown deepened as she scanned the area, lifting her head as if she was scenting the wind, which, for all I knew, she was. "Yet it was not trying to kill you."

I resisted the urge to say something trite like *Coulda fooled me*. Because, truth was, I knew she was right. "It didn't put up much of a fight," I agreed. "Maybe it was simply a warning?"

"The *graa* was foolish to attack you when I was present." She turned her gaze on me. "It had to have known that it would fail, and that its risk of destruction in this realm was great."

"But it could hardly wait for when you weren't around," I pointed out. Eilahn was never far from me. I ran a hand through my hair, growing more unsettled as more thoughts occurred to me. "And, of course, this means there's another summoner nearby, possibly working for the demonic lord who has it in for me."

"You are mistaken." The demon shook her head. "There is likely more than one lord with a desire to harm you."

"Thanks," I replied dryly. "You've really put me at ease." The whole reason we were tromping around the PD at night was because there'd been several attempts to summon me to the demon realm. Usually *I* was the one who did the summoning. I had the ability to summon to this world supernatural creatures known as demons from another plane of existence. Not hell—these weren't the demons of any sort of religious mythos, and the reason they were even called thus was lost to history. There were twelve species—or levels—of demons, and the higher the level, the more powerful they tended to be, both physically and in their ability to use and shape arcane power. And above the twelve levels of demons were the demonic lords—beings more on the level of demi-gods—who ruled the demon realm. Generally speaking, one did not summon a demonic lord without extensive preparation, planning, and loads of arcane power, since the lords had an annoying tendency to slaughter anyone who dared do so.

But eight months ago, or so, I'd summoned Lord Rhyzkahl by accident and survived. Since then—through a variety of circumstances and favors owed—I'd become his sworn summoner, bound by oath to summon him to this world at least once a month.

And someone in the demon realm didn't seem to be too happy with that arrangement. Or rather, several someones, if Eilahn was to be believed. And I had no reason not to trust her.

A cruiser pulled into the parking lot, and I quickly pulled my jacket back on to hide the blood on my arm. A moment later Tim stepped out with two laden plastic grocery bags, abject apology written all over his face.

"Ellen, I tried three different stores, but most everything is still closed, and all I could find was some cheap Kitty Kibble at the 24-hour drugstore, and so I got a bag of that just in case, but then I also got some tuna, and went to the all night deli and got some sliced turkey." He crouched and began unloading the bags onto the ground in front of her, like a cat presenting a dead mouse as a trophy. He looked up at her. "Y'think any of that might work?"

I turned away in a sudden "coughing" fit as the demon blinked in discomfiture. "I . . . cannot thank you enough for going to such effort," she managed after an odd few seconds of silence. The look she sent my way was nothing short of desperate, and I felt a brief surge of ridiculous satisfaction. As capable and kickass as the demon was, it was a relief to see that there were some situations that she had no idea how to handle.

"I think we're about done searching for the night, Tim," I said, stepping between the two since I wasn't sure if he was even physically capable of tearing his eyes away from her on his own. A gust of wind blew my hair into my face, and I shoved it back behind my ears. The eastern sky held ominous red and purple streaks as clouds churned across the coming dawn. "The weather's turning. It's time to pack it in for now."

Worry shadowed across his face. "What if she gets caught out in it?"

Oh, hell no. There was no way I was going to tromp around in the rain—and early December in south Louisiana meant it would be *cold* rain—on a search for a cat that didn't exist. Not no, but fuck no.

"Fuzzykins is a tough girl," I assured him. "She's just biding her time until she comes on out. I'm sure she has a warm box to curl up under."

He blinked and focused on me. "Oh, sure, Kara." He stood and looked down at the various supplies with a crestfallen look, and I felt a stab of guilt for sending him on this wild goose chase. "Well, maybe y'all can use all this next time you look for her?"

"I know we can," I said brightly. "Fuzzykins absolutely loves turkey. Isn't that right, Eilahn?"

"Loves it," she agreed.

He brightened at that. "All righty then!" He adjusted his gun belt, and I had no doubt that if he'd had a hat he'd have tipped it to Eilahn. "I'll see y'all around then!" Whistling, he returned to his cruiser. We watched him drive off, and Eilahn shook her head.

"Humans are weird," she muttered.

"Yeah," I agreed. "You pretty much nailed it."

My cell phone rang. "Now what?" I moaned. I didn't need to look at the caller ID to know it was the Beaulac PD dispatcher. I was on call for the weekend, and I'd yet to get through a Sunday on call without getting a message from the dispatcher. It wasn't always a murder—in fact it rarely was, fortunately—but it never failed to be something I had to actually go to the scene for. Luckily, I didn't pull weekend call more than once a month. Plus, it wasn't as if I had anyone at home who wanted me around on the weekends.

Well, except for my demon roommate, but she was pretty good at fending for herself.

I listened to the dispatcher's terse delivery, confirmed that I would be on my way, then hung up. "I guess we won't be finishing the warding up tonight," I said.

"We will finish it tomorrow," Eilahn stated, voice firm. "It is even more evident that you require multiple sanctuaries." With that she turned and strode toward the motorcycle parked beside my car. I frowned down at the blood on my jacket. I had a spare in my office that I could grab. That should be enough. And I had an umbrella in my car if it started to rain.

I even had a demon bodyguard. I was set for anything.

# Chapter 2

"This is wrong," I stated, infusing my words with as much emphasis as possible in order to convey to anyone listening just how intensely I felt about this. "So so SO wrong." I zipped my spare jacket higher as a shiver wracked me. "It's unnatural. It's worse than unnatural. It's ..." I struggled to think of an appropriate word.

"It's *snow*, you weirdo," Sergeant Scott Glassman retorted.

"This is the Deep South!" I wailed. Fluffy little flakes of madness swirled on the chill breeze and dotted the knit cap covering Scott's bald head. "It was nowhere near this cold an hour ago."

"It's called a cold front. Ninth grade science." He stood with a hip cocked and a thumb tucked into his belt by his gun, looking every inch the "good ol' boy" street cop that he was. We'd been teammates when I was on the road, and Scott had taught me more than a few tricks for dealing with the rural mentality. He made sergeant about the time I became a detective, and I had no doubt he'd someday be in charge of the Patrol division.

"Yeah, well," I grumbled, "we're not supposed to have snow down here!"

Scott let out a snort. "Would you rather have freezing rain?"

"I'd rather not have anything freezing, thank you very much." I scowled and dug my hands deeper into my pockets. "I put up with hurricanes and the misery of Louisiana summer so that I *don't* have to put up with snow or sleet or any other form of frozen wetness."

"My god, you're a weenie," Scott said.

"I don't like the cold!"

Scott turned to eye me, pursing his lips. "Well maybe you should try, oh, I don't know, dressing for the weather?"

I hunched my shoulders in a vain attempt to keep the nasty little snow-bits from wiggling their evil way down my collar. "I didn't know it was going to be this cold. Or *snowy*." I hissed the last word.

The stocky cop gave me a suitably withering look. "What, you don't own a computer to check the forecast? A smart phone? A television? And is that really a Members Only jacket? I didn't think anyone wore those anymore. Were you even born when that thing was made?"

I couldn't exactly tell him that I'd been too busy putting a magical security system on the PD to check the weather, or that my other—warmer—jacket had been clawed by a demon. "Bite me," I snarled instead.

His only reply was a laugh.

We were in the parking lot of the Beaulac Nature Center—which was a fancy name for a trail that wound through the woods and swamp. The "Center" part of it consisted of a shack not much bigger than a utility shed, and a Plexiglas-covered map of the immediate area. The lot was a mostly flat stretch of old gravel and sparse grass—barely big enough to hold the two Beaulac PD police cruisers, crime scene van, my unmarked and two other vehicles—an ancient and battered Peugeot, and a spanking new silver BMW.

The sight of the crime scene van pleased me. That meant that Crime Scene Technician Jill Faciane was already on the scene and doing her thing. A transplant from the New Orleans PD, who'd moved to Beaulac after Hurricane Katrina, she knew her shit, worked quickly and efficiently, and was my kind of smartass. Procedure dictated that crime scenes had to be processed before detectives could go tromping all over them, but if Jill was working I had solid hope that I wouldn't have to stand out in the cold any longer than necessary.

I dug into the pockets of my jacket in the desperate hope that I'd left some gloves in them from last year, but all I found was an old wadded up Kleenex that probably had some ancient germs on it. I didn't see any trash cans around, and I didn't feel right casually littering out here, so I reluctantly stuffed the old tissue back down into my pocket, hoping that any germs it carried were long dead.

"So what's the deal here, Sergeant?" I asked Scott. "Let me guess, I'm going to have to take a nature hike to get to the body."

He gave me a sad shake of his head. "You really are a weenie, aren't you?"

I grinned. "Go with your strengths!"

He lifted his chin toward an officer standing near the head of the trail. "I'll let Gordon give you the rundown. He'll be able to tell you a shitload more than I ever could."

I slid a look toward Officer Tracy Gordon. If I didn't have a rule against dating coworkers—and if my love life wasn't already *way* too complicated—I'd have been all over him. Tall and dark-skinned, he had a smart-hunk look about him that pushed my buttons in all the right ways. "He still your trainee?"

"Nope. He finished up last week, and I pulled every string I had to get him permanently assigned to my shift."

"Enjoy him while you can," I said, clapping Scott on the shoulder. "We'll be stealing him soon enough!"

He sighed. "I keep telling him that you detectives are joyless pricks and that going to investigations would be terrible for his career, but I'm not sure he's buying it."

"Imagine that!" I gave Scott a parting smile and then trotted over to where Tracy Gordon stood at the start of the trail. I knew it was the start of the trail because there was a deliberately crude sign that said "Start of Trail." I glanced quickly around. There were no other trails or paths or anything else that could possibly be mistaken for the nature trail, but I was willing to bet that the sign existed because at some point someone decided to simply charge into the woods and then complained that it hadn't been well marked.

Or maybe I was too quick to assume there were a large number of stupid people in the world.

"You need a better coat," Tracy said with a frown as he held the crime scene log for me to sign. "Scarf and gloves too. You're going to freeze your ass off dressed like that."

"Yes, Mom," I replied as I handed the pen back to him and stuffed my hands back into my pockets. Who was the stupid one now? "It wasn't this cold when I left my house," I added petulantly.

"Don't you ever check the weather?" he chided. "Cold front moving through today. This morning was the high temp for the day."

I scowled at the sky. Living in south Louisiana meant that snow was a rarity, but in the past few years there'd been a scattering of snow days—more than I'd ever remembered when I was a kid. Only two years ago we'd had a surprise dumping of nearly six inches—which had been awesome for everyone who didn't actually have to go out in it. St. Long Parish didn't have anything resembling a snowplow, and the best the parish officials had been able to do was spread salt and sand on the bridges and tell everyone to stay off the roads. As someone who usually *did* have to go out regardless of the weather, my dislike of driving in snow more than outweighed my inner six-year-old's desire to make a snowman. "I shouldn't have to put up with brutally hot summers *and* snow," I whined.

He chuckled. A rich sound. "It's not so bad if you actually dress for the weather." To my surprise he pulled off his scarf and draped it around my neck, looping it with practiced ease. He gave me a grin before I could speak. "I'm from Colorado. I won't freeze like you delicate southern flower types."

I knew I should protest the offer and at least try to give the scarf back to him, but it was lovely and warm and it stopped the breeze from diving down the collar of my coat. Plus it smelled very faintly of whatever his cologne was, and I had to resist the very unseemly desire to bury my face in it and take a deep whiff. "Thanks," I said instead. "I'll give it back on my way out."

"No hurry. So I take it you want the rundown?"

"Please."

He pulled a small notebook from his front pocket and flipped it open.

I quickly held up my hand before he could start speaking. "Just the Cliff Notes version for right now," I said. "I want to get through this before hypothermia sets in."

He smiled. "Fair enough. About a hundred yards down the trail is a small picnic area, along with our victim, white male. ID in his pocket says that he's Barry Landrieu, age thirty-seven. The Peugeot is his. No obvious sign of trauma on initial visual examination, though there appears to be blood around his nose. Coroner's office is on the way, and crime scene is already doing their magic."

Barry Landrieu. That name was maddeningly familiar, but my frozen brain didn't want to tell me why.

"The witness who found the body is in the shack," he continued before sliding the notebook back into his shirt pocket. "The BMW-Z4 belongs to him. I verified."

This was why I adored Officer Gordon. He saw the loose threads and checked them out without being told to do so. One of these days he was going to be a *fantastic* detective. "I'll deal with the witness after I see the body," I said. At least this witness was willing to stick around, which would save me the trouble of having to hunt him down later for a statement. Detention of witnesses was one of those things that was legal only under certain circumstances. "I'm afraid that if I go inside now," I continued, "I'll never be able to convince myself to come out."

The skin around his eyes crinkled attractively as he smiled. "Probably a good strategy."

I headed down the trail and, as described, in another hundred yards the trail opened out into a clearing that had been made into a picnic site. Beyond this area I could see that the trail continued on to a deck where one could look out over the marsh. A concrete barbecue pit held old ashes and a dusting of snow that was melting into slush. A pair of picnic tables had been there long enough to collect an assortment of carvings in their surfaces on the order of "Jenny wuz here" and "Buddy N Chelsea 4eva." And in the scruffy grass between the tables and the barbecue pit was the dead man.

A gangly male officer wearing a jacket with *Beaulac PD Crime Scene* emblazoned across the back crouched by the body, snapping pictures. Brown curls peeked out from beneath a black Beaulac PD baseball cap, and when he turned I saw a scattering of freckles across a slightly crooked nose. I didn't recognize him, but I sure as hell knew the slim, red-haired woman in a similar jacket standing beside him. This was Jill, one of my best friends and one of the very few who knew about the demon summoning. I had a feeling the crouching officer was a trainee of some sort—a guess that was somewhat confirmed when he straightened and looked to her for guidance.

His eyes shifted to me as I approached, and Jill turned, flashing me a smile. "Heya, darlin'," she said. "Lovely day for a nature walk!"

I couldn't help but note that she wore a dark blue knit hat, a black scarf wound around her neck and leather gloves. Apparently she *had* checked the weather before leaving her house this morning. And hadn't been distracted by a demon attack. "*Nature* and *walk* should

never be in a sentence together," I retorted, grimacing as
a burst of wind whipped through the trees and around us.
I hunched my shoulders in an attempt to bury my ears in
the borrowed scarf. "This sucks ass. Tell me what you've
found so I can finish up and get the hell out of here."

She laughed. "Okay, grumpypants. Tracy already gave
you the gist?" At my nod she continued, "It looks to me
like our vic has been here since maybe late yesterday, but
the CO folks will have to give the word on that. He
wasn't dressed for cold weather. No flies, but the cold is
probably keeping them away."

I crouched by the body. He was lying on his stomach
with one hand up near his face and the other down along
his side. One leg was cocked awkwardly over the other
in a way that made me think he might have stumbled
and collapsed. I peered at what I could see of his face.
Blond hair. A mustache stained red. "Looks like he had
a nosebleed," I said. "Not a whole lot of blood." I
skimmed my gaze over the rest of him, but there didn't
seem to be any obvious sign of trauma. No jacket, just a
long-sleeved Henley-style shirt, jeans, and boots. "Maybe
he overdosed, or had a stroke. Do those cause nosebleeds?"

Jill shrugged. "Ask Dr. Lanza," she said, referring to
the parish pathologist. "Who knows, maybe there's a big
knife that we can't see sticking into his belly. We won't
know anything for sure until the CO dudes roll this guy
over."

I nodded. There'd be no touching the body until the
coroner's office personnel got here and everything was
properly photographed and documented, which meant
there wasn't much I could do except interview whoever

found him. "Does his name sound familiar to you?" I flicked a glance up at Jill.

She frowned in thought then shook her head. "I don't think so. Why? Do you know him?"

"Not sure. The name Barry Landrieu rings a bell, and I kind of get the feeling I've seen him before, but . . ." I sighed and straightened. "Hell, I probably arrested him once or something." Though even as I said it I knew that wasn't it. Damn it, this was going to bug the ever-loving crap out of me until I figured it out.

I turned my attention to the gangly young man. "Hi. I'm Kara Gillian. I'd shake your hand but I don't want to take it out of my pocket."

He gave an awkward chuckle. "Drew Blackall. Nice to meet you."

"Drew's fresh out of the Academy," Jill informed me. "He told me he wanted to be just like the CSI people on TV," she added, face completely neutral.

He turned a bright shade of crimson, and I grinned. "And how long did it take for her to disabuse you of that notion?"

"About ten minutes," he admitted.

I was almost surprised it had taken that long. Jill had several ready-made rants about the inaccurate ways her profession was portrayed on TV and how such portrayals were detrimental to law enforcement and forensic labs.

Jill gave a pleased sigh. "Ah, I do love shaping young minds."

I snorted. "All right, I'm going to go talk to the witness. I'm freezing my tits off out here."

"He's a celebrity," Drew blurted out, then flushed as we both looked at him. "The witness. I mean, um, not like a movie star, but he's on TV and people around here know him. . . ." he trailed off, face coloring.

"Okay, I'll bite," I said. "Who is he?"

Drew gave an eager smile. "Roman Hatch!" he said. "He's on ESPN and he used to play for—"

"I know who he is," I interrupted, unable to completely hide the slight wince. "Roman Hatch. Former linebacker at LSU. They called him 'Hatchet Man.' Played for Green Bay and went to the Pro Bowl twice. Two years ago he had a career-ending knee injury, and now he's a color commentator for ESPN."

Jill cocked an eyebrow at me. "And here I thought you didn't know anything about sports."

I shrugged. "I *don't* know anything about sports. But I know Roman." I paused, shrugged. "I went to LSU. And I, uh, dated him for a couple of months during my senior year."

The look of astonishment on her face was almost enough to make me not mind the cold. "I think this shocks me more than . . . um . . . your house," she said. I was pretty sure she'd been about to say something about my summoning demons and had caught herself just in time. Luckily Drew didn't seem to be aware that Jill had censored herself. He stared at me in awe as if I'd just announced I was the new quarterback for the New Orleans Saints.

Jill shook her head and let out a low whistle. "Wow. You just don't strike me as the type who would ever date a football player."

"Yes. Because I'm *not*," I said emphatically. "Hence the reason we aren't still together."

Her eyes flashed with wicked humor, and I knew she

was dying to say something obnoxious about the type of men I currently had in my life. Good thing—for my sake—that the tech was here, and she was forced to restrain herself.

Any further commentary was cut short by the arrival of Coroner's Office personnel as they maneuvered their stretcher over bumps and debris in the trail.

The Coroner's Investigator gave me a dour nod before stooping to peer at the body. Clearly he was just as thrilled to be out in the cold as I was. He pulled on latex gloves then gave a nod to his assistant. Together they rolled Mr. Landrieu onto his back while Drew dutifully snapped pictures, and I stood back and shivered. The Investigator crouched again and ran gloved hands over the victim's skull and carefully examined the rest of the body.

"No obvious sign of injury or foul play," he finally stated. "Looks like the blood is from a nosebleed. Doc'll have to figure out if that had anything to do with the cause of death." He stood. "You need a looksee?"

"Yes, thank you," I replied. A shimmer of unease swept over me as I stepped toward the body and I shot a quick glance around, suddenly weirded out for absolutely no reason I could name. Nothing seemed out of the ordinary. No animals or movement. Anything with any sort of common sense was surely holed up in its nest. I shifted into othersight, but it didn't reveal anything sinister.

Still strangely unnerved, I crouched by the body. I felt as if something was pricking at my arcane senses, far too faint for me to be able to pinpoint. Too faint to even be sure that's what was bothering me. *Maybe I'm simply delirious from the cold.*

Familiarity tickled madly as I took a hard look at the man's face, but his features were distorted from the way he'd been lying. Impressions from leaves and dirt marred his cheek, along with the dull red tinge of lividity from the settling of the blood in his body. An ant casually traipsed across the milky white surface of his eye. Another was busy at the dried blood by his nose. The flies would be on him as soon as it warmed up. A few more days out here and the eyes, nose and mouth would be teeming with maggots, busily helping the decomposition process along.

"Kara . . . ?" Jill murmured. I abruptly realized that the Coroner's Office people were waiting for me to finish my observations so that they could get him into the body bag. Mumbling an apology, I stood and backed away a couple of steps while they rolled the body smoothly into the bag and zipped it closed.

Jill turned to Drew. "Why don't you go on back to the van and start in on the paperwork." He nodded and obediently trotted after the CO people as they trundled the loaded stretcher carefully back down the trail. As soon as they were out of earshot she gave me a penetrating look. "You saw something wonky, didn't you?" she asked.

I shook my head. "I thought I felt something strange, but I didn't see anything." I gave her a sharp look. "Why? Did you feel something?"

"No. It's just that your eyes go funny when you're looking for your woowoo stuff."

I frowned at her. "Funny? What do you mean?"

She shrugged. "Hard to describe. It's not like they glow or anything, but . . . they get super intense. I can almost *feel* it."

That was the first time I'd ever heard of anyone being able to tell when I was using othersight. Could Jill have some sort of sensitivity to the arcane? Or maybe it was simply that she knew what I was doing and thus read more into it.

"Where's your shadow?" she asked, and I knew she was referring to Eilahn. She knew about the demon and her role. That had been easy enough to share.

"Around somewhere," I muttered, still frowning. I didn't worry about Eilahn. I knew that if something happened she'd be at my side in less than a heartbeat. But I couldn't shake the feeling that something wasn't quite right with this scene. I kept thinking I saw flickers of movement at the edges of my vision, easily explained by the movement of the wind through the grass and the trees. Except . . .

*Except it feels off.*

I fought back a shiver as I scanned the area again with othersight. Jill stood silently and patiently while I opened myself as much as possible to any arcane sensations.

Nothing. It was simply woods. Sunlight fought to break through the clouds, scattering mottled shadows onto the carpet of leaves and pine needles. A branch scraped against a neighboring tree and droplets of moisture pattered down onto the picnic tables and the limp ashes in the barbecue pit.

I sighed and gave her a wry smile. "Guess I'm nuts after all."

She chuckled. "In other words, business as usual for you."

I fell into step with her as we made our way back up

the trail. "Life would be easier if I was nuts, I think," I said.

"Oh, just do what everyone else does—heavy drugs!"

I began to laugh, then stopped dead. *Barry Landrieu.* Now I remembered where I knew him from.

Jill turned back to me with a frown. "You okay?"

I gave a slow nod. "Yeah. Sorry. I, um, just realized why the victim's name seemed familiar."

She gave me a questioning look, but I hesitated. Had I ever told Jill about some of the more unpleasant parts of my past? *Screw it*, I decided. *If she can tolerate the whole demon summoning thing, she's not going to run screaming because of this.*

"After my dad was killed and my aunt became my guardian, I did a lot of acting out," I told her. "Experimenting with drugs and that sort of thing. Mostly it was just smoking pot and sneaking alcohol, but sometimes it was painkillers or ADHD meds."

Her brow furrowed but she simply gave me a *go on* nod.

"I used to hang with a girl named Tammy," I said. "Tammy North—and she had an older brother. Half-brother actually. He had a different last name, which is why I couldn't place it at first." I lifted my chin in the direction the stretcher had gone. "Barry Landrieu. Tammy and I would smoke pot that he gave us. But one day when I went over there Barry gave me something new to try. Heroin. I overdosed and damn near died."

"Jesus," she breathed.

I scuffed a shoe in the dirt. "Yeah, it pretty much sucked ass." Then I took a deep breath. "On the other hand, it was one hell of a wakeup call for me and my aunt."

"Is that when she tried to see if you could be a summoner?"

"Not immediately, but about a year later Aunt Tessa 'introduced' me to demon summoning. She also called the narcs on Barry and they busted him pretty soon after. I thought he was still in jail, to be honest."

"What happened to his sister?" Jill asked.

"Dunno. My aunt pulled strings and had me switch schools. I don't think I ever saw Tammy again." A sliver of guilt wormed through me. After recovering from the overdose I'd thrown myself into learning summoning, and I'd barely spared Tammy a second thought.

I blew out my breath. "Anyway. At least now I know why the name's familiar."

Jill reached and rubbed my arm. "You should go let the Hatchet Man console you in your time of loss," she said, then danced away, laughing, as I took a swing at her.

"You are such a bitch," I muttered, but I couldn't help but grin. However, my mood slipped a bit as we continued on to the parking lot. I knew the victim and the witness. What were the odds of that?

*Pretty high, actually, considering how small Beaulac is*, I decided. I should probably be surprised that it didn't happen more often. Sometimes a coincidence was just a coincidence.

Still, it was one of those things that would make me take a closer look at everyone involved.

Tracy was on his phone, and he simply gave us a slight wave as we passed him. Jill headed to her van while I hurried on to the shack. My haste had absolutely nothing to do with a desire to see Roman again—and everything to do with my desire to warm the hell up.

I stepped into the shack and quickly pulled the door closed behind me, breathing a silent prayer of thanks to whatever powers would listen to me that there was a space heater in here and that it was working at maximum efficiency. Beyond that there wasn't much appealing about the interior. A small metal desk against the far wall. Two office chairs that looked like they'd been in use during the seventies. Roman sat in one of the chairs, his attention on the phone in his hand. He had on jeans and expensive-looking cowboy boots, with a black sweater and a leather bomber jacket up top. He lifted his eyes to me as I entered, recognition flaring instantly.

"Kara?" he exclaimed, a broad smile spreading across his face as he stood. He was still as good-looking as ever—broad-shouldered and tall with hazel eyes set in a square-jawed face. His sandy-blond hair nearly brushed the rafters, and it was clear he hadn't slacked off on his workouts since leaving the Packers. His whole build pretty much screamed "former linebacker." I suddenly felt absurdly tiny. "Holy shit, what are you doing here?" His gaze swept over me, taking in my belt with the gun and badge.

I gave him a dutifully friendly smile. We hadn't parted with any sort of animosity. It was more of a *Holy crap we are SO not meant to be together* sort of thing, but still, the potential for awkwardness was definitely strong, especially since I'd been the one to end it. "Hi, Roman. How've you been?"

To my surprise he threw his arms around me in a hug before stepping back to give me a once-over, still grinning. "I've been awesome. You look great! And wow . . . a cop?"

"Homicide detective," I replied, a little proudly.

"That's fantastic!" he exclaimed. Then he seemed to remember where he was and what I was doing here, and he winced. "Sorry, I mean, it is, but it sucks that I have to find out like this." He shook his head. "Anyway. It really is good to see you, Kara."

"You too, Roman," I replied automatically, but I was surprised to realize that I actually kind of meant it. "Thanks for waiting around. I just need to ask you a few questions, if that's all right?"

"No problem," he said, dropping back into the chair. "Anything I can do to help."

Taking a seat in the other chair, I asked him for his driver's license and quickly jotted down his information. Michigan license. His cell phone had an out of state area code. "You in town visiting your folks?" I asked. We were both from this area, though he'd gone to a private all-boys high school on the other side of the parish while I'd suffered at Beaulac High.

"My maw-maw's doing a bit poorly," he said. "Nothing serious, but my dad needed some help moving her into assisted living. I also have a couple of investments I'm working on down here, and figured I'd check in on them."

"I'm sorry to hear that," I said. "I mean about your maw-maw, not about the investments," I quickly added. I'd only met his grandmother a couple of times, but she'd seemed nice enough. My grandparents had all passed away either before I was born or when I was too young to remember them. "Can you tell me what you were doing out here?" I asked.

He leaned back, exhaled. "I used to come out here all

the time when I was in high school. It was just some trails back then—it wasn't an official park or anything with the picnic tables and parking lot." A flicker of a grimace crossed his face, and it wasn't hard to figure out that he'd liked it better when no one else knew about it. "Anyway, whenever I'm home I try to get out here. I like coming out to watch the sun come up over the marsh. It's really pretty. Clears my head, y'know?"

I gave a smile of understanding. "Guess this time wasn't so head-clearing, huh?"

He scrubbed a hand over his face. "I didn't even see the body at first since it was still pretty dark. Passed right by him on the way out to the deck. Then on the way back . . . At first I thought it was just a bunch of trash or clothes that someone had dumped out here. I was all pissed off, and then I saw the guy's hand. I started to try and turn him over, but he was already stiff." Roman shot me a troubled look. "I probably messed up evidence, didn't I?"

"It was a natural reaction," I assured him. "I doubt you disturbed anything critical."

He blew out his breath, nodded. "I called nine one one and waited for the cops." He shrugged. "They told me to wait here. That's pretty much it."

"Did you see anyone else around?"

"Nope. It was dead quiet out here this morning." He winced. "Sorry. No pun intended, I swear."

"Don't worry. I've heard far worse from cops," I told him. "The ID on the victim is for a Barry Landrieu. Do you know him?" I watched him carefully.

He thought for a second then shook his head. "Doesn't ring a bell. Sorry."

As far as I could tell he was being truthful, but I still intended to run a check on both of them to see if there were any links. That was standard procedure. Sure, we used to date, but that didn't mean I was going to shirk on my job. Closing my notebook, I stood and so did he. "I appreciate your help. If I have any more questions I'll be in touch." I pulled out one of my cards and handed it to him. "And if you think of anything else, please let me know."

He glanced down at it before pulling out his wallet and tucking the card carefully within. "What happened to him? Was he murdered?"

"We won't really know anything until the autopsy," I said, "but right now I'm inclined to think it was natural causes."

"It was good seeing you again, Kara, despite the circumstances. You look great." He gave me a warm smile, reminding me why I'd gone out with him as long as I had. He was a smart guy with plenty of charm, and it had been tough to resist when he'd turned his attention to me. It had simply taken me a couple of months to get past the charm and realize that not only did we have nothing in common, but I was also never going to feel comfortable sharing the more private details of my life with him. Like the fact that I had never mastered shaving my legs in the shower and had to take a bath to accomplish the task. Or that I was absolutely addicted to my Water-Pik and actually *liked* getting my teeth cleaned at the dentist's office. Oh, yeah, and that whole demon summoning thing.

"Good seeing you too," I said. "I'm glad to hear you're doing well." I really hoped he didn't have anything to do with the death of Barry Landrieu. *Hopefully this case will be the nice, easy natural death it currently appears to be.*

He glanced down at my left hand. "Not married yet?"

My lips twitched. "Nope."

"Seeing anyone?" he asked, eyes on me.

Wow. How to answer that one? "Umm, sort of. Yeah." Did regular sex with a demonic lord count?

"I'm going to be in town for a couple of weeks," he said. "Maybe we could have lunch or coffee."

"I'd like that," I replied before I could think about whether or not I really would like it. "I, um, hate to chase you off, but I need to tie up the loose ends here and get started on the paperwork."

"No problem," he said. He pulled the door open and politely stood back to let me exit first. The cold was a knifing shock after the balmy comfort of the shack, and it took everything I had to force myself out into it and not suck my breath in dramatically or anything like that.

"I'll be in touch," Roman said, then surprised me by leaning down and giving me a quick kiss on the cheek before hurrying off to his car.

I watched as he started the BMW and drove off, then yelped at a hard smack on my arm. I turned to glare at Jill.

"Oh my god," she said, grinning wickedly. "You are a total hunk magnet!"

I thwapped her arm back. "Don't you start! I am not. Besides, you have a hunk of your own." Jill was dating Zack. Special Agent Zack Garner—who I'd recently discovered was a lot more than just a special agent.

Jill suddenly reached out and gave my arm—the same

one she'd just punched—a comforting squeeze. "Still nothing from Ryan?"

I couldn't quite suppress the wince as I shook my head. "Nothing worthwhile. I get spam that's friendlier." Jill heard from Zack several times a day, while in the past month and a half I'd received a grand total of three emails from Ryan—all oddly terse and almost painfully neutral. It was enough to give a girl a complex. And I was neurotic enough already, thank you very much.

However, part of my wince was guilt-induced. Jill seemed to be getting more and more serious about Zack. And I didn't have the faintest idea how to tell her—or even if I *should* tell her—that Zack wasn't exactly the perfect man she thought he was.

And that he wasn't a man at all, for that matter.

I was part of an interagency task force that supposedly dealt with financial crimes but actually handled situations that fell outside the definition of "ordinary." I'd met the other two primary members of the team— FBI Special Agents Ryan Kristoff and Zack Garner— during the investigation of the Symbol man murders, during which I'd confided to Ryan that I was a summoner. Shockingly, he'd known what a summoner was, and I subsequently discovered that he also had a fair amount of sensitivity to the arcane, though not as much as I did.

Or so I thought. But shortly over a month ago our little group began work on a case involving death threats against a local singer, and during the final wrap-up of the case—which turned into an ugly battle against a horde of golems—I discovered that there was a shitload more to Zack and Ryan than met the eye. Turned out that

Zack was a demon in human form. And Ryan? Well, the FBI agent who'd become one of my closest friends was very likely an exiled demonic lord, even though he had no memory or awareness of that fact.

The two agents had left for some sort of special training up in Quantico about a week after the battle with the golems. Meanwhile I was left to grapple with information I'd been told, stuff I'd seen, and things I'd deduced. Zack couldn't come right out and confirm my suspicions about the two of them, but he had repeatedly stressed that Ryan's safety could be jeopardized if he knew the truth. I still didn't know if Zack was Ryan's guard or his guardian, but I had an odd gut feeling that the training was a convenient excuse for Zack to get Ryan away for a while.

Jill's face twisted into a sympathetic expression. "Men are dicks," she announced, "and Ryan's being an emo dick, which is the worst sort."

I smiled despite my angst. "Ryan's never really struck me as the emo type."

She gave a snort. "Please. Zack says that he's being Mr. Moody—moping around or taking out whatever frustrations he has on anyone silly enough to be willing to train with him." Then her eyes softened—which wasn't an expression I was used to seeing on Jill. "Look, it really messed him up when he thought you'd died."

My stomach tightened again, and I had to work hard to keep a neutral expression on my face while I gave her a nod. The only reason I hadn't died was because of Ryan. And what he'd somehow been able to do.

*. . . he straightened, expression smoothing to ice, with only his eyes showing a devastating rage. He raised his*

*hands before him, and in the next heartbeat the space be-
tween his hands filled with white-blue potency. He lowered his head, lip curling as he unleashed the power at the
golem. . . .*

"I know," I managed to say. "But I didn't die." I
shrugged, wishing I could shrug off the tension and uncertainty as well. Was that why Zack and Ryan left? Did
they need to make sure that Ryan wouldn't go all
demonic-lord-smites-his-enemies again? "Whatever.
I've been through worse."

She gave a mock shudder. "Unfortunately, that's far
too true. You're such a drama queen!"

I grinned. "And you still hang with me."

"Makes me look good in comparison!" Then she lifted
her chin in the direction the BMW had gone. "So, you
and the football star, huh? Spill!"

"There's nothing to spill," I insisted. "We were in the
same Early Japanese Art class. We found out that we
were from the same town. He asked me out. He was nice.
We dated for about two months. We parted ways."

She eyed me. "And . . . ?"

I laughed. "Okay, he was also my 'first.' "

"Niiiiice," she said with an approving nod. "That's how
to get off to a good start." Then she cocked her head, eyes
sparkling mischievously. "So was it? A good start?"

"As good as any first time is, I suppose. He's a decent
guy. We just had absolutely nothing in common. And he
was a damn sight nicer than my second boyfriend. Complete asshat *and* sucked in bed."

Her lips twitched. "And now you date a demon."

"And now I date a demon." I shrugged. "Clearly I
haven't learned a damn thing."

# Chapter 3

The car heater did its best to pump out something resembling heat, but there was only so much that the poor Taurus could do for me. I could hardly blame it. It wasn't often that it was called upon to perform this sort of service. To its credit, it had a quite efficient air conditioner, which was usually far more important, since the summers were insanely brutal. Hell, I'd probably be needing the air conditioner again in less than a week. Weather in this area tended to be rather inconsistent.

After a few minutes of driving, though, I gave up and pulled into the parking lot of the first non-outrageously priced clothing store I could find that was open. Yes, I had real jackets and warm clothing at home, but that was more than a half hour away. I was freezing my ass off *now*.

My plan was to buy the cheapest, warmest jacket I could find and maybe a pair of gloves. But when I walked into the store the first thing that caught my eye was the mannequin by the door. Or rather, what was *on* the mannequin.

"Oh, sweetie," I murmured. "You belong on me." I

looked to the sales girl behind the counter. "I'd like to try that on, please."

I slid the coat on while the sales girl looked on approvingly.

"It's on sale, you know," she said slyly.

I ran my hands over it, inhaled deeply of the rich scent of the black leather. "Would it be wrong for me to say I don't care?" This mid-thigh length beauty fit snugly up top and skimmed over my hips, flaring out just enough to allow me to move and sit in comfort, with the side benefit of giving me something resembling a real figure. I didn't usually have anything close to a defined waist, and my bust was far from exceptional, but the cut of this coat gave me actual curves without making me look chunky. A stand-up collar blocked the cold without giving me the sense I was choking, and also looked satisfyingly tough. I swung my arms, pleased to see that even though it fit me like a second skin, I could still move freely in it. Fucking hell, yes. I was buying this coat. Who needed savings? At the rate I was going, I wouldn't live to see retirement anyway.

I ignored the whining of my credit card and my conscience. I bought black leather gloves as well, because what's a badass coat without badass gloves? It was a good thing the store didn't sell boots, because I had no doubt I'd have bought some. I had the brief urge to hand my Members Only jacket to the girl to dispose of, but my frugal side made a last-ditch rally and managed to slap a bit of sense into me.

Ten minutes later I was back in my car—and feeling not only warm but tough, because there's nothing like leather to make one feel invincible.

I didn't have any pressing need to go to the station since the report on the death of Barry Landrieu could certainly wait until Monday. However, two weeks ago the gods had decided that I was a good and just person and deserved to be compensated for the selfless works I had performed, and Grounds For Arrest had opened directly across the street from the Beaulac Police Department.

It was like Mecca and Nirvana and Valhalla all rolled into one. It was my Shangri La. They served coffee with chicory. And it was Good.

I parked in the detective's parking lot of the PD since the café lot was being converted into a drive-through. A gust of wind caught me as soon as I stepped out of my car, and I bared my teeth in a grin. This wasn't the icy wind from a possible summoning. This was simply winter. *But I'm dressed for it now, bitches.*

The clouds had successfully choked off the sun's pathetic attempt to infiltrate the day, and the sky was back to being grey and ugly. A battered pickup chugged desultorily down the street, while a cherry red Camaro following it blasted a heavy bass beat from behind tinted windows. Grill smoke from a hamburger shack down the street whipped past me, stirring my appetite, but in the next heartbeat the wind shifted, bringing with it the sour smell of the Dumpster behind the PD. A couple hunched against the wind as they made their way down the street, surprising me when they stopped to admire the display in the window of an antique shop. I didn't think this was the sort of weather anyone would want to go window-shopping in.

Squaring my shoulders in my kickass new coat, I crossed the street and ducked into the café. I pulled the door shut behind me and inhaled with pleasure as the scent wrapped me in its warm, pillowy embrace. Tugging my gloves off, I approached the counter.

The barista smiled as he passed a tall cup to me. "Morning, Kara. A pound of sugar, a gallon of cream, and a splash of coffee, right?"

"You're a very smart man, David," I replied with a grin as I handed over money.

"Well, you're my most regular regular so far," he said, then frowned. "That could be taken the wrong way."

Laughing, I took the change and dropped it into the tip jar. "If you ever start serving chocolate donuts," I said, "I'd probably never leave."

"Then for the safety of our fine community, I'll be sure to avoid ordering any."

"For the safety of my waistline as well!"

"Y'know, I actually had donuts here when we first opened," he said, picking up a towel and wiping down the counter as he spoke. "Had to stop carrying them because they didn't sell."

I nodded. "The stereotype."

"Exactly," he said, eyes flashing in amusement. "None of the cops who came in wanted to be seen eating donuts in public."

"It's my private shame," I said with a parting wink. I turned around and barely caught myself before spilling my precious coffee all over the front of Officer Gordon's jacket and my own. "Yikes! Sorry!"

Tracy gave me an engaging smile. "If I didn't know better I'd say you were stalking me."

"It's true," I replied. "I have a thing for men who keep me from freezing to death. Oh, and speaking of," I said as I tugged off the scarf and handed it back to him, "I can give this back to you now."

"Well, I knew that if you did freeze I'd be the one stuck writing the report about finding your body."

"I'm on call. I wonder if I'd have to investigate my own death?"

His mouth curved in amusement. "It's a bureaucracy. Of course you would." He looked to the patiently waiting David. "Sorry. Hot chocolate, please. Whole milk, with whipped cream."

Damn, that sounded good. I briefly regretted my addiction to coffee. But only briefly.

He returned his attention to me as David went off to make his drink. "New purchase? Surely you didn't have time to go back home."

It took me a second to figure out what he was talking about. "Oh, the coat!" I grinned. "Yep, just bought it. I couldn't resist."

"It's badass," he said with an approving nod.

I preened a bit, about to respond when a screech of tires on pavement pulled our attention. An instant later we heard the distinct *crash* of a car meeting something immoveable.

"That can't be good," I murmured as we both quickly moved to the broad windows at the front. The street and the detective's parking lot were in full view. My vehicle was the only one in the lot. Or rather, it had been. Now there was a dark blue Toyota Camry with its front end embedded in my car's driver's side.

I probably stared in disbelief for several seconds while the scene registered in my brain. "That's my car," I heard myself say. Then I shook myself out of my stupor.

"That's my fucking car!" Okay, so technically it was the PD's car, but still, it was assigned to *me*.

I spun and hit the door at a run, glancing up and down the street just long enough to make sure I wasn't about to get plowed by an oncoming vehicle. I was still holding my coffee, and the hot liquid splashed my hand through the little hole in the lid. I slowed to a brisk and angry walk as a blond woman made her stumbling way out of her driver's side of the Camry. She wasn't going anywhere fast. Not dressed in a pencil skirt and sky-high heels. She had the figure for it, I thought absently despite my current rage. Tall and slim and model perfect, even though she looked like she was in her late forties or so. Terrific genes. The bitch.

"Hey! You crazy, drunk bitch!" I shouted. "You just ran into the wrong car!"

She didn't seem to hear me. Blood streamed from her nose onto her white blouse. Clearly the airbag hadn't been very kind to her. Her unfocused gaze skimmed over me before she turned away from me and staggered to the middle of the parking lot. She stopped and looked up, spreading her arms as if she was waiting for aliens to snatch her up.

"Hey, lady!" I called out to her. "You need to get back over here right now."

The woman suddenly let out a scream of pain and grabbed her head. She turned to focus on me for the first time, her eyes wild and wide.

"Help me!" she whimpered.

*Drunk or high?* I thought sourly. "Don't worry, I'll get you plenty of help," I told her. "Now, step back over to the car, please."

She didn't move. Her eyes stayed locked on mine. I could see her fingers digging into her hair as if she was trying to hold her skull together. "Make it stop." Her voice cracked as if speech was an incredible effort. "Please!"

I stopped about a dozen feet from her. Last thing I wanted to do was tangle with a blood-covered bitch who was high on who-knew-what. "Make what stop? Come over here and have a seat by the car, and I'll get you some help."

She took a shaking breath, and for an instant I thought she was going to comply and make my life easier. Then in the next heartbeat her hands fell away from her head, her face went slack, and she dropped like a stone to the ground, hard enough for her head to connect with the asphalt with an audible crack.

"Shit!" I dropped the coffee and quickly closed the distance. Crouching beside her, I rolled her to her back and found a place on her neck that didn't have blood on it to check for a pulse. Not an easy task. *Two nosebleeds in one day?* I thought with a grimace. Coincidences like that made me itch. Especially on the same day a demon decided to attack me.

I whirled to signal for Tracy but he was right behind me and already on his radio, calling it in. "No pulse," I told him. "Tell 'em code three."

He nodded and relayed the information as I turned back to the woman, got my hands in proper position, and started giving chest compressions. I took the CPR class every year as part of my in-service training, but this was the first time I'd ever had to do it on a real person.

The woman's eyes were half lidded, and bubbles of

blood formed at her nostrils with every compression. The latest guidelines called for compressions only, no mouth-to-mouth, and I sent up a silent thanks for that. I was pretty sure I wouldn't want to risk giving breaths, even if I had one of those mask things. It was bad enough that my hands were getting blood on them. *I don't have any open cuts*, I reminded myself. I hoped.

I lost track of time, though it was probably only a minute or two before sirens cut through the air. An ambulance pulled into the parking lot, and a few seconds later EMS crouched beside me. I gratefully relinquished the duty to them.

I stood, legs a little numb from kneeling. I staggered a step and felt a strong hand at my elbow steadying me. I looked over to see Tracy, then gave him a nod of thanks as he handed me a sanitizing wipe. I scrubbed my hands thoroughly of every trace of blood then hurriedly checked my lovely new jacket to see if I'd gotten any on it. If so, I couldn't see it against the black leather. Yes, I knew I was being horribly shallow. But focusing on the little things kept me from losing my cool.

I returned my attention to the paramedics and their patient. "She was in the Camry," I explained with a gesture toward the two cars. "She ran into the other one, then got out and walked over here. She seemed a little unsteady, but then she just stopped and—" I paused, knowing it was going to sound strange. "She grabbed her head and said, 'Help me. Make it stop.' Then she dropped like a stone."

The one manning the ventilator glanced over at the car and frowned. "Could be a stroke. Doesn't seem like a bad crash, but you never know."

There wasn't anything more I could do then except stand back and watch. A glance over at the coffee shop showed a number of faces at the window peering out from the warmth. They were the smart ones. The paramedics continued to work on her, but it didn't seem to be doing much good. After a few minutes they loaded her up and screamed off with lights and sirens going.

I let my breath out as the ambulance departed then looked mournfully at my car. "Damn."

"At least you weren't in it," Tracy said with a rueful smile. "Then you'd have to go through the joy of a piss test as well."

"Yeah, small favors." I sighed, tugging my gloves out of my pockets and onto my hands. "I guess I shouldn't be whining about the car when there's a chance that woman might not make it."

Tracy shrugged, then looked back at the sound of approaching footsteps. I followed his gaze to see the barista, David, trotting up with a cup in his hand. He gave me a smile, then held the cup out to me. "I saw that you'd dropped yours and made up a new one."

"Oh my god," I said as I nearly snatched the cup from him. I took a big, scalding gulp and sighed in relief. "You are the perfect man!"

David laughed. "And you're quite easily impressed!" He gave me a wink and then headed back across the street to the coffee shop.

Tracy smiled. "The perfect man is one who brings you coffee? Makes me wonder how the men in your life usually treat you."

Men? Or demonic lords? I tried to cover my reaction

by taking another sip, but he took note of my sudden reticence and grimaced.

"I'm sorry," he said. "That's none of my business, and it was a dumb thing to say."

"No, no!" I hurried to reassure him. "It's all right." I made myself chuckle. "I'm not really the 'shower with gifts' kind of chick, and that's fine with me."

"Well, it looks like I get to write the report for this nonsense." He lifted his chin toward the two vehicles.

I peered into the open door of the woman's car. It looked like she'd recently had it detailed. There were vacuum marks on the passenger side carpet, and the dashboard had a slight sheen of Armor All. An air freshener wafer tucked into the console sent the scent of chemical pineapple through the vehicle.

I spied a dark red Coach handbag on the floorboard, wedged under the dash. "Her purse is here." I set my coffee on the roof of the car, and snagged it out. "Least I can do is help you inventory all this."

"Appreciated," he said.

After this I'd need to make some phone calls to my rank to see if I could score another car. I scowled as I dug through the woman's purse. Would I even be able to get a new one issued on a Sunday? I was most likely screwed until Monday.

I found the woman's wallet and removed the drivers license. "Her name is Evelyn Stark, and her address is. . . ." I trailed off. *Son of a bitch.*

"Kara?" I glanced up to see Tracy with his pen poised above his notepad and a frown on his face. I passed the driver's license over to him, fighting hard to maintain something resembling composure.

"Sorry," I managed "I know her. Knew her. I mean . . .
I knew who she was."

His brow furrowed in concern. "Friend of yours?"

I shook my head, chilled to the bone despite my coat.
"No." I took an unsteady breath. "No. Not at all. She's
the drunk driver who killed my dad."

# Chapter 4

I headed back over to the coffee shop after Tracy assured me he could handle the rest of the report just fine. I made a token protest, but he must have seen how dazed I felt and gently told me to get the fuck off his scene. The sun was making another valiant effort to break through the clouds, and the wind had died down a bit. Traffic had picked up some, and I paused at the street, waiting for a break. A silent ambulance went by. I knew it probably wasn't the same one that had taken Evelyn Stark away, but I watched it continue on down the street.

Would I have given her CPR if I'd known who she was?

*No.* I let out a shaking breath. *I'm not that good a person.* I couldn't get back at the ovarian cancer that had taken my mother from me when I was only eight, but I could sure as hell focus plenty of rage and grief on the woman who'd taken my dad three years later. When I first began learning about demons, I'd asked Aunt Tessa to send a demon after Evelyn Stark. Tessa utterly refused to aid me—not saying that such a desire was wrong but, instead, explaining how that sort of arrangement with a demon would be fraught with all sorts of peril because of their complex code of honor. Besides, she pointed out, the woman was serving a prison sentence, and it would be quite a tricky matter for a demon to get *to* her.

But the simple fact that my aunt had understood my pain and not dismissed my desire for revenge as petty or wrong had endeared her to me more than anything else ever could have. And by the time I became a summoner in my own right, and could potentially carry through with such a desire, my lust for that sort of revenge had faded.

But, no, I wouldn't have given Evelyn Stark CPR and gotten my hands all bloody.

The ambulance turned the corner. I shook myself out of the grim memories and made myself face the other thought clanging around in my head. *Barry Landrieu and Evelyn Stark died on the same day, both with nosebleeds.* I knew there was a connection between them, but I had no idea why anyone besides me would want to kill them. Hell, even I hadn't wanted them dead. Not anymore, at least.

I started to turn back toward the street, but movement on the roof of the PD building pulled my attention. Had the shadow of the AC unit moved? I held my breath, watching the shadow as my pulse thudded unsteadily. That was the *graa's* leaping-off perch this morning. Could there be another?

After a few seconds I let my breath out. No. Just my eyes playing tricks, and my paranoia working double-time. The sun was losing its battle again; the moving shadow had probably been a cloud.

A chill walked down my back, and I forced myself to look away. Too much weird shit in one day was making me jumpy as hell. I glanced back to see if Tracy was looking at me, but he was peering through the windshield of the Camry in an effort to get the VIN. Quickly shifting into othersight, I extended my senses as far as possible, but nothing untoward leaped out at me. No sign of any demon. No whisper of arcane power. Only the unfinished chain of sigils snaking around the PD building.

Letting out an unsteady breath, I hurried across the street and into the coffee shop. A table near the window gave me a good view of the PD and the parking lot. The coffee in my cup was still plenty warm, and I took a good long slug as I scanned the area. Nothing seemed out of place—other than the car that had attempted to intersect mine.

Still unsettled, I pulled out my phone and commenced with the various calls I needed to make. First was to my sergeant, Cory Crawford, to let him know that I was—again—in need of a new vehicle, though at least there was a possibility that my current one was fixable. My last car had gone into the Kreeger River when I'd been shoved off a bridge by a soul-stealing psychopath. My life was seldom dull.

I was getting ready to call Eilahn when I saw her pull in front of the coffee shop on her motorcycle. It was actually my aunt's bike, but she hadn't ridden it in months and was quite willing to allow Eilahn to use it—a relief to me since Tessa didn't have a motorcycle endorsement on her license. Neither did Eilahn, for that matter, but since all of the demon's identification were forgeries, it was a bit of a moot point. Besides, since Eilahn was in human form, she needed a way to get around, and the motorcycle gave her the most flexibility.

Eilahn parked the bike, pulled off her helmet and shook her hair out in a perfect imitation of a shampoo commercial. Sometimes I wondered if she did the drop-dead gorgeous thing just to annoy me. The level of conversation in the café dipped briefly as she strode in—wearing leather jacket and boots and holding a motorcycle helmet in her hand. Because, y'know, she didn't look like enough of a hot chick already.

She dropped smoothly into the chair across from me and set the helmet on the floor by her feet. "Something's wrong," I said, then glanced around to make sure there was no one close enough to hear what we were saying. Eilahn gave a slight smile, then traced a small glyph in the center of the table. Curious, I took a quick peek in othersight. It held a dull glow, but it didn't seem to be doing anything. It certainly wasn't a protective ward—at least not any kind that I'd seen before.

"Discourages eavesdroppers," she explained. "You and I can hear and understand each other fine, but anyone else will hear only mumbles, or snatches of phrases that make little sense."

"That is too cool," I breathed, staring at the glyph as I tried to memorize how she'd created it.

A faint flicker of pride crossed her face. "I will teach it to you later, if you wish. But for now we are free to discuss . . . matters."

I sipped my coffee as I tried to gather my thoughts. "There's a connection between the victim out at the nature center and the woman who ran into my car."

"I assume you mean more than the nosebleeds before their deaths?"

I let out a slow breath. "Yes. So I guess that means she didn't make it."

"She was dead before you could even lay hands upon her."

I didn't feel any elation or relief at the knowledge. I was more pleased that since she'd been taken to the hospital, and it wasn't a homicide, I didn't have to investigate her death. That was for the hospital and the Coroner's Office now.

"What killed her?" I asked.

"That I do not know," she replied. "I sensed the freeing of the essence, but I cannot tell the cause."

"I knew both of the victims."

She tilted her head, eyes on me. "You do not seem grieved at the passing of either."

"Probably because I'm not," I replied. I sat back and tunneled both hands through my hair. "Fuck. Barry Landrieu gave me heroin when I was fourteen, and I came within inches of dying of an overdose. And Evelyn Stark," I cocked my head toward the window and the view of the aftermath of the accident, "was driving drunk when she crossed the center line on Serenity Road and killed my dad."

Her eyes darkened with sympathy. "You were not in the car?"

I shook my head. "My dad got a call from a client who needed some papers notarized. He was a lawyer," I explained. "He knew he was only going to be a few minutes, so he left me at home while he went to meet the guy. . . ." I'd been so pleased that he thought that, at the ripe age of eleven, I was old enough to stay home by myself. When he still hadn't come home after two hours, I'd been worried sick and terrified to call the police because I thought I'd be getting him into trouble. It had been another hour before the knock on the door came.

"And then your aunt had the care of you," Eilahn murmured. "Which is how you learned to summon."

"Yep." I took another sip of coffee to give me a few more seconds to push the unpleasant memories back. "Not the way I would have planned it, given a choice."

"A tragic path indeed," she agreed, brow faintly furrowed. Then she spread her hands on the table and looked out the window. "And now these two people who did you harm both die on the day a demon attacked you."

"Oh, and I used to date the witness who found the first body," I added.

"Interesting."

I let out a small bark of laughter. "That's one word for it. I was thinking of a description more along the lines of 'fucking shit damn it all to hell this is a confusing mess plus it means there's another summoner who's trying to fuck my life up.'" The last time I'd been looking for another summoner had been during my investigation of the Symbol Man murders, and that case had not exactly been wrapped up nice and neatly. Sure, the Symbol Man had been stopped, but I'd ended up dead for a while, and my aunt had ended up in an arcane coma that had taken me weeks to get her out of.

Her full lips twitched. "'Interesting' is more concise."

"Stick with me a few more weeks, and I'll have you

cursing like a pro." Then I made a face. "Do you know of an easy way to find a summoner?" I asked, looking over at her with undisguised hope. "Are there any demons who can, um, sniff them out or something?"

She raised one dark eyebrow at me as amusement flashed in her eyes. "No."

I couldn't help but smile at her firm answer, even though it dashed my briefly shining hopes. "Okay," I pressed, "is there a way to ask other demons who's been summoning them?"

She pursed her lips, appearing to seriously consider the question. "In theory, yes, but in practice, it is nigh impossible," she said. "The demons are divided into numerous factions. It is a constantly shifting dynamic, affected by a number of factors, including which lord they serve. Simply answering a question would require payment on your part."

I winced at that. Summoning a demon wasn't like calling forth a genie who'd be at your beck and call no matter what the request. A summoning was a contest and a contract—first to show you were worthy to even call the demon by the level of skill used to create the portal and maintain the protections, and then to negotiate the terms of whatever service the summoner desired of the demon. Everything had a price and failure to abide by the terms—for either party—was a terrible breach of honor. If the summoner was the erring party, they usually ended up dead. There were no bad demons—only poorly worded contracts.

"So, I guess there aren't too many pollsters in the demon realm," I said glumly.

A smile curved her lips. "It is possible that you could

pose the question and accept free response. However, that has its own drawback."

"I might tip off this summoner that I'm looking for him or her."

"Precisely."

I let out a sigh. I didn't know of any other summoners in the area, but that didn't mean there weren't any. As far as I knew there were only a few hundred in the world, but even that was simply a slightly educated guess. We tended to be pretty private about our activities, for obvious reasons.

"Maybe the presence of the demon had nothing to do with the two deaths." I paused in consideration. "Maybe it's all a giant coincidence."

"I doubt that," Eilahn said, and I had to chuckle. She wasn't the type to snow me with pointless reassurances or allow me to wallow in comfortable delusions. Usually that was a good thing. But there were times when I could have used some pointless reassurances and some delusion-wallowing. "If it had wanted to kill you," she added, "it likely would have been a harder fight."

So why the fuck hadn't it? My arm still ached like a bitch where the damn thing had grabbed me. Had it been trying to do something else? Something Eilahn had managed to thwart? I had to fight the urge to thunk my head down onto the table. Fortunately the pinging of my phone signaling a text message distracted me from thoughts of self-injury. I read it with a growing sense of relief. "Ha! Since I'm on call Sarge is arranging for me to get another car." It would probably be a total pile of crap, but it would be a pile of crap for which I didn't have to pay a note or gas or insurance.

I stood and drained the last of my coffee. "I'm going to walk down to the motor pool and get my new wheels," I told Eilahn.

"I will walk with you," she said. "Too much is happening. I am unsettled."

That was the first time I'd ever heard the demon admit to anything less than total confidence. There went the last of my comfortable delusions.

# Chapter 5

The motor pool for the Beaulac PD was only a few blocks away. Well within walking distance. We'd barely made it past the PD building when we heard an eager shout from behind us.

"Kara! Ellen!"

We turned to see Officer Tim Daniels trotting up, wearing a grin that stretched from ear to ear. "I found her!"

I looked at him blankly. "Found who?"

"Fuzzykins!" His grin widened, if that was even possible. "Wait right here! She's in my car."

He took off at a jog. I felt rooted to the spot. "Okay," I said. "You get to break his heart and tell him it's the wrong cat."

The demon snorted. "The fuck I will."

I had to laugh. She was a fast learner.

Less than a minute later Tim returned, using both hands to carry a large cat carrier. A low throbbing growl began to emanate from it as he approached. "I had to come back by the station to fix my timecard," he said, breathless and exuberant. "And I was real worried about her being out in this cold and snow, so I tried to think like a cat. Like, where would I go to be warm, y'know?" He set the carrier down. The growl changed pitch briefly, and I could see some sort of creature shifting within. "Then I remembered what you said about the turkey, and so I said to myself, 'Self, if you were a cat who liked turkey and wanted a warm place, you'd probably end up over by Kelly's Deli.'"

"Um." I swallowed and tried again. "Are you sure it's the right cat?"

Chuckling, he crouched and peered inside the container. "Great big calico Manx, right? And it's a female. I checked, just to be sure, even though male calicos are pretty darn rare."

"You're kidding," I blurted, staring at him. No way he'd found a cat matching my random description. I didn't even dare look at Eilahn.

He gave an earnest nod. "It's true! It's a genetic thing with the way the X-chromosomes carry the coat color." He shrugged, ducked his head almost shyly. "I like biology."

I decided not to clarify what I thought he was kidding about. Slowly I lowered myself to peer into the carrier. I saw plenty of teeth and narrow-slitted eyes as it hissed and spat. But beyond that I could see calico fur. Nor was there any sign of a tail.

"That's Fuzzykins, right?" He was so damn proud of himself. And I could hardly blame him. And what the hell was I supposed to say? It was the goddamn cat I'd described. This was getting ridiculous. Just how many co-incidences was I going to encounter today? I could only hope to hell that most of these events truly were pure happenstance. Or maybe I simply needed to go back to bed and start this day over.

"Yes," I heard myself saying. "That's Fuzzykins." I mustered a weak smile. "That's a good Fuzzykins. Good kitty."

Fuzzykins gave me a *fuck you* glare accompanied by a I-want-to-claw-your-face-off hiss. I quickly stood. "Um . . . she must be traumatized from her time on the street." Great. A feral fucking cat. What the hell was I supposed to do with this thing?

Eilahn crouched and peered into the carrier. To my shock the growl stopped and the cat gave a perfectly normal *mrow?* The demon smiled and stuck her fingers between the wires of the carrier door. I wasn't worried about her fingers getting bitten off—not with demon-fast reflexes, but apparently Eilahn didn't have to worry about that. The damn creature rubbed her cheek against Eilahn's fingers and started up a purr that shook the carrier.

Eilahn turned her gaze up to me—no longer the confident, kickass demon, but this time a hopeful eager child with a "can I keep it, pleeeeeeease?" expression on her face. I blinked in surprise. This was a side of her I'd never seen before. I hoped she didn't want to eat it.

I resisted the urge to sigh and instead forced a smile. "You rock, Tim. Thanks for finding her for me."

Super. My demon had a cat. Because my life wasn't strange enough already.

I had to bite my lip to keep from grinning at the exuberant joy Eilahn took in the cat as we walked to the motor pool. Every hundred feet or so she set the carrier down so she could coo at the creature and let it rub against her fingers.

And the questions. Good grief, the questions.

"Is the food that Tim obtained of sufficient quality?"

"We will need to acquire a cat box, yes? What is the proper litter to be used?"

"Veterinary care! I must make an appointment for inoculation. That is how it works, yes?"

"Catnip. Felines require catnip, I have heard."

At least she wasn't asking about recipes for kitty gumbo.

We finally made it to the motor pool, and I asked her, "How do you know so much about cats?" On the one hand she seemed incredibly wise and knowledgeable, but on the other she was like a nine-year-old.

"I have read about them," she said, her brow drawn down into a slightly puzzled frown as if to say, *How else would I know about them?*

I masked a smile and proceeded to deal with the various paperwork I had to fill out to take possession of the replacement vehicle. Once that was done there was a bit of a delay while the demon fretted over the best configuration for transporting the damn cat.

"I do not wish her to grow upset," Eilahn said, frown puckering her forehead. "I have heard that cats do not care to ride in cars. If I am in the front and she in the back, will she not grow distraught? Perhaps I should hold her in my lap."

"Um, that's a pretty darn big carrier to hold on your lap," I pointed out.

She blinked. "I did not intend to have her in the carrier. Why can I not simply hold her in my lap so that I can stroke her fur? Will that not calm her?"

I had a vision of a psychotic cat careening around the inside of the car—followed by an image of my mangled death in the ensuing wreck.

"No," I stated. Firmly. "The cat stays in the carrier while she's in the car." For an instant I thought the Eilahn was actually going to pout. "It's safer for the cat," I added. At that she gave a reserved nod.

"Then I will sit in the back seat," she said. "And I will turn the carrier so that I can reassure her." She nodded to herself again, clearly pleased with her solution.

I had to smile. "If you want we could stop by the store on the way home and pick up some supplies. I mean, it'd probably be easiest to do that now."

The smile that spread across her face was radiant. "You truly do not mind the addition of a feline pet to your household?"

I shrugged. "I'm cool with it." Hell, I wasn't a hundred percent on board with the concept, but it sure seemed to make Eilahn happy. It felt kind of nice to be able to pay her back somehow.

We made it home without any more incidents, other than shoving my credit card balance a bit higher. Eilahn had insisted on bringing Fuzzykins into the store, though again, I had to put my foot down and insist that the cat stay in the carrier. I had no doubt that if Eilahn had her way, the cat would be riding on her shoulders. The demon had looked longingly at an outrageously priced "Kitty Kondo"—a carpet-covered monstrosity for cats to supposedly play and lounge upon—but Eilahn seemed to understand that such a thing would be pretty far outside of my budget. I was stretching my finances already with the amount of stuff we had to get.

Eilahn nearly skipped up to the porch with the carrier and wasted no time opening it up and gathering the enormous cat into her arms. I unloaded the majority of the cat supplies onto the steps, then moved to give the cat a pet. It gave me a foul glare and hiss, then turned and bumped her head against the demon's chin. Eilahn gave a delighted laugh and sat down with her, utterly entranced as the cat twined around her and rubbed against her, purring madly.

I shook my head in bemusement. "I think we bought a brush," I told Eilahn. "She probably likes being brushed."

The demon gave a delighted cry and dug through the bags. As soon as she located the brush she fell upon the cat with it like a master groomer. I only *thought* the cat had been purring loudly before.

"I'm going to get the mail," I told her. She gave an absent nod of acknowledgement and continued showering affection onto the cat. I grinned as I turned and started the hike to my mailbox.

My driveway was long and winding—a slog of well over a quarter mile. It opened up into a broad area in front of the house that could conceivably hold half a dozen cars but had probably never held more than three at any one time. I wasn't exactly known for throwing wild parties at my place. I lived in a single-story Acadian-style house that sat in the middle of ten acres of woods and on enough of a hill to allow me to have a basement. It couldn't be seen from the highway, and I liked it that way, since my "hobby" of summoning big, scary, supernatural creatures probably wouldn't go over too well with the Bible-belt mentality of south Louisiana.

I'd had new gravel put down the week before, which made the trek to the highway more challenging since it was like walking in shifting sand. I was usually a lazy-butt and drove to the mailbox, but I knew if I did that I'd earn an intensely withering look from the demon. Plus, she'd probably make me run ten times the distance in penance.

A chill wind wrapped around me, bringing with it the tang of pine and damp. Tugging my gloves back on, I cast a look up at a sky that had gone from light grey to dark and yucky in the past hour. The tops of the pines that surrounded my house swayed with a rising wind accompanied by a rush of sound like a distant roaring crowd. I didn't have to check the weather forecast to know that more snow or other nastiness was on its way. This would be a fine day to stay inside and do energetic things like sit on my ass and catch up on TV.

The air went still when I was about a hundred yards from the house. The crunch of the gravel beneath my feet seemed to shout out into the sudden silence, and I slowed. Looking up again, I frowned as I saw that the trees had gone utterly still. *That's odd. Even if the wind died surely they'd still be swaying a bit—*

An icy wind slammed into me before I could finish the thought, nearly buffeting me off my feet. I continued to stare stupidly at the trees. *Still as stone. Why aren't they moving?*

"Kara!" Eilahn's shout yanked me out of my absorption. I swiveled my head to see her running hard toward me, arms and legs pumping like a cheetah on steroids. "Run!" she yelled.

That wind. *Oh fuck.* Realization and horror slammed into me, and I dug my feet in and started sprinting for the house. Now I could feel the arcane menace in the unnaturally cold wind. I'd felt that before. I needed to get behind the safety of the wards *now.*

The house wasn't all that far away, but running in the fresh gravel was a nightmare of uneven footing and shifting purchase. I briefly debated running along the side of the driveway but quickly abandoned that idea. There were so many sticks and pine cones and who-the-hell-knew-what-else that I'd be more likely to trip. Eilahn was still running all-out toward me, and I kept my focus on her as my lungs began to burn. I was a reluctant runner at the best of times, and speed had never been my strong suit.

But right now I could feel the lick of the arcane at my heels as it reached for me, and it spurred me like nothing else ever could. This was a summoning—of me. And I knew without a doubt that if it succeeded, I was well and truly fucked.

Eilahn reached me and spun in a move that no human could ever duplicate, managing to grab me and throw me over her shoulders at the same time. I let out a shocked *Oof!* but I didn't resist. Right now I didn't give a shit that I was in an exceedingly ignominious position. The pull seemed to be clawing at my essence and I could see the portal forming behind Eilahn—a slit in the fabric of the world surrounded by a greedy vortex of power. Tendrils of power began to snake out from the portal, gaining substance with every second, like tentacles in the maw of a kraken. The air seemed to shriek in protest, groaning like a building on fire. I tasted sulfur and ozone. I'd seen hundreds of portals, but I'd always been on the calling end. It looked a lot different from the you're-coming-with-me-now end, and I didn't like it one bit.

A tongue of energy whipped out and snaked around one wrist, and I let loose a girly yelp of horror, shaking my wrist to try and shed it. But this wasn't a physical thing that could be dislodged. "Eilahn!" I shrieked. "It has me!"

Yet even as the words left my mouth Eilahn performed another inhuman move—somehow twisting and pulling me off her shoulders and launching me into the air.

My girly shriek shifted to a shocked scream as I hurtled through the air in a collision course with the porch of my house. I had barely enough time to remember to tuck my limbs in, and then I was through the wards and crashing into an ungainly, rolling tumble onto the porch.

I came to a stop and gasped for breath, distantly aware that several parts of my body hurt, but far more viscerally aware that the horrible pull was gone. A heartbeat later Eilahn gave a magnificent bound and landed in a crouch beside me. I shot a worried glance down the driveway, only to see that the tendrils had pulled back into the portal, and it was already beginning to spiral closed. Within three heartbeats it was gone, blinking out of existence with a *pop* that I felt more than heard.

"Are you hurt?" Eilahn asked, worry darkening her eyes. "Forgive me for throwing you. I could think of no other way to get you within the wards in time. Another few heartbeats and the portal's hold would have been too strong to break."

"S'okay," I managed to croak. "Rather be broken than summoned."

Eilahn's lips pressed together as she ran her hands over me. A moment later some of the concern in her face cleared, and she sat back on her heels. "Nothing appears to be broken, though you will be bruised." Then a whisper of a smile touched her lips. "It is good that I have been teaching you to fall, yes?"

I let out a strangled noise and cautiously pushed myself up to a sitting position, absurdly glad that the rocking chairs I'd purchased a few weeks ago with the grand intention of creating a "picturesque" front porch were still sitting in the shed out behind the house waiting to be assembled and painted. Being thrown into those would have sucked the big one. Who the hell was I trying to be picturesque for anyway? No one ever came to my house, and that was usually more than fine with me.

"You have no idea how much it kills me to admit this," I said, "but, yeah. That whole tuck and roll crap paid off." Oh, the joy of being thrown to the ground by a demon. Over and over and over.

The demon chuckled low in her throat. "Your praise brings me great joy." Then she suddenly turned with a cry of dismay and scooped the cat up from the steps. As I watched, she cradled it to her chest, murmuring in an unfamiliar language, though I was pretty sure she was saying the demon equivalent of, *"Oh, my poor widdle fuzzywuzzykins! Were you scared by that silly flying lady? You poor baby. Mommy will protect you and make it all better! Oh yes, she will!"*

After a few seconds of reassurance she set the cat

down, then turned to gaze down the driveway, a mixture of unease and anger in her expression. "The danger to you grows. Yet I am not convinced this attempt is connected to the attack from earlier this morning."

"It's fucked up, no matter what," I said, leaning back against my house. This was the fourth time I'd barely escaped being summoned. Two weeks ago I'd been walking to my car after getting groceries when I'd felt that blast of icy wind. Eilahn had appeared out of nowhere, tossed me into the backseat of my car, and taken off like a bat out of hell—leaving behind a grocery cart filled with a week's worth of food. "Am I wrong, or does it seem like whoever's doing this is getting better at it? I used to be able to just run away from it. This one felt like it was right on top of me no matter what."

She turned to me, worry darkening her eyes. "You are not wrong. With each attempt they refine the summoning. I do not think it will be possible to simply run from them anymore. It would not have worked this time, save that I was able to quickly get you within strong wards. Soon it will take only seconds to lock onto you and bring you through."

The words were like a punch in the gut. "So, basically, if I step outside the safety of wards, I risk being summoned?" I heard the anger in my voice, and I hoped she knew it wasn't directed at her.

Eilahn shook her head. "No, they will not be able to attempt another summoning for a while. It is not a constant threat."

"Define 'a while.'"

"A dozen hours at least."

I pinched the bridge of my nose. "Okay, that's not the

cheery news it could have been. I was really hoping for several *days* at the very minimum. Or years."

Eilahn's expression remained grave. "I truly wish I had more encouraging news for you. But it is not a completely hopeless situation. The house is warded, and I will complete the warding on your place of work tonight." She reached down and helped me to my feet. I was glad of the assistance as I discovered all the places that were going to have impressive bruises by tomorrow. "There are also other . . . options," she said.

"Such as?"

She released me as soon as she was certain I wasn't going to topple right back over. "There may be certain physical artifacts that can aid in shielding you. Plus, you can continue to work on the mental exercises I showed you."

I made a face as I hobbled my way inside and down the hall to the kitchen. "Those are more unpleasant than your lessons in falling." Eilahn had been trying to teach me a way to turn my *othersight* inward in order to cloak my arcane signature, but all I'd managed to do so far was give myself spectacular headaches. It was like the "imagine a white wall" trick to the nth degree, and I had a feeling it was something that came far more easily to demon minds than my own.

"I will attempt to locate an artifact," Eilahn said. "But the best hope is that Lord Rhyzkahl will be able to determine who is seeking to interfere."

*Interfere.* That was a nice way of putting it. Someone in the demon realm was attempting to summon me—bring me through in the same way that I was able to summon the creatures native to that world. The scary part—for me at least—was that if I were to be successfully summoned, the summoner would most assuredly be powerful enough to bind me to his will, make me a slave. If I wasn't simply killed outright, that is.

I really had no idea whether the ultimate goal was to kill me or not. *And why did the* graa *attack me? What was its goal?*

I sank into a chair at the kitchen table and clasped my hands together in my lap to hide the fact that they were shaking slightly. Not sure why I was bothering, since the *syraza* was definitely perceptive enough to see how off-kilter I was. She placed a mug of coffee in front of me, confirming my suspicion that she was well aware of my mental state. I gave her a weak smile of thanks and wrapped my hands around the mug, exhaling in relief as I took a sip of the most wonderful substance known to mankind. No wonder I hadn't been able to run faster. I'd been practically uncaffeinated. I shouldn't be expected to function on only one cup of coffee.

"I hate this," I confessed. Eilahn tilted her head and frowned. "Not the coffee," I quickly amended. "It's perfect. I hate this whole stress and worry and always waiting for some sort of attack. I mean, I know I'm not the toughest chick on the planet, and I'm not some sort of supercop . . . but I *am* a cop, and I've survived a lot of shit, and I really fucking hate this constant nagging fear that I have going on." I scowled down into my coffee. "It sucks, and I don't know what the hell to do about it."

"You are due to summon Lord Rhyzkahl within the next week," she replied quietly. "I suggest you do so tonight, since the moon is full. He needs to know about this latest attempt."

My scowl deepened. "Yeah, well I hate that too—the

whole waiting-to-be-rescued crap. I'm not some weak-kneed damsel in distress."

Eilahn gave a low laugh. "No one who knows you would ever accuse you of being weak in any way." She stood and turned to the counter while I blinked in surprise at the compliment. "But I do understand your sentiment and why it chafes." She shot me a glance over her shoulder. "Perhaps some comfort food is in order. I can make a late breakfast if you wish."

I grinned despite my mood. "You've only been with me for a month and a half, and you already know me way too well. I could definitely do with some comfort food right about now."

The sound of gravel crunching under tires pulled my attention. Reaching out mentally to the wards, I couldn't sense a direct threat, but someone was definitely attempting to come down the driveway and failing. I glanced at Eilahn. She seemed studiously unconcerned which gave me a pretty good idea of who was attempting to get near the house.

Pushing up from the table, I winced at how much I'd managed to stiffen up in such a short time. I hobbled down the hall and grabbed my coat, pulling open the door to see a dark blue Crown Victoria backing up. I closed the door behind me and watched as it backed up to the first curve, then stopped and came forward again. At about fifty feet from the house the car stopped again and began to back up. Laughing, I made my way down the steps and waved my arms to get the attention of the driver. A second later the car stopped again and Special Agent Ryan Kristoff stepped out, sweeping an annoyed and frustrated glare over the house and the environs.

He didn't look any different. He still carried himself like a federal agent. His hair was perhaps a bit shorter than normal, in a brush cut that couldn't quite hide the fact that it tended to curl when it got longer. He had on his usual casual attire of khaki pants and oxford shirt, and the black pea coat he wore over them couldn't hide the broad shoulders that tapered down to a slim and muscled waistline. But I knew he *was* different. At least, different from what I'd assumed him to be for so long. It felt odd that he looked the same as always.

A sharp and icy breeze dove down my collar, and I quickly zipped my coat up.

"What the hell have you done to your house?" Ryan demanded.

I stared at him then burst out laughing. This, at least, was the same old Ryan. Moody, mercurial, and charming. "Having some trouble?"

He glowered at me, but a hint of a smile played at the corners of his mouth. "I can't get to your damn house! Did you do something to the wards? I have this over-powering urge to go run some errands first." He peered at the house, and I had a feeling he was using his own othersight to check out the protections. Ryan had the ability to see and sense arcane power, though as far as he was aware he simply had limited skills that he'd inherited from his grandmother. Of course I knew his true skills were anything but limited, though I had to wonder why he'd been left with any power at all when his memories and abilities had been stripped from him. *Maybe it's impossible to completely shut it down*, I mused. *Maybe throttling his power down to idle was the only option.*

"Yep, Eilahn tightened everything up and tweaked the aversions," I said. Aversions were specialized protections that simply reduced or altered a person's desire to cross a particular boundary. They could be overcome if a person had a stronger-than-usual will to get past them, but they effectively deterred most intruders. "Just keep your eyes on me as you drive up and don't think about the house," I told him.

He gave a curt nod then smiled. "It's good to see you."

"You too," I said, probably more fervently than I meant to. Our eyes met, and for an instant I forgot about the cold and the drifting flakes.

Only for an instant, though, because another breeze swirled snow into my eyes. "Arggh! Yes, good to see you, but I'm freezing my ass off in this *fucking* snow. Just keep your eyes on me!" I retreated to the porch without waiting for a response, though his laugh followed me. He got back into his car and slowly drove toward me as I motioned him forward, feeling a little like the people who direct planes on runways.

As I watched, the tension in his face gradually cleared, and a few seconds later he stopped in front of the house and got out of his car.

"It won't be so hard next time," I told him. "The wards will figure out that you're welcome here and should adjust."

He trotted up the stairs to me. "Nice to know I'm welcome."

"Well, how are you supposed to stalk me if you can't get to the house?" I said with a wink. I yanked the door open and ducked inside, closing it as soon as he was all the way in. "Oh, and by the way, this weather sucks ass."

He laughed. "I've been seeing far too much of this up north. I was really hoping to avoid snow down here."

"So it's your fault," I retorted.

"Apparently so. By the way, that coat looks great on you." He swept an approving gaze over me. "Is it new?"

"Bought it today," I said, giving a spin to show it off before slipping said coat off. "Wearing it is the only thing that makes this weather even remotely worthwhile."

"You look tough in it," he said. "I figured you'd be wearing that god-awful Members Only jacket of yours."

"Don't make me regret letting you through the wards!" I warned. "That jacket has a special place in my heart."

"It belongs in a special place in the eighties!" He laughed and pulled me into a hug, and I let myself relax into it. We were already back to our usual banter, the old patterns of behavior.

*This can work if I just don't think too much about it. Right?* Because I couldn't tell Ryan what I knew about him. Zack had made that clear. Ryan's memories and abilities had been blocked for a reason and what little I'd been able to pry out of Zack had been enough to convince me that Ryan was safer not knowing.

But that didn't mean I had to stop looking for the truth.

I pulled back, then punched him hard in the chest. "Why didn't you call? Or text? Or email? Or anything?" I demanded.

He grimaced and made a show of rubbing his chest, but I knew that the flicker of pain I saw flash across his face had nothing to do with my punch. "I'm sorry. I'm a dick. I just. . . ." He faltered.

"Don't do it again," I said, relenting. "Okay?"

Relief shimmered in his eyes. "Okay. I promise."

On impulse I gave him another hug, and this time I could feel that some of the tension had left him.

"Come on," I said, turning to head down the hallway. "Eilahn said something earlier about a very late breakfast."

"Do I dare eat her cooking?" he replied as he followed me. He knew Eilahn was a demon. He also knew the demons didn't like him, though he said he had no idea why. For that matter, neither did I, other than that they called him a *kiraknikahl*, or oathbreaker. Though it didn't take a genius to figure out that it probably had something to do with my theory that he was an exiled demonic lord.

"She knows you're a friend and off-limits as far as any sort of permanent damage is concerned. I think the worst she might do is hock a loogie into your omelet," I said as seriously as I could manage.

I snickered as I heard him groan. "You're evil," he muttered.

Eilahn was already at the kitchen counter and pouring batter onto a waffle iron. I had no doubt that she'd been completely aware of Ryan's presence in the driveway and of our conversation in the foyer. I wasn't at all surprised that she hadn't allowed him inside the protections. She kept her hostility in check at my request, but it was definitely still there. *And what the hell could a demonic lord do to deserve exile?* I wondered for the millionth time. *What oath did he break?*

And how much of a fool was I being by continuing to associate with him? The lords were dangerous, and Ryan clearly had enemies. *But I can't simply abandon him*, I thought with a touch of defiance. *He's still my friend, damn it. At least until I have a damn good reason to feel otherwise.*

The *syraza* gave Ryan a slight nod as he entered the kitchen. "Good afternoon, Ryan," she said, tone not *quite* chilly. "Will you be joining us for a late breakfast?"

He smiled broadly and plopped down at the table. "Why yes, I believe I shall, and thank you for the invite!"

"*I* did not invite you," she replied before returning her attention to the waffle iron. I winced at the reply, but Ryan merely smiled wider. Great, it was going to be like this.

I headed toward the coffeemaker. Thankfully, she had also made coffee. "I didn't know I had a waffle iron."

"You did," Eilahn replied with a slight smile. "It was at the back of one of your cabinets. Still in the box."

I wasn't terribly surprised. I went through phases where I was convinced I was going to learn how to cook, or at least learn how to make cool things like waffles or margaritas. Those phases usually passed quickly, and the related appliance ended up forgotten somewhere. In contrast, in the relatively short time she had been living with me, I'd discovered that Eilahn was an enthusiastic and skilled gourmet. I had no idea if she'd already possessed these skills, or if she picked them up while here, but I wasn't about to complain. I'd never eaten so well in my life.

*I need to figure out some way to give her an allowance or something.* I almost asked her if she needed funds then stopped myself. This wasn't something I wanted to get into with Ryan around.

I busied myself with getting my coffee the way I liked it and poured a mug for Ryan as well. Ryan knew who and what Eilahn was and knew about her role here as my protector. But I felt strangely protective toward her—which wasn't logical in many ways, since she was the badass demon.

*But the demons hate him for a reason. And even if he doesn't remember or realize it, he's pretty damn powerful.* I couldn't . . . *wouldn't* risk Eilahn if I could at all help it. No matter how much I cared about Ryan.

*I do care about Ryan,* I told myself as I handed him his mug. He met my eyes and smiled as he took it from me, his fingers briefly brushing mine. I returned the smile but I couldn't fight back the uncertainty. *I care about Ryan . . . the Ryan I knew. Who the fuck is this?*

I set my own coffee down on the table, then pulled the chair that faced the hallway out and around to exchange it with the chair across from Ryan. He gave me a puzzled look at my antics. "This chair wobbles," I explained with a lift of my chin toward the one I'd just switched out.

"So, why don't you sit somewhere else?" he asked with a lift of one eyebrow.

I plopped my butt down in the replacement chair. "Because I don't like sitting with my back to the hallway. It gives me the willies."

Amusement lit his eyes. "The willies?"

"The willies," I confirmed, with an accompanying sticking out of tongue. "Eilahn does *not* get the willies sitting there, so that is her usual seat. And you are actually in *my* usual seat, but I am being nice and not telling you to move." I smiled sweetly at him and took a sip of my coffee.

Ryan gave a chuckle. "Gotcha. It all makes perfect sense now."

Eilahn placed a waffle-laden plate in front of me, then removed a second large waffle from the iron, placed it on a plate and took her seat. She paused for a heartbeat, then looked to Ryan with a guileless expression. "I left the waffle iron on for you. There is more batter in the pitcher beside it."

"I think I need to complain to the management about the service here," he said as he pushed back his chair, but he gave me a wink as he headed to the counter.

*He's back less than an hour, and I can already see where the dynamic between them is going.* Demons or not, I was going to nip this shit in the bud.

"Just so the two of you know," I said, stabbing my fork into my waffle. "I'm really not into the whole passive-aggressive teasing back and forth bullshit that masks real antipathy, and that the parties involved think is oh-so amusing. Yeah, it's funny sometimes, but it kind of fucking stresses me out. So, Ryan, stop antagonizing Eilahn. And Eilahn, I don't expect you to serve him, me, or anyone else, but by human standards telling a guest in your house to cook their own meal is considered rude." I lifted my head to smile sweetly at them. "And now I'm going to eat my waffle."

Ryan had the grace to look chagrined. "Sorry, Kara."

Eilahn inclined her head. "I apologize as well."

"I have no problem making my own waffle," Ryan said. "Please go ahead and eat, Eilahn."

I didn't detect any trace of sarcasm and apparently neither did Eilahn, for she murmured thanks. I breathed a silent sigh of relief and dug into my comfort food.

\*     \*     \*

After we finished eating I told Eilahn I'd take care of cleaning up. She didn't put up an argument. She retreated outside, leaving Ryan and me alone in the kitchen. An awkward silence fell as I ran the water and waited for it to turn hot.

"Any new and interesting cases?" Ryan asked after a moment.

"Sort of," I said, dabbling my fingers under the running water. "Not a murder but something kind of strange." I quickly explained about the deaths of Barry Landrieu and Evelyn Stark and how I knew them. I wasn't about to share the details of my connection to the two victims with the entire Beaulac police department, but I trusted Ryan.

He leaned against the counter, crossed his arms over his chest, and frowned. "Coincidences make me twitchy."

"You and me both," I said. The water was still cold, so I shut it off. Grabbing a towel, I dried my hands as I walked down the hall to a utility closet. "My water heater's ancient," I explained as he followed me. "Sometimes I have to relight the pilot manually."

He wrinkled his nose in sympathy as I crouched and stuck the long lighter into the appropriate hole in the bottom of the tank. "It looks like you've done this a few times," he said.

I listened for the sound of the gas firing up, then stood and nodded. "It's on my list of things to replace when I can afford it," I said with a sigh, closing the closet door. I didn't bother returning to the kitchen, since I knew it would take a while for the water to warm up, and instead headed to the living room.

"There's more," I said as I plopped down into the armchair instead of my customary spot on the couch. Yes, I was a chickenshit, because what if he sat next to me? Then I might have to actually think about how I felt about him and whether his sitting next to me meant anything or nothing as far as his own feelings. And then I'd have to consider the fact that I suspected stuff about Ryan that I didn't dare share with him, as well as consider the possibility that this whole "Ryan" that I knew was a total sham anyway.

No, much better to sit in the armchair and give myself more time to try and figure all of this crap out.

He didn't seem to notice my hesitation over the seating arrangements and simply sat on the end of the couch closer to the chair. "More?" he frowned. "Tell me."

I did so, giving him a rundown of the *graa* attack as well as the summoning attempt.

"Fucking hell," he breathed after I finished. "So there's another summoner involved, there are two deaths that seem to be connected, and someone in the demon realm is still trying to summon you."

I nodded.

"Are any of these related to each other?" he asked.

I spread my hands and shrugged. "I have no fucking idea."

He gave a dry chuckle. "Is your life ever dull?"

I could only laugh. "Not in the ways that count!"

He reached for my hand and gave it a squeeze. "I have your back," he said. "In any way I can. You know that, right?"

The memory of the being who'd blasted the golem

with arcane power rose up. I could barely reconcile that creature and Ryan as the same person.

"I know that," I said. He released my hand and gave me a warm smile.

A quiet fell, undercut by the muted rush of the water heater. "Where'd you grow up?" I asked, feeling as if I was taking a hammer to the smooth glass of the silence. It sounded more abrupt than I'd intended. "I mean, you're not from the South, are you?"

A slight smile creased his mouth. "Depends. Are you going to call me a damn Yankee if I admit I was born in upstate New York?"

"Nothing so nice," I replied with a small laugh.

He folded one leg over the other, resting his ankle across his knee. "I guess I'll have to brave the insults then. Saratoga, New York. Went to high school at Saratoga Springs High then left for the bustle of the big city."

"New York City?"

He grinned. "Cleveland."

This time my laugh was genuine. "Oh, my. Culture shock!"

"In more ways than one."

I tucked my feet underneath me. "What about your folks. Do they still live in Saratoga?" I knew what the answer would be. Or rather, I knew what he needed to tell me.

He shook his head, a shadow flickering across his face. "My mother passed away right before I started college. My dad about five years later."

I made the appropriate sympathetic expression. He believed it. Surely nobody was that good an actor. "Any brothers or sisters?"

"Nope. I have some cousins I never see, but that's about it."

Hunh. I'd expected him to say that both his parents had been only children or some such thing. But maybe whatever caused him to have these fake memories also made him have no desire to seek out the rest of his mythical family.

*His memories are fake. They have to be. Is his personality fake as well? Is this the real Ryan? If he ever remembers who he is, will this person go away? Will he still regard me in the same way?*

I already knew the answer to that. There was no possible way he'd see me in the same light. Except . . . somehow he'd acted with the instincts and abilities of his former self when I was hurt and the golems were threatening. Were those instincts always running in the background? Or was that a one-time chink in the armor that held him? I could keep on grilling him about his past, but what was the point? I had zero doubt that if—no, *when*—I verified this info it would all check out. Whoever had taken the effort to insert this nuanced memory and background would have surely taken steps to make sure the paper trail jived as well.

Fuzzykins chose that moment to stalk into the room. She leaped nimbly onto the end of the couch and stared balefully at Ryan.

"When did you get a cat?" he asked. He reached out a hand to give the cat a scratch, then yanked it back as Fuzzykins snarled and swiped at it with a claws extended.

"It's Eilahn's." I quickly explained the circumstances surrounding the acquisition of the cat. "Don't feel bad. She hates me too. But she completely adores Eilahn."

"That's pretty funny," he admitted. Then, "Are you summoning tonight?"

I blinked, surprised both at the abruptness of the question and that he would want to know at all. He didn't like Rhyzkahl—okay, "hated" was probably a better word—and he didn't usually want any reminder that I had any sort of contact or relationship with the demonic lord.

My surprise must have been evident because he gave a little shrug of apology. "It's a full moon," he said. "I figured it'd be tonight—unless you already did for this month?"

I shook my head. "Not yet. I was planning to tonight." I eyed him, mentally bracing myself for his usual gritted-teeth tolerance that barely masked his dislike of the arrangement. I frowned when it didn't come. "You seem oddly cool with this."

He placed both feet on the floor and exhaled. "I did a lot of thinking while I was up at Quantico. I didn't like some of the things I realized."

"Such as?"

"Such as the fact that you're one of my best friends, the fact that I care about you considerably, and the fact that you're in a situation that I have no right to judge, and that I need to grow the fuck up and actually be supportive." He gave me a wry smile. "I realized that it's not enough for me to simply not be vocal about the fact that I hated what was going on, because you're not stupid, and you can certainly tell I disapprove whether I say it or not. But instead, I needed to change my damn outlook and accept what is and look for the positive in it. In other words, I need to stop being so much of a dick. That was kind of the reason I didn't call. I was trying to process everything."

I had to smile. "In other words, you were a dick because you were thinking about how to stop being a dick."

He chuckled. "Well, when you put it that way. . . ."

"It's okay," I said. "I appreciate it, no matter how it came about."

He put his hands on his knees and gave a nod, seeming relieved. "Okay, well, I should get out of your hair then, but how about we catch up tomorrow—I can bring over pizza and some DVDs of shows that I'm sure you've never seen but I think you should."

I groaned. "You're still trying to make me a nerd, aren't you?"

"No," he said with a dramatic sigh. "I think there's no hope of that. But it won't stop me from trying." He stood, and I followed suit. "So, tomorrow?"

I nodded. "It's a plan."

He smiled, gave me a close hug. I allowed myself to relax against him before we separated. For a brief instant I thought he was going to do something like kiss my forehead or cheek or something else that fell within the affection-between-friends boundary, but he merely smiled at me before turning and leaving.

I watched through the window as he drove off. We'd broken through a huge barrier in our relationship. He'd come to accept the presence of Rhyzkahl in my life. I could stop with the cycles of guilt and angst and all that.

Except that I felt as if it wasn't real. *Is this all part of the act? Am I just another facet of his cover?*

# Chapter 6

After Ryan left I made a glancing effort at cleaning the kitchen that extended to loading the dishwasher and nothing else. A nap followed shortly thereafter, and even though I'd only intended to sleep for a couple of hours, it was nearly ten p.m. when I woke.

There was a note on my bathroom mirror from Eilahn—written with a dry-erase marker in a flowing, elegant script—telling me that she was running some errands and that I was to stay inside. She never left my property without informing me first—not because she felt she had to report to me, but because she wanted to reassure me as to my safety, and to be sure I knew to stay within the wards.

I let out a small sigh of relief. This was the second time I'd summoned Rhyzkahl since she'd become my guardian, and I never knew whether she'd expect to be in the summoning chamber with me. But the last time I summoned she had errands as well, so apparently she was fine with making herself scarce. Not that I was worried about anything going wrong with the summoning itself because of her presence, but time with Rhyzkahl was . . .

Well, let's just say I preferred privacy for those summonings.

I'd learned not to worry when I couldn't find her in the house. Most of the time she was roaming on the rest of the ten acres that made up my property. The majority of it was woods, and I had a suspicion that wherever she called home in the demon realm was heavily wooded, because she moved through the trees and undergrowth with an uncanny silence and grace that spoke of a deep ease with her surroundings.

I headed to the kitchen to make a pot of coffee. Did Eilahn ever get homesick? As confident and assured as she seemed to be, surely there were chinks in that armor somewhere. For that matter, did she have family? A mate? I dumped the water into the top of the coffeemaker, troubled that this was only now occurring to me.

*There's too damn much that I don't know about the demons and their world.* I readied my mug with sugar and creamer as I pondered that. The demons were usually deliberately mysterious and evasive when it came to questions about their world—at least, that's what I'd always been taught and had come to understand from the reading I'd done during my studies to become a summoner. In fact it was considered a waste of effort to ask those sort of questions, since the asker would likely end up paying for an answer that didn't actually give any information.

Even though it had never particularly bothered me before, I found that it bugged the crap out of me now. Why wouldn't the demons answer those type of questions? *Or maybe the question should be, why are summoners discouraged from asking them?*

I poured my coffee and sat. I had a demon at my disposal now. Maybe it was time to start finding some shit out.

After I finished waking up I showered and began my usual mental preparations for summoning. I was only summoning Rhyzkahl, but I didn't want to get out of the habit of being in the proper frame of mind.

I laughed as I toweled my hair dry. *I'm "only" summoning Rhyzkahl.* He was supposedly one of the most powerful of the demonic lords in existence, and I was now an old hand at bringing him through. Of course, if he wasn't willing to be summoned, it would be an entirely different matter. Such a summoning would require several summoners working together to be certain that the lord could be contained long enough for whatever was required so that they could avoid being slaughtered. Rather like the summoning of Szerain that had accidentally turned into a summoning of Rhyzkahl. Over thirty years ago six summoners had teamed up to summon the demonic lord Szerain, in an attempt to obtain healing for the breast-cancer-ravaged wife of one of the six, Peter Cerise.

My hands slowed then stopped, and I let the towel drop to the floor. Szerain was willing. That's what Tessa had said. That's why those six summoners had decided to summon him instead of some other lord. *But if he was willing, why did they need six summoners?* Why else would they all be there? This had been gnawing at me in the background for the last month and a half. And now I was seeing more ways that it just didn't add up. Was Szerain willing, or simply more open to such things? But again . . . why six summoners?

Before heading downstairs I considered the various things I could possibly ask Rhyzkahl. I was limited to two questions per summoning. And I was obligated to summon him no less than once a month. *But there's nothing that says I can't summon him more often than that.*

I mused on that as I changed into the gray silk shirt and pants that I wore for summonings. There were only two problems with the simplistic math of summon-the-demonic-lord-more-often-and-get-more-questions-answered option. First was that summonings took power. The simplest and most common source of power was the natural potency that filled the world—strongest and easiest to draw during the full moon. I'd learned of a way to store that potency, which gave me more flexibility as to when I could summon, but even that had limitations.

The second problem was that once I summoned the demonic lord to this sphere, he was most certainly not under my control except for the terms of our agreement. One of the reasons my summonings of him were easier was because I didn't bother attempting to maintain the sort of bindings and protections that could hold a being of his power. Our deal was that he would stay no longer than half a day and would abide by the same judicial laws of this sphere that applied to me.

That still gave him a shitload of wiggle room, and I didn't want to push my luck any further than I had to.

*Maybe that was why they used six summoners . . . to bind Szerain?* But if they'd truly had sufficient protections in place, then how was it that Rhyzkahl had been able to break through the bindings and slaughter them? He'd caught them with their guard down, which seemed to indicate that there'd been no major protections—

which would mean that their goal had *not* been to bind Szerain. So, what was it?

I had plenty of questions for the demonic lord. Most of the time he was the best—and often only—source of information, as long as I knew how to phrase the question. I always had the option to wade through the unorganized nightmare that was my aunt's library, but right now I had a resource that was, if not at my beck and call, at least available to me—and I'd be a moron not to try and tap it as much as possible while I could.

And then there was the other reason to summon Rhyzkahl.

The sex.

Holy hells, but the sex was fantastic. My usual pattern was to angst over the fact that I had this "demon with benefits" relationship, but a tough talk from Jill not too long ago had managed to shift my thinking on that somewhat. I was a grown-up. I was allowed to enjoy sex. And I damn well intended to.

Pausing at the door to the basement, I took off my robe and folded it carefully by the door. One of my many quirks was my superstition about changing into my summoning garb: I always walked naked down the basement stairs and got dressed at the bottom. The few times I'd dared to mix it up something had gone wrong with the ritual. It was a damn chilly walk into the frigid basement tonight, but I wasn't about to start making changes to my routine.

At the bottom of the stairs, I quickly pulled on the grey silk pants and shirt and, as soon as I was dressed, immediately moved to the other end of the basement to get a fire going in the fireplace. I breathed a sigh of relief as the warmth began to spread throughout the room then moved on to the task of setting out my implements and lighting the candles. Even though my storage diagram was close to being full of power, I intended to do this the "old school" way and use the natural available potency of the full moon. No sense wasting what was stored, and this way I still had plenty of power in reserve in case I needed to summon another demon in the next few days.

And with everything that had happened today, I had a feeling I'd be wanting to do just that.

I didn't need to make any significant changes to the large diagram that dominated the center of the room. Still, I checked it carefully to make sure the symbols were crisp and nothing had become smudged or marred in any way. Much like a preflight checklist on an airplane. Too much was in play during a summoning for me to take chances.

Standing at the edge of the diagram, I took a deep, settling breath and allowed the energy to fill me before I carefully redirected it into the diagram and the portal I needed to form. I chanted steadily, using the cadence of the ancient words to shape my will. I bypassed the protections that would normally protect me from the demon I intended to summon. Instead, I took that power and augmented the protections that shielded me from the energies of the forming portal. One could never be too careful on that front.

Within a dozen heartbeats the portal snapped into place. I spoke the demonic lord's name, calling him with my will and my voice. Another dozen heartbeats and he was through, crouching in the center of my diagram as the portal closed smoothly behind him.

I released the breath I was holding as my vision cleared, and I could see the crouched figure in the center of the diagram. I'd summoned the demonic lord close to half a dozen times, and had yet to shake the persistent worry that something could and would go wrong.

Then again, that was probably something I shouldn't shake. The day I stopped worrying would also probably be the day I stopped being as meticulous and careful, and even the slightest error during a summoning could spell the kind of disaster that ended with the summoner in teeny-tiny bits.

*It's a wonder that anyone takes the risk.* Yet, it was so incredibly worth every second of risk, at least to me. Even before I'd decided to use the summoning as a supplement to my police work, I'd always felt a draw, a hunger to see and learn more. Every summoning was an accomplishment, a trial I'd overcome.

As soon as one full moon was over, I'd dive back into my studies and begin preparing for the next. It was almost like an addiction. Perhaps that was part of the talent? The hunger for it? After all, why take the risk, otherwise? If someone were to "design" a summoner, it would sure be useful to make them want to do it.

That was an oddly disturbing thought. I quickly chased it from my head as the demonic lord straightened. Then I could only stare, blinking like an idiot at him.

"What are you—" I clamped my lips shut on what I was about to say and hurriedly reworked it so that I didn't use up one of my allotted questions. "Your clothing is . . . um . . . not your usual, er, style."

I was accustomed to seeing him in clothing suited

to . . . well, a Renaissance festival—breeches, flowing shirts, boots, that sort of thing. I'd always assumed that he wore that style of clothing because that's what demonic lords *wore* in the demon realm.

But . . . now he had on black jeans that hugged the muscled contours of his legs without looking sprayed on, a crisp tailored shirt so white it nearly made his silver-blond hair look dark in contrast, and a grey jacket that looked like it was some sort of exceedingly expensive silk-wool blend.

And his hair. Holy shit, the hair! His hair had formerly hung to his waist, but now it ended just past his shoulders. Even the normal alabaster hue of his skin looked like it had been replaced with the faintest touch of . . . a tan?

He looked like an action hero on the red carpet. He looked *hot*—in a completely new and different way from what I was used to. And I didn't know what the hell to make of it. What game was he playing now? There was no possible way this had been done solely to impress me.

The light from the fireplace bathed his skin in a warm glow. A smile twitched his lips, and his crystal blue eyes found mine. "Smoothly performed, as usual," he said with approval, and it took me a few seconds of mental floundering to realize he was referring to my summoning technique. Normally I'd have basked in the glow of such a compliment—especially since he never gave empty compliments—but at the moment I was still attempting to recover my composure at seeing this transformed version of him. And—what?—he wasn't even going to respond to my statement or explain the change in his look? He knew I didn't dare waste a question on that.

He stepped out of the circle and slid his arms around me, bending his head to kiss me. But to my surprise he kept it light and released me barely a second later.

"There has been another incident?" he asked, eyes narrowing as he looked down at me.

Was my worry that obvious? "Several," I said, pushing aside my curiosity about the overhaul of his appearance—at least for the moment. "A *graa* attacked this morning." I shoved my sleeve up and showed him the wicked bruise and the shallow puncture its claw had left. "But Eilahn said she didn't think it was trying to kill me."

He frowned and absently stroked his hand over my arm, eyes still intent on mine. "Go on."

A lovely warmth spread along my bicep as the ache faded. "And two people are dead whom I had every reason to hate, though I don't know for certain there's a connection."

"But your instincts tell you there is," he stated.

"They do," I replied. "Both had nosebleeds, and I'll bet my next paycheck that the autopsy will show that they died of the same thing—whatever that was."

"And there is more yet?" he asked.

"Yep. After we got back home there was another summoning attempt," I told him. "Eilahn saved my ass—threw me through the wards of the house."

An eyebrow lifted. "Threw you?"

"Pretty much," I said with a smile. "Luckily she's been teaching me how to fall."

"Good that she foresaw the need." He ran his hands lightly from my shoulders down my back. Tingling warmth followed his touch along with a decidedly pleasant cessation of aches and pains. "You suffered no serious injury," he stated.

I obligingly pressed closer to make it easier for him to examine me. "Just bruises." I tipped my head back to look up at him. "Pretty sure I have a few lower down."

Amusement shimmered in his eyes as he slid his hands down to cup my ass. "I would not wish for you to be suffering in any way." Then he lowered his head to nuzzle my neck. "Unless I'm the one making you suffer . . . and scream," he murmured against my skin.

I laughed breathlessly as heat flashed through me, but I forced myself to temper my ardor. He was still utterly beautiful, with a body like a Greek god, and he still had that demonic lord presence. But now I could actually picture him going out in public without drawing any more attention than any other incredibly gorgeous man would. And I realized with an abrupt shock that it was oddly unsettling. Here I'd finally wrapped my head around the idea that I didn't need to feel guilt or angst about enjoying sex with him. I felt that Rhyzkahl and I had settled into an understanding of our relationship. He was my fantasy fuck-buddy, and since there was no chance that it would ever spill over into the "real" world, I didn't have to worry about strings attached—other than the ones binding me to him as his sworn summoner.

But now . . . *This shit just got real.* Sure, I was a grown-up and I was allowed to have sex with anyone I wanted. But that also meant I didn't have to be ruled by my hormones.

"You have questions," he stated, a slight smile on his face as he eyed me. Could he tell how off-balance I was?

"I would not wish to succumb to distraction and not give you the full measure of our agreement," he added.

I took a breath and did my best to clear my thoughts. Okay, so the goalposts had been moved. I knew these changes were important, but unfortunately I had other stuff to deal with that was a lot more pressing. "Will questions about threats to me originating in the demon realm count against my two questions?"

A sparkle of amusement flashed in his eyes, and before he could open his mouth I jabbed a forefinger at him and narrowed my own eyes. "And don't you dare count that against me, either," I added.

He inclined his head slightly. "And now you seek to rework the terms of the agreement. Shameful."

Normally I'd have been deeply frightened at the insinuation that I was being less than honorable, but he still looked amused. Or so I hoped. "Merely seeking to clarify what might be seen as a loophole," I replied. "Since it is our very agreement that puts me in jeopardy, it seems to me that questions concerning matters that might affect it negatively—like me *dying* or some such thing—go beyond the scope of the usual boundaries where I ask questions merely to further my own education or base of knowledge."

"You are becoming skilled in the manipulation of words and meaning," he said, and this time he actually gave a slight smile.

I gave a soft snort. "Yeah, well, spending so much time with a demon will do that to you." Living with Eilahn was like a verbal chess match sometimes.

"Among other things," he said cryptically. "I trust that

all is well between you and the *syraza*? She is proving to be suitable to the task I set her?"

It was my turn to incline my head in a nod. "All is well. In fact she's a very considerate roommate and is currently attempting to train me in self-defense." I couldn't quite hide the grimace. I wasn't exactly a future ninja chick. We'd finally agreed that I'd simply do my best in order to buy her time to do whatever she needed to do. *Then again,* I realized, *I didn't do too badly against the graa.* Maybe there was hope for me yet?

"Most excellent." He gave a satisfied nod. "You need not risk wasting your questions regarding your safety, dearest," he said. "I am presently dealing with the matter."

I scowled, even though I'd half-expected a bullshit answer like that. A don't-you-worry-your-pretty-head-about-this kind of thing.

"It is quite complicated," he added in a low voice, stroking a thumb over my cheek. "I know this answer does not satisfy you."

"No, it doesn't," I replied. "I really hate being kept in the dark."

"You are a detective. A seeker of knowledge. This lack of information chafes at your very nature. But some matters cannot be directly explained or revealed, lest the peril to you increase." He moved away from me and draped himself elegantly into the armchair by the fireplace.

An odd flush of anger swept over me. "That's bullshit," I said. "Oh, great, it's for *my own good* that you can't tell me anything! I'm so goddamn sick of this shit!" His eyes narrowed, and I knew I needed to shut the hell up, but I couldn't seem to stop the words pouring out of my mouth. "I never know what the fuck is going on. I summon you, and we fuck. I'm just some kind of sextoy or something to you. Then you sneak upstairs and use my computer—" I had to take a breath then, and somehow I regained enough control of myself to clamp down on the bizarre fury. What the hell was I thinking going off on him like that?

My gut clenched as Rhyzkahl regarded me from where he sat. The leaping flames in the fireplace cast stark shadows across his beautiful features, giving him an even more dangerous and menacing appearance. Not that he needed shadows for that. He was a demonic lord, one of the most powerful creatures that I knew of and certainly the most powerful that I'd ever encountered.

So why the hell had I gone off like that?

"I . . . I'm sorry," I said. I shook my head, frowned. "I didn't mean all that."

"I did not sneak," he finally said.

I blinked in confusion. This wasn't the retaliation I'd expected. "Huh?"

The demonic lord's lips twitched ever so slightly. "Your computer. I did not *sneak* upstairs."

Shit, had I asked that as a question? I hurriedly cast back to my memory of my off-balanced rant. I hadn't planned on wasting my questions on that, since the response he'd just given me was pretty much the response I'd expected. I didn't have any other possible suspects, and I knew that he would never in a million years lie to me—not with that demonic sense of honor ruling his words and actions. No, I decided after a few seconds of mental rummaging, I hadn't actually asked a question.

Therefore, if he was willing to keep talking, I was more than willing to continue on this tack.

"You waited until I was asleep," I pointed out.

He lifted a perfect eyebrow. "I do not recall having to wait at all. You fell asleep rather quickly after you received your fill of pleasure."

I flushed, even though it certainly hadn't been the first, or last, time he'd "pleasured" me. "You could have just asked me if you could use the computer," I said, far more sullenly than I'd meant. Fucking hell, was I PMS-ing or something?

He lifted one shoulder in an elegant shrug, amusement lighting his eyes, which did *not* make it easier for me to get my mood under control. "I was unaware that there were portions of your house that were off-limits to me," he replied.

My scowl darkened. He was enjoying this, the jerk, and I was only making it more amusing for him by continuing to nag him about this stupid detail. I folded my arms across my chest. "I just . . . I have personal shit on there, y'know. It would be like you reading my diary or something. And you could have just asked. And how the hell do you know how to use a computer anyway?"

He was on his feet and in front of me holding my shoulders in the time it took me to blink. "I had need of information," he stated, no longer looking amused. "And if I chose not to share my need for this information with you, then that is my prerogative." His grip on my shoulders was firm, though not to the point of hurting me. Yet. I knew he was powerful enough to shatter me before I could twitch.

"You stated none of this need for privacy when we set

the terms," he continued. Then his eyes narrowed. "Think you that I could not strip all of your secrets from you in the time it takes your heart to beat thrice?"

My mouth had gone dry, but I made myself look up at him, forced myself to meet the ancient potency that simmered behind his gaze. "You don't *own* me," I stated as boldly as I could, though the tremor in my voice kind of ruined my show of strength. "I don't *serve* you. The deal was that I'd summon you once a month, and you'd answer two questions for me. I'm not going to bow or grovel or . . . or . . ."

He released me and spun away, hissing what sounded like an expletive under his breath. "Have I ever demanded thus from you?" His hands tightened into fists, and he looked back at me. He was angry, but it was a different anger than I'd ever seen in him before. I'd seen him filled with the kind of fury that made me mewl in terror, and I'd seen him with a dark anger that could only precede a slaughter. But this anger was . . . strangely personal.

His jaw tightened. "Have I ever required obeisance from you?"

I shook my head in a jerky move. "No," I muttered.

He lifted his hand, and I didn't have to shift into othersight to see the power coiling into his control. Fear spasmed through me, along with the desire to flee, but before the thought could translate into action the potency wound around me, stilling me. In the next heartbeat I was on my knees before him, forced there by his will.

"I could wring such servitude from you if I wished," he continued, voice resonating in the stone of the basement as my pulse slammed.

"Stop this," I managed to gasp. Then my gaze was torn from him as my head bowed. "Stop it!" I said, voice shaking more with anger than fear. "I'm not going to fucking beg you to stop, if that's what you're waiting for. You're being a fucking asshole!"

A second later I nearly sprawled face first as he released me. I barely caught myself on my hands in time, then I jerked my head up to see him standing with his head tilted back and his eyes closed, breathing deeply. He opened his eyes and met mine.

"And I will *not* force this from you," he stated quietly. "I swear to you I will never do this to you again, unless there is some other pressing and dire need for this manner of display other than my own vanity."

I didn't say anything to that. I was so angry I was shaking, and I could tell that I was about to cry. I hated that. I cried when I got angry or frustrated, and that had been happening way too much lately.

He stepped to me and crouched, then pulled me to my feet and enveloped me in his arms before I could think to protest. "Forgive me," he murmured. "That was a churlish display, and you did not deserve it. I was . . . an asshole."

I almost laughed at the admission but managed to hold it back. But I did surreptitiously wipe my sniffly nose on his jacket.

"Apology accepted," I said. "It didn't help that I was being a bitch." My anger was gone now, thankfully. It bugged me that I'd lost control like that. *He's not human. He could have slapped me down a lot harder.*

But he hadn't. That had been a demonic lord version of shouting back at me. In fact he'd shown incredible restraint. I sighed inwardly. Someday I would figure out this fucked up dynamic between us.

I pulled back enough to look up at him. "I, um, find it interesting that you know how to use a computer," I said, carefully not phrasing it as a question.

To my surprise he kissed me tenderly on the forehead. He'd been doing more of these oddly affectionate moves, which only managed to confuse the living fuck out of me. "Once summoned," he said, "a demonic lord is able to bring another demon through to this sphere, though it is not simple and requires a great deal of effort. There is a *luhrek* who is gifted with matters of technology. She performed the work I required."

*He brought another demon through?* Okay, that was a big ol' whopping shocker, and I knew it showed on my face. Yet, again, there was nothing in the terms of our agreement that barred him from doing anything like that.

I could feel a simmer of anger at the edges of my mind, and I took a shaky breath. I had to keep control of it this time. I couldn't count on him being all nice and understanding if I went mental on him again. I was safe with him only because of the oaths that bound us both. I could fool myself all I wanted about understanding the dynamic between us, but the truth was that I had no idea where I stood with him. Or where I wanted to stand with him. And what if I started seeing someone—like an actual boyfriend? If I ever decided I wanted to stop sleeping with Rhyzkahl, how would he react? Was being my lover part of a plan, or was there any spark at all of true desire to be with me? And if the latter were true . . . how did I feel about that?

"I want to know why you changed your look but I don't want to waste a question on that," I blurted. He lifted an eyebrow, but I bulled onward before he could speak. "I know this is going to seem stupid, but it's kinda freaking me out because it makes me wonder what you're up to. And even though I know I can't really trust you beyond the oaths you've given me, I feel more comfortable around you than I feel around most humans, and in some ways I really care about you, and the thought that this whole thing is just you playing me as part of some bigger game is a pretty awful one." I clamped my lips shut as I felt the flush rise up my neck. Shit. I'd gone mental again with the verbal diarrhea but in a different direction. *Did I really just tell him that I didn't trust him* and *that I cared about him?*

"I mean . . ." I started, but then trailed off. What the fuck was I supposed to say that could serve as any sort of useful damage control? I needed to simply shut the fuck up.

His expression remained inscrutable as he regarded me. "When I watched television with you I realized that it might be useful and worthwhile to more closely conform my appearance to current standards." He paused. "You are right to be wary of me and to trust cautiously, but I will tell you that some of the decision to change my clothing was based on my observation that you found these styles . . . appealing. I do hope that on this, at least, you will believe me."

I managed to give him a smile in response. I wasn't about to tell him that his changing to please me was the part that was freaking me out.

Rhyzkahl bent his head to kiss me. I returned it, then

pulled back and looked up into his face. "I don't want to fuck today."

He dipped his head in a slight nod. "Then we will not."

"I mean, it's not you at all, and you're still crazy-hot and sexy, but I just have too many things going through my head today and—"

"Then we will not," he gently interrupted. "There is never a need to explain or defend such a wish."

He sure did make it hard to distrust him. *The best con men always seem trustworthy*, I reminded myself. I leaned my head against his chest and closed my eyes. His hand stroked over me, a warm tingle following its path.

"You like to win, don't you?" I murmured.

"I do not care for the consequences of losing," he said.

"Winning has consequences as well."

"But one tends to have more control over consequences when one is the victor."

I opened my eyes to look into his. "Do you ever lose?"

"Yes. It is how I know that I prefer to win." An expression of regret skimmed across his face and was gone. "You have yet to ask your questions, dear one."

I pulled away from him, moved to the table, and hitched myself up to sit on it. Rhyzkahl's eyes were intent upon me as if he knew what I was going to ask. For that matter, it was possible that he *did* know. I desperately wanted to know about the summoning of Szerain. But there was another question that haunted me more.

"I know Ryan Kristoff is a demonic lord," I said, watching him. To his credit he didn't twitch, but the hopeful part of me thought it detected just the faintest flicker of interest. I also noted that he neither confirmed nor denied it.

"Why is he on earth, posing as a human, and with no apparent knowledge or memory of being a demonic lord?"

The air seemed to grow heavy as he regarded me. I could hear my heart thumping as I waited for his answer, any answer.

When he finally spoke his voice was low and rich, tinged with an emotion that I couldn't process. "I am bound by oath, Kara," he said, shocking me by the use of my name. I couldn't remember the last time he had spoken it. It was usually "dear one" or something of that ilk. He stepped to me, let out a low sigh, and touched my cheek lightly with the tips of his fingers. "I know this frustrates you beyond measure. But I cannot answer this question. Ask another."

*Frustrated* was putting it mildly. "You can't tell me anything?" I asked, struggling to hold back my disappointment. I'd finally pinned him down and asked the damn question right, and all I got was "I am bound by oath"?

"I cannot answer this question," he repeated.

A flare of annoyance rose. I opened my mouth to make a retort, but then I closed it and processed what he'd said. Part of my agreement with him was that, in return for summoning him no less than once a month, I could ask two questions, and he would answer them to the best of his ability. However, I'd also discovered that I had to be extremely careful about how I asked a question. If I didn't phrase it properly, and he didn't feel like answering it, he'd find a way to wiggle out of it. In other words, asking a yes/no question would get me a yes/no answer, and not a word more.

But he'd said that he could not answer *this* question, not that he couldn't answer questions about Ryan.

I thought for a second. The demonic lord waited quietly, almost patiently as I worked out what I could ask that might give me a useful answer.

Sitting up, I took a deep breath and tried again. "What sort of offense could a demonic lord commit that might cause the other lords to strip him of his memories and exile him?"

"There is none," Rhyzkahl stated, eyes never leaving mine. "The lords do not censure their own."

Well, crapping hells. That didn't make any sense. "So why . . . ?" I stopped, shook my head. No, he wasn't going to answer a direct question. I made myself think about the answer. Okay, the lords wouldn't censure. So who would? Was there another level beyond even the lords?

I needed to think about that one some more. No sense wasting a question. Maybe time to go back to my other big question.

"Why was Szerain willing to be summoned by Peter Cerise and the five other summoners on the night that you were summoned by accident instead?" I was trying to be as specific as possible without knowing the exact date—not that the exact date would probably mean anything to the demonic lord.

Rhyzkahl turned away from me to face the fireplace. He stood with his hands clasped lightly behind his back, silent, but I had the impression he was gathering his thoughts. I waited, struggling to control my impatience. I had a strong feeling I'd just asked a doozy of a question.

He finally spoke.

"Because two of the summoners present were bound to him in much the same way that you are bound to me."

Wow. I fought back the urge to pepper him with further questions. *Which ones? Then why were there six summoners? How did it go so wrong? Was my grandmother sworn to Szerain? What was Szerain's goal? What was your goal?*

"Why did you kill them?" I blurted. "My grandmother ... and the others?" I'd never known my grandmother—she was simply a name. I'd never felt any sort of connection to her, and I'd somehow managed to compartmentalize her cause of death into a category similar to poking bears with sticks. She'd been involved in something insanely dangerous, and when it had gone bad I'd somehow decided that it was tragic but not really Rhyzkahl's fault. He'd reacted as expected, that's all. Maybe it made me a terribly callous person, that I could have become intimate with the one who took her life, but I was a summoner. I knew the risks. Surely, so did she, and she'd accepted them. *If a summoning goes badly wrong, you die. It's worth it, though, because ...*

*Because* ... I frowned, forgetting Rhyzkahl's presence and my unanswered question. Summoning was so incredible and satisfying. I felt clear-headed and alive and powerful after every ritual. Once I'd started summoning, I'd never once been tempted to go back to drugs. I hadn't thought about that until now. How had I done that? Who the hell shook an addiction that easily? Right now I couldn't imagine *not* being a summoner.

Was summoning an addiction? Now that I had the storage diagram I never went more than two weeks without conducting a ritual, even if it was simply a lower-level demon summoned for "practice."

But I couldn't ask him. The question about killing my grandmother and the others still hung in the air, and I didn't expect him to answer it. He'd already answered two questions for me.

"It wasn't revenge for being summoned," I said, feeling a need to fill the silence as I worked it out. "I mean, not totally. You saw an opportunity to take away his advantage. Kill the two who were bound to him."

He tilted his head back and closed his eyes, inhaling deeply. "It was not so simple as that," he said. He looked toward the summoning diagram, and for an instant I could have sworn I saw agony mar his beautiful features, but it was gone before I could be sure. "I slew them for revenge," he said, voice so low I could barely hear him. "But not for the errant summoning. I sought to hurt Szerain in the opportunity presented to me, by destroying his summoners and slaying the ones who would have supported his plans." I was shocked to see his hands tighten into fists as anger slashed across his face. "It was the only vengeance I was allowed to take, and so I did, even though it was paltry and insufficient." His eyes returned to mine, and the anger in them faded. "The women did not suffer in their deaths. I give you my oath on that. I simply freed their essences. They felt no pain."

My throat felt tight and hot, and all I could do at first was manage a short nod to acknowledge what he'd said.

"What did he do?" I was finally able to croak out. "What did Szerain do for you to want revenge?"

Rhyzkahl moved to me, gently placed his hands on either side of my head and kissed my forehead in a move so tender I could only stare at him in complete bafflement.

"You have already asked your questions, dear one, plus a third," he said softly. "But I will answer this one as well. Szerain stole something from me. Something deeply precious and priceless. He stole it, and then he willfully destroyed it, because he knew what the loss would do to me." And with that he took a deep breath, kissed me on my lips, then straightened and was gone.

# Chapter 7

I stayed down there, sitting in the armchair and staring at nothing in particular until my legs threatened to fall asleep and the rest of me as well. For once I'd come away from a session of "two questions" feeling almost overwhelmed with information—very little of which made any sense. Szerain had been some sort of asshole and took something from Rhyzkahl. In turn, Rhyzkahl killed the summoners to disrupt Szerain's plans—out of revenge. So, what were those plans? What did Szerain take?

Fragments of memory spun in my head like leaves in a breeze, coming to rest in patterns I could almost begin to recognize. A name shouted in a moment of desperation. An ice cold visage. . . .

The house was dark and quiet when I made my way back upstairs. Eilahn's motorcycle helmet was by the front door, which told me she was back from wherever she went, but she didn't seem to be in the house. Maybe she sensed that I needed to be alone with my thoughts for a while. My jangling, chaotic thoughts.

If so, she was wrong.

I went out to the living room and sat on the couch. I tucked my bare feet underneath me and pulled the throw over my legs. "Eilahn . . . ?"

Less than a minute later I heard a soft thump, the front door opened, and the *syraza* came in, followed by Fuzzykins. The demon gave me a soft smile as she closed the door, then settled into the recliner, tucking her own feet up in an echo of my pose. The cat jumped onto the back of the couch and proceeded to wash her butt in my direction.

"You must not have been far," I said to Eilahn.

"I was on the roof," she replied. "The sky is lovely tonight, and the air is fresh."

I started to ask her how the hell she got onto the roof in the first place, then realized that was a stupid question. "Is it anything like this on your world?"

"Similar," she said. "The air is a bit drier there, and it gets much colder, but there is much forest. There are mountains not far away. And we can see more stars."

"No ambient light," I replied with a nod. "You must not have big cities full of light pollution."

She tilted her head. "There are cities. But they do not cast as much light."

A tug of longing pulled at me. I'd been to the demon realm only once, after Rhyzkahl brought me there to live out the last few seconds before I died—allowing me to return to this plane of existence in one piece, much like what happened to demons when they were killed on this world. I'd spent less than a minute there, but what little I'd seen had left me wanting to see so much more. "Did you leave any, um, family behind to come here?"

"I am unmated," she replied, a slight smile curving her

mouth. "I would not have agreed to come had I other commitments."

"Oh, so, you had a choice?" I said, then instantly hated how it sounded. "I mean. . . ." I trailed off, grimacing. "I'm sorry. I guess I'm completely ignorant of how things work over there. With the demons and the lords."

She pursed her lips and was silent for a moment. "It is a complex dynamic," she finally said. I waited to see if she was going to elaborate on that, but she remained silent.

Time to get to the meat of things. "When we were out at the landfill," I said, "fighting the golems . . . when that one golem hit me, you yelled to Ryan. That's when he turned around and, um, saved me."

The demon was still as stone. She didn't nod or acknowledge my statement.

I was suddenly nervous. Little things were starting to click into place, though I knew I was still missing most of the big picture. It was like the moment when working on a picture puzzle that you put three pieces together and suddenly realize it's a face. Maybe you still don't know where it's supposed to go, or what the final picture looks like, but at least you have something more than hundreds of scattered pieces.

I knew that once I started putting it together, I wouldn't be able to stop until I had the whole picture, whether I liked the end result or not.

"You didn't call him by his name," I said, taking the plunge. "I mean, the name you yelled wasn't 'Ryan,' was it?"

She shook her head, a slow deliberate movement. Her eyes never left mine.

My pulse beat an unsteady staccato. "It was 'Szerain,' right?"

"It was," she said in a low voice.

I blew out an unsteady breath. It was true. *Fucking hell. He's a demonic lord. He's* that *demonic lord.* So what the hell happened? "Can you, um, get in trouble for doing that?" I asked after a moment of mental floundering. "Using that name, I mean?"

She seemed to consider the question. "I should not have done so, but there were circumstances. I doubt I will receive much censure."

I licked my lips. "Ryan is . . . Szerain?"

Her look was full of apology. "I am oathbound. I cannot answer that."

I let out a breathless laugh. Zack had said something very similar when I'd asked him if Ryan was a demonic lord. "Right. I understand." I suddenly felt calmer than I had in a long time. So what if the answers I'd been given only raised more questions? It was a shitload better than being completely in the dark. "I just have one more question," I said. "Were . . . are they enemies? Rhyzkahl and Szerain?"

Eilahn pursed her lips, appeared to consider the question. She was silent for long enough that I was about to retract the question when she took a breath to speak.

"'Enemies' is a strong word," she said, looking off into an unknown distance and speaking as if she was measuring each word carefully. "It implies that the two parties have conflicting goals." She shifted her gaze to me. "What if they have the same goal? What would they be then?"

"They'd be allies," I said.

Eilahn's smooth forehead creased in a frown. "Yet what if they disagreed on how to reach said goal?"

I turned the question over in my head, and finally shrugged. "I dunno. Bad allies? Rivals?"

A smile whispered across her mouth. "Some things are difficult to define." She stood, and I knew that was the most I'd be able to get out of her regarding the dynamic between Rhyzkahl and Szerain.

*In other words, It's Really Fucking Complicated,* I thought wryly.

"I was able to finish the warding on your place of work," she said. "I was also able to obtain something that may be of assistance." She reached for a backpack at the end of the couch. "Come to the kitchen. I have something to give you."

I obediently followed. "Somehow I get the feeling this isn't an early Christmas present."

"Alas, no," she said as she sat at the table. Out of the backpack she pulled a plain cardboard box, big enough to hold a coffee mug, and set it in front of her. "But, speaking of the Christmas festival—when do you plan to obtain a tree?"

I blinked as I took a seat opposite her. "Um, well, I hadn't really planned on getting one."

"Oh." She looked almost forlorn. "Are your beliefs different? Do you object to the symbol of the tree?"

I shook my head. "No, it's not that. It's just that it's usually only me here, and most of the time I figure it's not worth the trouble or time." I paused. "My aunt always puts a tree up though, if you want to see one."

The demon inclined her head. "I would like that." She still looked disappointed though.

"Or we could get one," I said, oddly pleased at the thought.

A smile spread across her face, and once again she was the kid who wanted the pet cat. "Could we? I have read about such things, and was hoping to be able to participate in the traditions."

I grinned. "Yeah, sure. Maybe we can go later today and get one." And a tree stand, and decorations, and lights. Good thing there was still some room to go before I hit my credit limit.

I gave a slight nod toward the box on the table. "So, what's that?"

She pushed it toward me. "You may open it."

The top of the box was closed with a thin strip of masking tape, easily torn. I expected there to be some sort of packing material to go through, but there was only one item in the box—a bulky and rather ugly bracelet.

I took it out and turned it over in my hands. It was a lot lighter than I expected, made of some pinkish-coppery metal, though I was fairly sure it wasn't copper. It looked old, too—pitted and scarred, as if had been knocked around for a few hundred years. Overall, "ugly" really was the best way to describe it. "It almost looks like an old-style shackle," I said, tugging it open easily. "Except there's no place for a chain to attach." Peering closer, I could see an opening that could possibly be a key hole.

"It needs no chain, and it is a shackle—of a sort. It was quite difficult to acquire."

I set it down on the table. The thing made me vaguely uncomfortable. "And you're giving this to me . . . why?"

"This will offer you an added level of protection above what I can provide." Eilahn said, eyes steady on me.

"What, is it some sort of arcane artifact?" I asked, switching over to othersight to peer at the thing. To my disappointment it appeared perfectly mundane.

"The opposite," she replied. "It suppresses the arcane, and it will make it nigh to impossible for you to be summoned as long as you are wearing it."

I let out a breath. "That's fantastic!" Then I saw that her expression was guarded. "What's the catch?"

"It dampens all arcane. Including yours," she said, tone serious. "You will not be able to summon or use othersight while wearing it, nor will you be able to sense arcane that you are accustomed to sensing. And you cannot wear it for extended periods, lest you become ill from it."

I swallowed. "Ill how? Like, sick to my stomach, or like cancer?"

"You will feel tired and then generally unpleasant. I believe an appropriate analogy would be the feeling of having influenza. But that would only happen with extended wear. The sensation should disappear as soon as you take it off. Which you would *only* do when you are within wards," she added with a warning tilt of her eyebrow.

That wasn't quite so bad then. As long as I wasn't wearing a piece of uranium on my wrist that would give me some sort of lymphoma somewhere down the road.

"Put it on," Eilahn said gently, and I realized I'd been frowning at it for at least a dozen heartbeats.

I glanced up at her. "You said it was a shackle. What did you mean?"

"Artifacts of this type have been used to keep practitioners of the arcane from using their abilities, or to control *when* they used them"

"In the demon realm?"

"In both worlds," she stated. "I borrowed this from the storage room of a museum in New Orleans."

"Borrowed?"

The demon gave a light shrug. "I suspect that none there knew of its true nature, else it would not have been in a storage room with only a padlock for security. I will return it when you no longer have need of it, or I will make appropriate recompense."

I'd have thought the demon sense of honor wouldn't have allowed "borrowing" without asking, but apparently there was wiggle room in there according to whether the borrowed item would be missed. Apparently I still had a lot to learn about their honor. Hopefully I wouldn't need the artifact for very long, and she could return it before anyone missed it. "Why couldn't you just ask Rhyzkahl to bring one with him the next time I summoned him?"

She shook her head. "Because of its nature, it is not something that can be transferred through a portal without extreme effort."

I winced. "Oh. Right. Something that mutes the arcane would screw up a portal pretty good, huh."

"Precisely." She watched me steadily. "The lock has been disabled. You will be able to remove it whenever you wish."

I gave an unsteady smile. "I know. I'm just a little weirded out by the idea of putting on what's essentially a slave cuff."

She lowered her head, eyes steady on me. "You can wear this cuff here, or you can truly be made a slave in the demon realm after being summoned and bound," the demon said, voice abruptly hard.

I clenched my jaw, then gave a curt nod. I was being a weenie. Lifting the cuff, I quickly snapped it onto my wrist. I expected to feel something unusual—a tingling, or, well, anything. But the cuff could have been made of plastic for all I felt.

"I don't feel any different," I finally said.

She gave a satisfied nod. "It will take a little time for you to feel any effect. But I would not have you wear anything that caused you harm or made it so that you were unable to function."

I lifted my wrist and peered at the cuff. "It's seriously ugly though. I guess I can just wear long sleeves and keep it covered."

The demon traced a sigil on the surface of the table. Even without othersight I should have been able to see it, but I couldn't see a damn thing, and I found that it was impossible for me to switch into othersight.

"Now I kind of feel like my ears need to pop," I said. "I mean, not really my ears, but it feels like the same thing."

She gave a slight nod. "With your arcane senses instead of your physical. I understand."

"And I can't be summoned as long as I'm wearing this?"

Her lips curved in a slight smile. "That is correct. It will be impossible for the ritual to 'lock onto you,' so to speak."

It seemed to remain oddly cool against my skin.

"Couldn't I just wait until I feel a summoning beginning and then snap it on?"

"No, in fact that could be quite dangerous," she stated. At my frown she continued. "The cuff will prevent a summoning from locking onto you. You may have noticed that each summoning attempt has been stronger and more focused than the last. Soon it will be impossible to simply run as a means of escape. If a summoning locates you, and you then put the cuff on, you will still be summoned. But the cuff will alter the portal—"

"And I'd end up in tiny bits," I said with a wince.

"Correct." She reached across the table to touch the back of my hand. "You will not have to wear this forever," she said. "Lord Rhyzkahl is doing his utmost to eliminate the threat."

I nodded and resisted the urge to do more mopey whining. "Yeah. It's cool. I can handle this. It's just a piece of damn jewelry." Even so, I pulled it off, breathing a sigh of relief as everything seemed to leap back into focus.

"I have something else for you," she said, dipping into her pack and pulling out a thick envelope.

"Matching earrings?" I said with a deliberately cheeky grin.

She chuckled. "No. I did not think you wished to wear yet more ugly jewelry." She pushed the envelope toward me. "I am aware that your finances have been stressed with the additional expenses incurred by my presence. Since it is hardly worthwhile to protect you and yet have you fall into financial ruin, I am hoping that this will ameliorate the situation somewhat."

Stunned and wary, I pulled the envelope to me and

peered inside. I didn't pull the bills out to count them, but at a rough estimate I figured it was about five thousand dollars in hundred dollar bills. "Wow," I managed after several heartbeats of trying to figure out what to say. "Um, how did you get this?"

She gave a pleased smile. "I borrowed forty dollars from your wallet and went to a casino on the Gulf Coast. The advertisements on television stated that one could win large sums of money at such places." Then her brow puckered. "However, I must say, their advertisements are terribly misleading. One must have excellent skills at observation, physics, and mathematics in order to compete with a minimum of disadvantage. Fortunately, I am in possession of all of those skills, but I would venture to say that very few humans have the necessary aptitudes." She inclined her head. "No offense intended."

I grinned. "None taken. The casinos pretty much count on people being stupid."

"And they are seldom disappointed, I am sure," she said. "I could only remain and partake of the gaming for an hour, but I am hoping the monies within the envelope will help your situation. And the original forty dollars are in there as well."

Pulling the bills out of the envelope, I counted off five hundred and then handed the rest back to her. "Thank you for worrying about me, but you're really not a very expensive roommate. However, you do need your own money."

She paused before taking the envelope back. "Are you certain? If you need more funds, you need only ask."

"I'm sure," I said.

A smile spread across her face as she tucked the envelope into her backpack. "My thanks. I do indeed have some purchases I wish to make."

Somehow I had the feeling that it wouldn't be long before Fuzzykins was the proud owner of a shiny new Kitty Kondo.

# Chapter 8

"I can't think of a better way to start the day," my aunt's boyfriend said as he looked down at the corpse before him.

I cocked an eyebrow at him. "You really need a life."

A smile ghosted across his lips, which on him was equivalent to a full-belly laugh. Carl was the morgue assistant to Dr. Jonathan Lanza, the parish pathologist. Tall and lean, with short, almost colorless hair and hazel-brown eyes, he managed to avoid looking like the archetypical morgue worker by having a semblance of a tan and a fairly athletic build. However, he was reserved to the point of appearing emotionless, which tended to swing him right back into the stereotype. In the past few months I'd had the chance to get to know him some, and I'd come to learn that he was anything but emotionless. He was a keen observer and tended to think carefully before speaking, but moreover, he was my aunt's boyfriend—and that right there told me there was something very special about him. My aunt was . . . odd. But he seemed to understand her. Better than I did, to be honest.

We were in the cutting room of the St. Long Parish

Morgue. On the metal table before us was the naked body of Barry Landrieu. The scent of formalin and Pine-Sol mingled, and my stomach gave off an unfamiliar twinge of queasiness. I'd only been wearing the cuff for a few hours, and I was already feeling the effects. *As long as I don't puke during the autopsy I'll be all right,* I tried to reassure myself. I would never live it down if I lost my breakfast.

"You don't normally come to autopsies of natural deaths," Carl said as he readied instruments on a side table. Scalpels, scissors, syringes, a bone saw. And one that always made me wince—long-handled pruning shears, used to cut through the ribs so that the pathologist could better examine the internal organs.

"Two deaths with nosebleeds in the same day?" I said. "I tend to be suspicious of coincidences." Out of habit I tried to shift into othersight to give the body a once-over and silently cursed as it proved impossible with the stupid cuff on.

He gave a mild nod. "It does seem odd," he agreed. "And you sometimes have more reason than most to dislike what appears to be coincidence to others."

I was silent for several heartbeats. "I knew them both. Barry here was the one who gave me heroin." Carl knew about that incident already. "And the other one, Evelyn Stark, was the drunk driver who killed my dad."

"Ah," he said, and in that one syllable was a paragraph's worth of meaning.

"Plus, Eilahn and I encountered a *graa* early yesterday morning," I added. Carl knew a great deal about the arcane and demons, but I didn't know if that was because of his relationship with my aunt or if he had prior knowledge. I knew that wards didn't seem to have any effect on him, and he'd once been attacked by an assailant with the ability to suck out a person's essence, yet he'd been completely unaffected. But despite not knowing a damn thing about him, I trusted him.

*But should I?* I was suddenly suspicious of any sort of blind trust. Yet, Tessa cared deeply for him and clearly, she trusted him. And I'd never seen the barest whisper or hint that Carl had anything but fond adoration for my aunt in return. Maybe there were times when blind trust was necessary. I sure as hell needed to be better about trusting people.

His hazel brown eyes flicked to me. "Should I assume it was not a pleasant encounter?"

"You could say that," I replied with a dry laugh, "though Eilahn's convinced it wasn't trying to kill me." I lifted my shoulders in a shrug. "Obviously, I need even *more* weird shit in my life."

A smile touched the corners of his mouth. "And yet you weather it well."

"I'd hate to see what my life would be like if I weathered it badly!"

"And you don't think your aunt summoned this demon?"

That hadn't even occurred to me. Why the hell hadn't it? She was a strong summoner. She was the one who had trained me. "I'm pretty confident that she wouldn't send a demon to attack me," I told him. Still, I should have asked her. What if the attack had been some sort of misunderstanding? "*Did* she summon it?"

His eyes held mine briefly before he looked back down at the instruments. "No."

Carl was a hard man to read, but I could have sworn I'd seen relief, or something awfully close to it, in that brief look. I let out a breath and resisted the urge to ask him why the hell he'd implied that she had. Carl usually had good stuff to say, but he didn't always come right out and say it—usually preferring for me to come around to it on my own. "I don't know if it had anything to do with the deaths of these two people," I said, "but it sure as hell got my attention."

"Interesting," he murmured, then turned back to the body and began a meticulous search for scars, tattoos, or injuries. "If the *graa* wasn't there in connection with the two victims, why would it be there? Do you think your aunt can give you advice or counsel about that?" He didn't look up at me, but I still felt pinned down by his attention. I resisted the urge to squirm.

"I don't want to worry her," I finally said. "She's been through a lot of shit lately . . . most of it my fault."

"It is the role of parents—and guardians—to worry about their loved ones," he pointed out.

My throat felt tight. Was I keeping things from my aunt to protect her or to protect me from her ire? My relationship with her had been a tempestuous one for most of our time together. She was acerbic, and odd, and generally didn't care what people thought of her. And while I could appreciate that mentality more now that I was older, back when I was young it was yet another hurdle to overcome. It was bad enough that both my parents had died, but now I had to live with my crazy aunt who did weird shit and didn't seem to care that the other kids at school laughed at her—and me. Tessa hadn't cared about fads—in fact she tended to hold anything that was fashionable in complete disdain, and had subtly, and not-so-subtly, pushed me to be "unique" and to "forge my own path."

But as a thirteen-year-old, I wasn't ready to be unique. What I'd needed was to fit in, to be a little invisible until I could find my comfort zone. That was impossible with Tessa. Was it any wonder that I'd rebelled and found a different way to hide and feel comfortable? Or at least, what felt like comfort.

Carl remained silent, but it didn't feel judgmental. It simply seemed as if he was waiting for me to digest his comment on my own, and he'd be there to pick up the conversation when I did. I felt an odd surge of gratitude toward him. I had a few friends who knew that I summoned demons, but somehow talking it out with Carl was different, and it felt oddly freeing to be able to discuss bizarre shit like this.

"She's different," I said at last.

"That she is," Carl agreed.

I shook my head. "No, I mean . . . since she woke up." My aunt's essence had been stripped from her body by a serial killer, and it had taken me several weeks to find a way to call her back to herself.

His eyes met mine. "I know."

"I don't think she wants to summon anymore."

"I think you're right."

I tilted my head. "Do you know why? I mean . . . has she said anything?"

"Not to me."

Our conversation was cut off by the entrance of Dr. Lanza. A slender man about my height with distinct Italian coloring and features, he had an easygoing manner that had done much to put me at ease when I was still learning the ropes of investigating homicides. *And now I'm an old hand at this whole find-the-murderer thing*, I thought with mild amusement.

Dr. Lanza shot me a warm smile as he pulled protective clothing over his jeans and New Orleans Hornets T-shirt. "You must have some dark suspicions, Kara," he said, his smile teasing.

"C'mon, Doc, I *always* have dark suspicions," I replied with an easy grin, automatically slipping away from the confiding and open mood of the conversation with Carl and into the tone that I maintained with everyone else—the ones who had no clue that there was more to our world than what was apparent to the usual five senses. I was used to it. Humor, and lots of caution about what I said and asked. But I was damn grateful that there were people with whom I could discuss the more bizarre details.

"Luckily, that's part of your job description," Doc said as he lifted a scalpel and started in on the Y incision. "So, yes, your two victims both had nosebleeds, but those can be caused by a lot of things," Doc said as he filleted the skin and flesh away from the ribs. I retreated even farther as Carl stepped up to cut through the ribs with the pruning shears. "I'd be willing to bet that the second victim's was caused by the air bag."

I simply gave a nod and a slight shrug. I had no intention of sharing the other, more personal connection. At least not until I knew more.

I waited patiently while Doc went through the procedures, and I did my usual escape from the room when Carl used the bone saw to cut through the skull. He wore a breathing mask for this part, since the saw kicked up all sorts of bone dust—which, of course, had blood and other yuck in it. Not only did I have no desire to breathe it in, I didn't want it in my hair or anywhere else. Nasty.

As soon as the brain was revealed, though, I ducked back in, not hiding my eagerness very well as I waited for Doc to do his examination.

He took the brain from the scale and began to slice it into neat sections. I watched as he narrowed his eyes and frowned. "Well, this one definitely stroked out." He let out a low whistle. "Fucking hell. Looks like he had several at once. I've never seen anything like this. This guy never had a chance." He motioned me over with the bloody scalpel. "Come see, Kara."

I really didn't want to see it, but I knew I had to look, for my pride as much as for my own personal education. I moved to his side and peered at the pink and grey convolutions. He didn't even have to point anything out. I had no trouble seeing the damage and clots of blood. "What could have caused that?"

He blew out his breath. "Not sure. Perhaps a cancer . . . ." He trailed off, mumbling under his breath about occult large cell carcinoma and some other stuff I couldn't make out. His brow drew together in a frown as he continued his examination. "No obvious sign of cancer, though. I'll have to take a look under the microscope later."

I wasn't surprised when he asked Carl to preserve the brain, and the sections he'd cut, in formalin. Doc seemed perplexed but also a little excited, as if he couldn't wait to dig into the mystery of why this man had died this way. Heck, it was probably a welcome change from the usual boring parade of drug overdoses and heart attacks. Doc continued the autopsy, peering carefully at the quick test that showed if any of the most commonly abused drugs were in the victim's system.

"Clean," he muttered. "But I'll order a comprehensive toxicological screening."

He retreated to write up his notes while Carl put the body of Barry Landrieu back into the cooler and got Evelyn Stark prepped and ready to go.

Carl laid the woman's body out on the table and snapped pictures, then removed her clothing and took more pictures, expression emotionless and clinical. He wiped away the blood on her face, but I could still see it clotted up in her nostrils. Evelyn had been an attractive woman, but it was clear she'd been awfully close to that point in life when even the best of genetics weren't enough. She had a slim, leggy build, but the skin of her belly sagged and her thighs were flabby and had no muscle tone.

He glanced up at me after he set the camera aside. "Can you give me a hand?"

"With what?" I asked, narrowing my eyes at him in distrust. He had a habit of asking me to do gross and nasty things during autopsies.

He silently held out a syringe. His face was expressionless, but humor danced in his eyes.

He was asking me to get the vitreous—the fluid in the eyeball. The process for this involved sticking a needle into the side of the eye. Needless to say, it squicked me out big time. I usually shied away from this. Emphatically.

But this time I took the syringe from his hand. He

cocked an eyebrow at me in mild astonishment, then smiled and gestured to the body. "You know how to do it?"

I gave him a stiff nod. I'd seen it done a few dozen times. *Time to stop being a weenie.* The needle slid in with barely any resistance. A shiver raced down my spine at the sight of the needle tip going through the pupil, but it came with an absurd sense of satisfaction. I'd finally won a round of "make Kara do something nasty." I carefully drew out the fluid, pulled the needle back out, and then carefully handed it to Carl.

"Don't *ever* ask me to do that again," I said.

He burst out laughing, then quickly squirted the fluid into a tube. "I won't. I promise." He put the tube away, then turned back to me. "Do you want to try cutting the head open?"

"No!"

He grinned. "Your loss," he said.

"And on that, I will gladly accept defeat," I told him.

We suspended our banter as Doc returned to the cutting room. He remained largely quiet during the autopsy of Evelyn Stark. I had the feeling that his mind was already running through possibilities on why Barry Landrieu's brain had exploded, so to speak.

I watched his face as he began to cut through Evelyn Stark's brain, could see the instant he saw it from the way his face went still and pale. He gave his head a slight shake of disbelief, then yanked his gaze up to me. "What's the connection?" he asked. "There has to be some sort of connection. This isn't possible."

I could completely understand how he felt. "I don't know, Doc," I said, the lie bitter in my mouth. "But I gotta say, I'm glad to know my hunch was right."

His gaze grew hard for an instant, then he shook his head again. "That was one hell of a hunch, Kara." He gave me a smile, but it had a guarded, curious edge to it.

I spread my hands and tried to look baffled.

"Hunh." He turned his attention back to the body. "Maybe it's some sort of designer drug. Something that's not showing on the quick test. Or a virus." He grimaced. "Of course, if it is a virus, we're all fucked."

"I was on both scenes and gave CPR to her," I jerked my chin toward the body. "And my brain hasn't exploded yet. So we're probably all right."

Doc gave a humorless chuckle. "It's also only been one day. Hardly enough time for anything to take hold." He blew out his breath. "I have a feeling I'll be spending the rest of the day looking through a microscope."

"Barry Landrieu was a known drug user," I said. "And Evelyn Stark was an alcoholic."

He gave a nod. "My investigator told me that Landrieu went to jail a few years ago, and when he got out he supposedly cleaned up and was doing the whole straight-and-narrow thing."

"You don't see that very often," I said.

"Well, apparently his little sister died of an overdose while he was in prison. Guess that was his wakeup call."

Shock and regret coiled through me. *I made it out of that life and never looked back.* But what could I have done for her? Given her pep talks? Pressure her to get into rehab? No way to know if anything would have helped, but once I had my own act together surely I could have *tried*.

Doc was still talking, thankfully oblivious to my reaction. I yanked my attention back to him and did my best to shove down the guilt.

"Anyway, I'll put a rush on the tox screen. Let's keep our fingers crossed that's what it is."

I gave him a dutiful nod in response. He had his avenues of investigation, and I had mine. Now I knew for certain that the two deaths were related and not simply by coincidence. My next hunch was that the presence of the *graa* was connected. Now I simply had to hunt down a summoner.

Easy.

# Chapter 9

I left the morgue, still wondering how the hell I was going to accomplish my grand goal of finding this other summoner. We were private people out of self-preservation, and there wasn't exactly a local directory. I fully intended to check and see if my aunt had any leads, but other than that I didn't know what else I could do except wait for the summoner to tip his or her hand again.

By the time I made it to the station the sky had cleared to the kind of brilliant blue that only happened in southern winters when it was stupid-cold outside. No snow anymore, which was a relief, but the chill wind that swept around the building was anything but brisk and refreshing. Stabbing-icy-knives-of-death wind was probably a better description.

I made sure the cuff was concealed under my coat sleeve as I hurried up to the building. The last thing I wanted was to deal with questions about it. Actually the last thing I wanted was to have to keep wearing the damn thing. This whole mild nausea thing was a real downer.

I gave myself a mental slap and scowl as I entered the door marked "Investigations." Yeah, I didn't care to feel crummy. But getting summoned to the demon sphere? That was a whole 'nuther level of Do Not Want. I could deal with a bit of queasy stomach.

Warm air wrapped pleasantly behind me, and I quickly pulled the door closed to block out the wind.

"Damn, Gillian, afraid of a little cold weather?"

The nasal tenor startled me. I spun to see Detectives Boudreaux and Pellini sitting in the cramped waiting area usually reserved for people who had appointments to see one of the investigators. I straightened, instantly annoyed that I'd allowed my surprise to show.

"I'm a delicate southern flower, Boudreaux," I said to the detective who could best be described as weasely. Skinny to the point of emaciated, he looked like a meth addict, but not as healthy. It didn't look like he'd shaved in at least two days, but he was in no danger of growing anything resembling an actual beard. The patchy stubble on his chin looked like a fur coat left for a month in a moth factory. The stains on his khaki pants indicated he was in the long habit of wiping his hands on them instead of a napkin, his shirt had more wrinkles than a smoker's lips, and his tie looked like it had been knotted with a square knot. Yet despite his complete lack of professional demeanor, he managed to close enough cases to stay on in Investigations. He was lazy, couldn't investigate worth a shit, and was annoying as all hell, but rumor had it that he was a brilliant interrogator and could finesse information and confessions out of the most hardcore and stubborn types. "The chill does terrible things to my sunny disposition," I added.

Pellini shifted on the ancient couch and pulled his belt further up under the pudge of his belly. "Delicate, my ass," he said with a snort of sour amusement from beneath his mustache. "You could take Boudreaux here down with your eyes closed."

I blinked. Had that been a compliment? From Pellini? Our conversational exchanges usually involved various insults, not-so-veiled slurs, and generally disagreeable banter. I had no doubt that he would have been more than happy in the "old days" of police work when respecting a suspect's civil rights was a laughable concept. "What are you two doing sitting out here?" I asked, deciding to pretend the possible compliment hadn't happened. Too many weird things were happening lately. A Nice Pellini would put me right over the edge.

"Our office is about thirty degrees," Boudreaux said, face twisted in annoyance. "Maintenance is supposed to be coming by 'any minute now.' They said that an hour and a half ago."

And I had no doubt that they intended to avoid all semblance of work until the climate control was fixed. I decided to not point out that they could have brought their laptops out to the lobby so that they could get caught up on their reports.

"I hear you had a fun weekend," Pellini said.

"Yep," I said. "A guy died out at the Nature Center. Barry Landrieu. Then a lady crashed her ride into mine and dropped in the middle of the parking lot out here."

Pellini's mouth pursed beneath his mustache. "Nature center guy . . . you said his name was Landrieu? White guy? Blond hair and a mustache?"

I nodded warily. "You know him?"

A frown curved his already dour face. "Neighbor of mine. Was it a thirty?"

He was asking me if it was a Signal 30. A homicide. "Nah. Just got back from the autopsy. Natural death." It wasn't a complete lie. It did look like a natural death. I wasn't going to tell him that the woman had died in the exact same way. Pellini and Boudreaux already thought I was plenty weird. No sense giving them more reason to think so. I was probably already pegging out their "whackadoo" meter. I also wasn't about to mention my own history with him. "Buddy of yours?" I asked.

Pellini shook his head. "Nah. Just a guy who lived down the street—about four houses down. Big-time jogger. Every fucking day, rain or shine."

I tried not to show my surprise. Maybe it wasn't the same guy?

"Dude was an ex-con," he continued, putting the lie to my brief suspicion that it was someone else. "But he didn't seem like a bad guy. Looked like he was trying hard to start over."

I did my best to hide my shock. Pellini was being understanding? Showing a measure of actual empathy? "That's pretty cool," I said.

Pellini shrugged. "Yeah, but this week he got weird. Had issues with some of the neighbors."

I leaned against the doorframe. I was pretty sure this was the longest conversation I'd ever had with Pellini where I didn't have the urge to throw something heavy and dangerous at him. "Any issues with you?"

Pellini gave a low bark of laughter. "He tried. I was in my garage the other day and he comes walking up the driveway, stopped right before the door and starts going on about how the Saints didn't deserve to win the Super Bowl, and that Green Bay was going to take it all the way this year."

Boudreaux gave a snort. "Did you bust his ass?"

Pellini shrugged. "Nah. I kinda wondered if maybe he was trying to bait me and get me to take a swing at him—figured he probably had a buddy of his ready with a camera."

I was more than a little impressed at the level of restraint and understanding Pellini had shown, but then he spoiled it by continuing.

"Instead I went by his house later that night, let all the air out of his tires, and pissed on his front mat," he said with a satisfied smile.

"Okay, even *I* think that's funny," I admitted. "Well lemme go write this shit up so I can get out of here and leave you two to your little camping trip."

"You only wish you were cool enough to hang out with us," Pellini called after me as I continued on down the hall.

My office was frigid as well, but unlike Boudreaux and Pellini I was used to having a shit office and was prepared for it. Luckily it was about the size of a utility closet, which meant that it only took about ten minutes for the space heater in the corner to bring the ambient temperature up to the point where I could shed my coat. I pulled off the cuff as well and stuffed it into the pocket of my coat, breathing a deep sigh of relief as the simmering queasiness eased.

I plopped into my chair, then swept a frowning glance around the office as a sudden urge to rearrange the furniture seized me. I'd had it in the current configuration ever since getting this office. Maybe it was time for some change?

Easier said than done. I stood and spent several frustrating minutes trying to figure out how to turn the desk ninety degrees before realizing it was physically impossible. The desk had probably been assembled in the office, and I had a feeling that it would have be completely taken apart in order to change its position. I sat back down, annoyed at being thwarted by geometry. *Maybe this weekend I can bring some tools up here and get that done.*

In the meantime, I had things I wanted to check on. Ruthlessly pushing aside a stab of guilt at what I was about to do, I pulled up a search engine on my computer and typed in "Saratoga Springs, New York public records." Within a few minutes I found records stating that a Ryan Walker Kristoff had been born to Julius Kristoff and a Catherine Rathbun Kristoff. Okay, birth records successfully faked. But how deep did the history go? Would a bit of scratching reveal the charade?

Pretty deep, I began to realize after about fifteen minutes of searching. He had a full genealogy that went back at least four generations—which was as far back as I bothered searching before giving up and looking for other details. There were school records and assorted newspaper clippings for Ryan, his parents, and his cousins, one of whom had been arrested twice for driving under the influence. A bit of finagling pulled up Ryan's college transcript and his yearbook pictures, and more public records searches turned up name checks for various cases he'd been involved in.

In other words, it was, in every way, shape, and form,

as real a background and history as anyone could possibly have. I sat back, baffled. *There's no way this is faked. So what the hell does this mean?*

I glanced up at a tap on my door, surprised to see Roman Hatch standing in the doorway, carefully balancing a box that looked like it might very well contain donuts, with a coffee cup on top of that. "Morning," he said with a wide smile. "This is the proper sort of gift for a cop, right?"

Grinning, I motioned him in, then accepted the coffee cup he handed me. "It's a good start," I said, pulling the lid off. It already had cream in it and I glanced at him. "You added sugar?"

"Sure did," he said, setting the box on the desk. "I remember you used to like it pretty sweet."

"Just like me," I said with a bat of my eyelashes. Taking a sip, I discovered our definitions of "pretty sweet" were quite different. At most there might have been three sugars in it. More likely two. Still, it was a nice gesture, and I wasn't about to throw it in his face or anything. Besides, it was heaps better than the coffee here at the station. "Have a seat." I indicated the beat up chair that was squeezed into the corner of my tiny office. I leaned forward and tweaked open the box. Donuts, though not my favorite—the chocolate kind. Still, I was cool with regular glazed as well. "And now you will get to see me at my most glamorous," I said as I snagged one out.

"How long have you had this office?" His gaze swept the miniscule area.

I had to finish chewing and swallowing donut before I could reply. "Almost a year. I don't mind how small it is since I don't have to share."

"Sure, but don't you believe in decorating?"

I made a show of looking around. "It is decorated! See, I have a poster." I was quite proud of my fake "Magic Eye" poster. I'd lost count of the number of people who struggled to see a 3-D image in it that didn't exist.

He chuckled but didn't rise to the bait of the poster. "I stand corrected. You should consider opening your own interior design business."

"Nah. I like being a cop. I get to drive fast and tell people how stupid they are." I licked icing off my fingers and grinned.

"Anyway," he said, shifting to a smile that he probably thought was disarming. "I was wondering if you could help me out with something?"

I gave him a properly inquisitive look, though the slight curl of disappointment in my belly already had a good idea of what he was about to ask. Some sort of trouble with his neighbor maybe, or a ticket that he was hoping I could help him take care of.

He tugged a folded piece of paper from his pocket. A ticket. I hated that I'd been right. No real interest in me after all. I shouldn't have been surprised. Back in college he'd always seemed more interested in having either a hot girlfriend he could show off or a super smart one he could use for free tutoring. I hadn't really fallen into either category, which was one of the reasons I'd been astounded that he'd asked me out in the first place.

Unfolding the ticket, his expression morphed into "sheepish." I wasn't buying it. He probably practiced these expressions in the mirror in order to get what he wanted. He was smooth.

But I'd been dealing with demons for the past ten years.

I didn't say anything as he set it on the desk. Didn't even look at it. Just continued to gaze at him with the same inquisitive, slightly puzzled expression. Two could play this game.

He broke first, tapping the ticket with a finger and clearing his throat. "There's this road near my parents' house with a hill, and I didn't realize how fast I was going. He got me for sixty in a forty-five."

"Okay," I said as guilelessly as possible. "You need to know where to go to pay it? Or are you going to contest it in court?"

He leaned back, rueful smile still in place. "It's a pretty hefty fine," he said. "I was wondering if you knew any way I could get it reduced?"

"You want me to see if I can fix it." I didn't make it a question. "You want to see if you can spend a few dollars for donuts and coffee to see if you can save over a hundred." If I was more of a bitch I'd throw the coffee right back at him.

Now he winced. "I didn't mean it like that, I swear. I just wanted to see if it could be changed to seatbelt or—" He let out a choked cry and staggered to his feet, staring down in shock at the coffee covering his front.

I stared in shock as well, then yanked my eyes to my right hand—which was holding the empty coffee cup. I barely even remembered throwing the coffee at him, but I knew I had. I'd thought about it, then done it. No hesitation.

"Oh my god, Roman. I . . . I . . ." I dropped the empty cup on my desk and yanked open my top drawer to grab out some tired napkins from a long ago fast food meal. I thrust them toward him, and he eyed them almost uncertainly before taking them and making a futile attempt to blot up the coffee.

"I guess that's a 'no' then" he said, mouth twisting in a grimace.

"Shit, Roman, I swear I—"

"Everything cool here?"

I jerked my head around to see Cory, my sergeant, standing in the doorway of the office, frowning beneath his mustache, brown eyes taking in the details.

I opened my mouth but suddenly had no idea what to say. *I threw my coffee on him because he asked me how to get a ticket reduced.* So fucking what? That kind of stuff happened all the time.

"I'm a klutz," Roman spoke up while I was still floundering. He turned the wry smile onto Sarge as he wiped his hands on the soggy napkins. "I was trying to give Kara her coffee, and we bumped hands." He laughed, an easy sound. "I was the loser."

Damn, but he was good. I'd have totally believed him if I hadn't actually been here when it happened and done the actual spilling. Throwing, rather.

Sarge's face cleared, and he gave a brisk nod. "Gotcha. There's a restroom down the hall if you need to clean up." He shifted his attention to me. "I'll see if I can get a trustee in here to mop."

I just gave him a nod. I wasn't sure if it was safe for me to speak yet.

Roman simply gave a self-effacing chuckle. "I think I got the worst of it. I'm going to have to head home to change anyway." He shot me a perfect imitation of an apologetic look. Or maybe he really was apologetic? "I'm really sorry about getting coffee everywhere, Kara."

I gulped. "Um. 'S okay," I managed. Why the *fuck* had I thrown my coffee at him?

He caught my eye, and for the first time I saw what I thought might be true emotion—a confusing split-second flash of regret, anger, affection, and relief. Then he was out the door while I stood with my hands clenched to keep them from shaking.

Sarge watched him go, and as soon as the outer door closed he turned to me, eyes narrowed. "What happened?"

I shook my head as if that could get my thoughts back in order. "I threw my coffee at him."

He made a *hmmf*ing sound. "No shit. I'm not any sort of blood-spatter analyst, but—" His gaze raked the coffee on the wall. "—even I can tell that was more than a 'bump' of hands. Now tell me whether I need to go after him and defend the virtue of one of my sisters in blue."

A snort of laughter escaped me at the thought of anyone defending what little virtue I might still have. I unclenched my hands, sighed. "He didn't do anything like that. All he did was ask if I could get a ticket reduced." I grimaced and rubbed at my eyes. "I have no idea why that set me off."

He pursed his lips. "You cool now?"

I nodded vigorously. "Like ice." Spazzing out on the inside, but I could fake cool.

Maybe I couldn't, because Sarge simply snorted and turned away. "I'll go get that trustee."

I wanted to sink into my chair and wallow in a mild freakout, but I couldn't afford that sort of luxury right now. I needed to go see my aunt.

I waited long enough for the trustee to wipe down the wall and mop up the worst of the coffee, then I shooed him out, locked my door and headed down the hall to my sergeant's office.

"By the way," I said as I stood in his doorway, "both the vics from yesterday had mega-strokes."

He lifted his head and leveled a frown at me. "Does Doc have a reason why yet?"

I shook my head. "I need to go check out a few things, if that's okay."

"Do what you need to do," he said, then dropped his attention back to the paperwork on his desk. I masked a grin as I left. Cory knew that a number of my cases had some supernatural aspects, but that didn't mean he had to like it. Or openly acknowledge it. Or anything else that gave him the screaming willies. Poor guy. He tried, though. I had to give him that.

I stepped out of the back door and then let out a shocked cry as someone slammed me up against the outside wall. Or rather, I would have let out a shocked cry if I had any air left in my lungs.

Eilahn glared at me as she pinned me against the wall with her forearm. With her other she fished the cuff out of my coat pocket and held it up in front of me.

"Don't forget," she said in a mild tone that belied the fury in her narrowed eyes.

"Oh, yeah," I managed to rasp. "Sorry . . . ?" I offered her as groveling a smile as I could manage.

She *hmm*fed and released me but only to grab my wrist and snap the cuff around it. "Don't forget," she repeated.

I took a shuddering breath as the faint queasiness returned. "I won't. I'm really sorry."

Her expression softened, and she laid a hand on my shoulder. "I am not wroth with you. But this is a habit that you must form."

"I will." I took a deep breath in a futile attempt to settle my stomach. "Thanks for watching out for me."

She smiled. "It is my pleasure." And with that she turned and walked off. I watched her until she turned the corner, then I continued on to my car. If I'd ever had any doubts about her ability to be at my side in a split second, they were gone now. Not that I'd ever had any, to be honest.

My demon bodyguard kicked ass. Unfortunately, every now and then that ass was mine.

# Chapter 10

I gave the door of Tessa's house a cursory knock, then entered, a split second ahead of her shout of "Kitchen!" At least that much was normal—or as normal as anything to do with my aunt could be. I paused, slipped the cuff off, and stuffed it into my bag before shedding my coat. My aunt's pristine white, century-old house was warded to the teeth; I had no fear of being attacked or summoned while in here. Situated in a historical district on the lakefront, Tessa kept her house in exquisite condition, with carefully maintained landscaping, eggshell-blue gingerbread molding along the porch, and a set of white rockers that, unlike mine, had actually been taken out of the boxes they came in and assembled. The inside of her house was just as lovely—brilliant hardwood floors, crown molding, and flowered wallpaper in a subtle pattern of rose and gold. Not that she ever let anyone inside to see it whom she didn't trust completely. Even the "Welcome" sign on the door was a standing joke, at least in my opinion. The aversions were such that only someone who was welcome—or seriously determined— would ever get close enough to the house to see it.

Continuing on down the hallway, I entered the kitchen to see Tessa and Carl sitting at the table playing some sort of card game. Staying true to her incredibly eclectic and weird sense of style, she had on a thigh-length black sweater dress embroidered in gold spider webs, with gold lamé leggings underneath that and knee-high boots—with what had to be five-inch heels. Her wild, kinky blond hair was pulled back from her face by a white scarf. As usual, it totally worked on her. It helped that she was a tiny little thing without a spare ounce of fat on her body.

Tessa gave me a cheery smile, then returned her attention to the richly colored cards displayed in front of her and in her hand. "There's hot water in the kettle if you want tea," she informed me.

"I'm good, thanks," I said, pulling myself onto a stool at the counter. "Are those tarot cards?"

Tessa let out a bright peal of laughter. "Oh, heavens, no. Nothing that silly. We're playing 'Magic, The Gathering.'"

After umpteen years of living with my aunt, somehow she still managed to confuse and surprise me. "Um. Okay. That's like 'Dungeons and Dragons' or something, right?"

She shook her head, then shrugged. "Not quite the same thing. This is a complex trading card game simulating battles between fantasy armies, complete with dragons, angels, elves, goblins, and magic."

"Ah. Of course." Through sheer will and love of my aunt I somehow managed to keep from rolling my eyes.

"Besides," she continued, "*Thursday* nights are our D&D games. Carl and I are just passing a little time."

She cast a fond look at the man across the table from her. In response he reached out and touched the back of her hand. It was a tiny gesture, made with barely a change in his expression, but somehow it conveyed so much tenderness that my throat briefly closed from the utterly simple beauty of it.

"Would you like to join us?" Tessa asked me, but there was enough of a twinkle in her eye that I knew she wasn't serious. Not that she wanted to exclude me or anything of the sort, but she was all too aware that I was far from the type to play role playing games or indulge in any other sort of geekiness. I had enough of the real thing in my life, thank you very much.

"Gee, maybe next time," I replied, and this time I *did* roll my eyes. "Do you mind if I take a stroll through your library instead?"

"Not at all," she replied without the slightest hitch or hesitation. I was watching for anything like that and was almost surprised at the ease of her agreement. "Does this have something to do with a case?"

"Possibly," I said, thinking of the presence of the *graa*. "I went out on a scene yesterday . . . ." Now I was the one to hesitate. We didn't talk much about the Shit Years—which was how I thought of that time between the death of my father and my entry into the world of demon summoning. My relationship with my aunt had consisted mostly of screaming matches and sullen resentment—on both sides—and once we finally managed to find common ground we were both glad to put that time behind us. I had less problem talking about my wayward past with people like Jill and Carl, probably because they weren't involved.

Carl set his cards down and stood. "I'm going to enjoy the backyard for a little while," he remarked to no one in particular, then silently quit the room.

I could totally see why my aunt adored him. I did too at that moment. Taking a steadying breath, I asked, "Do you remember Tammy North?"

"I do," Tessa said, slight frown puckering her forehead. "You and she used to hang out."

"If by 'hang out' you mean 'do drugs,'" I corrected, grimacing.

She gave a soft sigh. "Yes, that too.

"Found out today that she died a while back." I paused. "Overdose."

Her eyes shadowed. "You're not surprised," Tessa stated.

"I feel like I should have . . . I dunno, gone back for her somehow." Sighing, I ran a hand through my hair. "I know it probably wouldn't have done any good, but . . ." I trailed off, not sure what I wanted to say. "I was lucky." I didn't have to elaborate, but I did anyway. "You had my back."

A smile whispered across her face. "Still do, sweets." Her eyes grazed across the arcane tattoo on the inside of my left forearm for a hundredth of a heartbeat, then returned to mine. I knew that my aunt could see the Mark on my arm. Even through the fabric of my long-sleeved shirt, she could surely sense it. I also knew she was fully aware of what it meant—that I was sworn to Lord Rhyzkahl. I'd expected some sort of argument or confrontation about it, but it had never materialized. Yet in that ever-so-brief flick of her eyes, we'd had the discussion about the mark and what it meant. She wouldn't stop worrying, but I knew she supported me, no matter what.

"I know," I replied, suddenly all full of warm fuzzies. I cleared my throat, about to embarrass myself by welling up with tears or something equally dorky.

Tessa saved me. "Who was the victim at your scene?" she asked.

I straightened my shoulders and got control of myself. "Her brother. Barry."

Tessa's mouth became a stiff line. "Yes. The one who thought you were ready to try heroin at the tender age of fourteen."

"That's the one."

"You'll pardon me if I'm not consumed with grief over his passing."

I gave a low snort. "No, I get it." Even though that brush with death had been a wakeup call for my aunt and me, Tessa would never forgive the man for nearly killing me. Frankly, I was a little shocked that he'd never received a visit from a demon.

I didn't like the unpleasant thought that popped into my head. Carl had said she wasn't summoning anymore, but how much did he really know? "Tessa, did you ever send a demon after him?" *Like, very recently?*

To my surprise she gave a sharp laugh. "Oh, how I was tempted. But I accomplished far more by sending the narcs after him and making sure he went to jail."

Reassured, some of the tension eased out of my back. She wouldn't lie to me about something like that.

"Now tell me why you think there's something off about his death." She cast a narrow-eyed gaze my way.

I shook my head. "First I have to tell you about the other death." I quickly recounted the incident with the car crashing into mine and the driver's subsequent death. "The driver was Evelyn Stark," I finished.

She closed her eyes briefly. When she opened them they were dark with sympathy. "She was drunk again?"

"No. At least I don't think so. But here's where it gets weird. Both Barry and Evelyn died of multiple strokes."

Her eyebrows rose.

"And here's where it gets even weirder," I said with a humorless smile. "Yesterday morning Eilahn and I were attacked by a *graa* while we were placing wards around the PD building."

Her eyebrows dove into a dark frown. "Which means there's another summoner in the game."

"Right. I don't know yet how much of a part this summoner has, but I figure my best course of action right now is to track his or her ass down."

My aunt grimaced. "Not an easy task."

"What about that librarian you met in New Orleans when you were first starting out—the one who hooked you up with Katashi?"

She sighed. "No, she passed away quite some time ago." Her brow furrowed in thought. "I'll get in touch with Katashi, see if he knows of anyone working in this area." Pain flashed quickly through her eyes and was gone. "He owes me anyway," she added softly.

I knew Katashi, the summoner who'd trained my aunt. I'd gone to Japan last year for a couple of months to study under him—a complete waste of time and money. He was ninety if he was a day, and a condescending, sexist asshole. I could barely tolerate him for two months. I had no idea how my aunt had put up with him for close to a decade.

"I appreciate it," I said.

Her chin dipped in a nod. "I wouldn't hold your breath waiting for Katashi to respond. You'd best get to your research, if you want to have any chance of results."

I smiled wryly. "I guess I'd better."

"Let me know if you need anything," she said, then looked back to her cards as Carl walked back into the kitchen and sat back in his chair as if he'd never left.

I slipped off my stool and made my escape to the library.

Ages ago—or so it seemed—Ryan had asked me why I summoned the demons. And my reply to him was something flip, on the order of, "Because I can." But, in truth, there was so much more to it than that. It wasn't simply the fact that I had this ability. It was the fact that the summoning gave me something in my life that I didn't have and probably never would have. It gave me purpose and a sense of accomplishment, and it was something that I'd earned. No one had anointed me as a summoner. Other than the innate ability to open the portal, I had to work and learn and study and bleed to get to my current skill level. I wasn't heir to some incredible power or fortune that had been bestowed upon me, and it wasn't as if some supernatural accident had occurred that had made me this way—like the stories where a homely girl is turned into an all-powerful vampire or werewolf or some such thing. No, I'd fucking earned this. This power, this ability was mine.

That's why I summoned the demons. Because I could.

But right now, standing in the middle of Aunt Tessa's library, I almost wished I couldn't. Because then maybe I wouldn't have to deal with this nightmare of a room.

My aunt insisted that there was a method to the madness in her library. And, to her credit, there was something about this place that somehow allowed me to find what I needed to find, even if it wasn't always what I was looking for. Yet I continued to insist that it could not truly be called a library. Those were places of order, with some sort of system in place for keeping track of the contents. When one thought of a library, one might imagine a room with bookshelves from floor to ceiling, perhaps a table and some chairs. And yes, this room had all that. But the shelves were crammed—sometimes literally—with books, not always with the spine out, and certainly not with even a passing nod to alphabetization or any other comprehensible system. And the tables and chairs were also stacked high—books, papers, and the occasional scroll or big, horking tome. Shoved into the corners were more books, maps, and the occasional curio that I could never tell if it was some sort of valuable artifact or something that had caught her eye at a garage sale. To complete the bizarre image, the room was lit by an enormous crystal chandelier that took up most of the ceiling.

Only one corner of the room was clear—a heavily warded spot that I now knew held a portal of sorts between our world and the demon realm. It wasn't the type of thing that a sentient creature could come through, but if left unwarded plenty of other things could come through—or be pushed through, as I'd found out the hard way. The best guess was that it acted as some sort of "pressure valve." Regardless, we now knew that it needed to stay warded and well-protected. I was perfectly fine with leaving it the fuck alone.

Putting the portal out of my mind, I began my search for anything that might help me figure out how to track down another summoner, as well as any references to humans being summoned to the demon realm. I even kept my eyes peeled for any references to strokes, though with my limited knowledge of anatomy and physiology, it was likely that I'd skim right over something pertinent without even realizing it.

After an hour of pulling books and papers off the shelves at random I'd learned that pineapples are classified as berries, that if one should desire to summon a *nyssor* by the name of Votevha the best possible offering is bacon, and that a whale's penis is called a "dork."

Sighing, I did my best to replace everything where I'd found it. Not only was I no closer to finding this summoner, but now I was craving a BLT like crazy. And I didn't even like tomatoes.

When I came out of the library, Tessa wasn't in the kitchen. I finally found her sitting cross-legged on a red velvet fainting couch in the front room, with a book in her hand and reading glasses perched on her nose. The boots with the sky-high heels lay in a tumble on the floor in front of the couch. Her eyes flicked up to me and she smiled. "Find anything useful?"

My answer was a shrug. "Hard to tell. You know how it is."

She pulled her glasses off and folded them closed. "Sometimes it takes a while for things to click into place."

"Yeah." I paused, took a seat in an armchair that faces the front window. "Is Carl still here?"

She shook her head, eyes on me. "What's on your mind, sweets?"

I said it quickly before I could change my mind or lose my nerve. "Do you hate Rhyzkahl for killing my grandmother?" I caught myself before adding "your mother" to clarify. Tessa knew who I was talking about.

Tessa marked the place in the book and set it aside. *Dragonflight*, I absently noted. "There was a time when I did," she said, voice even. Then a smile flickered across her mouth. "And to answer the question you left unasked," she continued, "no, I have never felt any sort of anger or ire toward you for your arrangement with the lord."

Arrangement. That was one way of putting it. I had no doubt Tessa was fully aware what sort of relationship we had. "So, um, you don't hate him anymore?" I asked, frowning. Would I be so forgiving? I sure as hell wasn't toward Evelyn Stark. Then again, for some reason it had never bothered me until recently that Rhyzkahl had killed my grandmother. I'd somehow assumed that was a failure of character on my part, but now I couldn't help but wonder—had Rhyzkahl deliberately suppressed thoughts I might have had about my grandmother? He'd sworn not to compel me against my will, but making sure I didn't think unpleasant thoughts wasn't "compelling." The idea left a sour taste in my mouth. *I have no proof*, I reminded myself. *I never knew my grandmother, and she was involved in dangerous practices.*

Great. So either I was a cold bitch, or my lover had been playing tricks with my head. Fucking hell, but I sure hoped a third option came along soon.

Tessa didn't seem to notice my inner turmoil. She turned her head to look out the window, mouth slightly pursed and forehead creased. She stayed silent for nearly a full minute, but I had the feeling she was choosing what to say in response to my question. I did my best to wait patiently for her answer.

"When I was in the void, I . . . learned things," she said, nearly whispering, forcing me to strain to hear her. "I don't think there's any way to describe it, because it was more a sense of how things are and how they are meant to be rather than any particular nugget of information. But in the time since I woke I've been trying to assimilate it all." She lifted a shoulder in a shrug and glanced at me with a wry smile. "And somewhere in there I could not maintain my anger at Rhyzkahl."

"But why?" I persisted.

"Because what he did was necessary." She shook her head, seemingly dissatisfied with the answer. "I'm sorry, sweets, it's difficult to explain."

"Does that mean you're all right with me being his summoner?" I asked with a touch of disbelief.

She laughed. "Oh, powers above and below, no! But not because of who he is or what he's done."

"Because he's a demonic lord," I said.

She hesitated, nodded, an odd expression of dismay and resignation whispering across her features before she smoothed them out and answered me. "That's as close an answer as I can give you."

# Chapter 11

I remembered to snap the cuff around my wrist before I stepped beyond the wards, thus avoiding being tackled by Eilahn. I knew the *syraza* was always nearby, but the amazing thing was that I never felt as if I was under any sort of surveillance, and it was remarkably easy to forget about her. As a guardian of someone who was jealous of their privacy, she was perfect.

A wave of queasiness hit me as I drove past a fried chicken stand, and I gritted my teeth against it. Sure, the cuff gave me a great deal of peace of mind, but this constant simmering nausea *sucked*. If pregnancy and morning sickness were anything like this, I wanted no part of it.

A cold stab of apprehension went through me. I'd been blithely assuming the nausea was because of the cuff. Was I engaging in unhealthy denial? Nausea, check. Mood swings, check. *Shiiiiiit.* I'd read enough novels where the woman felt sick and seemed somehow oblivious to the connection between regular booty calls and getting knocked up. I was definitely getting the former. *But I'm also on the pill*, I thought, almost desperately. I'd slept with Rhyzkahl the night before, but when was the last time prior to that?

At the next stoplight I retrieved my phone from my bag, and pulled up the calendar. Since I was on the pill I had a pretty good idea of my cycle. I chewed my lower lip as I looked at the dates. The pill wasn't infallible; I knew that. And the dates could *possibly* work out. But it didn't seem very likely. Still, my gut remained tight as I stopped at a drugstore and bought two pregnancy tests — just to be sure — while praying to any gods willing to listen that I wouldn't run into anyone I knew. Wouldn't *that* set the rumor mill spinning!

My luck held, and I made my purchases without anyone but the bored checker knowing. Even made it home without puking. But that's where my tenuous hold on luck failed me. The crunch of gravel came from behind me as I ran up the steps. I turned, my hand on the doorknob.

The dark blue Crown Vic pulled up and parked next to my car. Ryan gave me a smile as he stepped out, and I fought to give the same in return, hyper-aware of the pregnancy tests in my messenger bag. I glanced down to make sure that the zipper on my bag was closed and spied the cuff on my wrist. *Shit.* I didn't want Ryan asking about that. He'd worry, or get pissed, or something else I didn't feel like dealing with. I knew I'd have to tell him at some point . . . just not right at this moment. Luckily I was inside the wards now. I hurriedly slipped it off, dropped it in the outer pocket of my bag, and shoved the velcro flap down.

The queasy feeling receded as soon as it was off my arm, and I took a deep breath of relief. *Okay, maybe not pregnant after all*, I thought a little shakily. At least I hoped that was the cause. Still, I planned on testing to be sure.

I yanked my thoughts away from that topic as Ryan approached. I knew too much about him now. *Can he read my thoughts? Even subconsciously?* I was pretty darn sure that Rhyzkahl could, which meant that—if Ryan truly was a demonic lord—he might be able to as well. *Think of something innocuous, like a white wall, or a purple giraffe.* Ugh, I had no experience in trying to avoid having my mind read. *Purple Giraffe. Purple Giraffe!*

"Hey, Kara," he said, smile relaxed and easy as he climbed the stairs. No sign on his face that he was picking up any of my stray thoughts. Instead he cocked his head, smile widening. "You forgot, didn't you?"

I blinked at him, only now realizing he had a pizza box in one hand and a boxed set of DVDs in the other. I grimaced. "Oh, right. You're going to attempt to turn me into a nerd."

He laughed. "It's a gradual process, but I fully intend to wear you down."

The tension eased out of me. This was familiar ground again. I entered my house and dropped my bag by the desk near the door, nudging it lightly underneath in what I hoped was a casual manner and not an obvious attempt to keep it out of sight.

He didn't seem to notice anything and moved into what passed for my living room, setting the pizza and DVDs down on the coffee table. Curious, I picked up the DVD box and peered at the cover.

"Seriously?" I said, casting a doubtful look at him. "This spaceship looks like a chicken."

He gave me a mock scowl. "It's a beautiful ship."

"Is this guy trying to look like a cowboy?" I continued, purposely needling him. "A space cowboy?"

Giving a tragic sigh, he snatched the box out of my hand. "Just watch the show."

I chuckled and plopped onto the couch. "Fine. I'll watch your space cowboy chicken ship show. But only because you brought pizza." At least the nausea was pretty much gone.

Ryan shot a glance down the hallway. "Where's your roommate?"

I shrugged. "She's around. She doesn't usually hang out inside. I think she feels closed in or something. Or maybe she just likes giving me space."

"Ah. Makes sense," he said, sliding a disc into my DVD player. "I guess it's an adjustment for you." He moved to the couch and sat. Friend distance, I noted. Not right next to me, but not on the other end, either. "Have you ever had a roommate?" he asked. "I mean, besides your aunt, which I figure doesn't count."

"Had one in college. We pretty much ignored each other."

Ryan grinned. "The best kind."

He started the DVD, and we lapsed into comfortable silence while we munched pizza and watched. To my chagrin I found myself intrigued by the premise and the characters, though I didn't dare admit it. He'd be way too satisfied if I did that.

He was entranced with the show, and I found myself watching him surreptitiously. He was a damn attractive man, though with a completely different kind of look than Rhyzkahl. Where Rhyzkahl was utterly beautiful and perfect, Ryan had more of a rugged, "man's man" thing going on. He had a great mouth, too. What would it be like to have that mouth on mine? And damn, what I'd give to run my hand down his chest. A slow flush of warmth crept through me. Why did I have to be careful around him? That was absurd. It didn't matter who or what he was. There was nothing at stake. Ryan was sexy as all hell, and the fact that I suspected he was a demonic lord only made him hotter.

Somewhere deep in the back of my mind I knew there was a good reason to keep Ryan in the "friend zone," but it didn't seem terribly important right now. Why hold myself back from what I wanted?

I shifted and reached to the back of his head, running my fingers through his hair the way I'd been wanting to ever since I met him. He twitched in surprise at the touch and turned his head to look at me, brow drawing down in question and confusion.

"Kara . . . ?"

"I like your hair," I murmured, sliding my other hand across his thigh. His breath caught, and I smiled, enjoying his reaction. "I like all of you." I moved in closer, shifting to nuzzle his neck. "You smell *great*."

"Jesus, Kara." His voice was suddenly rough, and his hands tightened into fists as a shudder ran through him. The scent of him wrapped around me, and I ran my tongue lightly up the side of his neck. "Kara, wait . . . are you sure—?"

I didn't let him finish the sentence. Shifting quickly to straddle his hips, I kissed him, groaning softly as my tongue found his. He tasted great too, and now I wanted more.

His hands on my shoulders gently but firmly pushed me back, breaking the kiss. I couldn't understand the expression on his face. I knew he wanted me too, so why would he look distressed? Maybe he simply wanted to be sure. "Fuck me, Ryan," I breathed, grinding myself against him. I gave a throaty laugh. He did want me. Some things were obvious. "Come on. Right here. I want you inside of me."

A distant part of me clamored for attention, but it seemed terribly dim, and the desire for what I wanted overpowered it easily. I slid my hands up his chest. "You want me. I know it. You want to fuck me." I pushed his hands away and captured his mouth again.

I heard the front door slam open, but I didn't pay any attention. All I wanted was the feel and taste of Ryan. Something seized me by the back of my shirt, and I let out a snarl as whatever it was hauled me away from Ryan. Twisting, I tried to strike out at the interloper, but Eilahn blocked my blow easily and delivered a sharp and stinging slap across my face.

"You fucking bitch!" I howled, flailing out another attempt to strike the grim-faced *syraza*. She said nothing but struck me again, this time hard enough for me to see stars. I staggered and sprawled on the arm of the couch as I dimly heard Eilahn ordering Ryan to go outside. I turned to look at him and caught sight of the oddly tortured expression on his face, though I couldn't figure out why that could be. Surely he wanted to fuck me too, right? What was wrong with that? Why the hell was Eilahn interfering? She had no right! Had Rhyzkahl ordered her to keep me away from other men? With a snarl of rage I threw myself at her, swinging a punch for her head, but she stopped me cold and seized my throat in a grip that felt like steel. She wasn't cutting off my air—instead she had her fingers placed perfectly to cut off the blood to my brain. I clawed at her fingers, panicked as the blood roared in my ears, and my vision narrowed. Flailing, I watched the grim and worried set of her face as the blackness swept in.

"I am sworn to protect you," I heard her say through the roaring. Then I heard nothing at all.

"What happened?"

"I do not know."

"I wouldn't have. . . ." That was Ryan's voice. "You do know that, right?"

My head throbbed hideously, and the voices seemed to stab through my ears.

"I do." That was Eilahn. I cracked an eye open uncertainly. The memory of the last few minutes before I lost consciousness was horribly clear. Humiliatingly so. Eilahn crouched before me, and I did my best to focus on her. I knew that Ryan was nearby, but I didn't dare try and look at him. Oh fuck, I never wanted to look at him again.

I burst into tears instead, which, of course, only served to increase my total humiliation. To my complete shock she pulled me into an embrace. I'd been sitting on the couch with her kneeling before me, but in a graceful and impossibly strong move, she shifted so that she was the one sitting, and I was somehow cradled in her lap. Somehow it didn't feel demeaning at all. Good thing, since I was utterly aghast at what I'd done and couldn't stop crying. But the demon merely held me close like a child and hummed softly.

Gradually ease stole through me, and I was finally able to stop shaking and get control of the racking sobs. But I made no move to pull away. I wasn't ready to face Ryan.

"You were overtaken," the demon murmured. "You must not feel shame for what happened."

*But it was what I wanted*, I thought miserably. *I wasn't being controlled.*

"Something affected you," she continued. "You know in your essence that you would never have acted thus on your own volition."

She had a point there. Even if I did want Ryan to . . . I cringed. I couldn't even think it without flushing in embarrassment at my behavior. Which, of course, helped prove Eilahn's point. I wasn't quite the type to jump on him, no matter how much I might secretly lust after him. And especially now that I knew how much more could be at stake. An unpleasant chill snaked through me. *I am sworn to protect you.* That's what Eilahn had said right before I lost consciousness. Was she protecting me from Ryan? From Rhyzkahl? Would she have done the same if I'd made a pass at, say, Tracy Gordon?

I lifted my head unsteadily. She slid smoothly aside and shifted so that I was sitting properly again, though she remained beside me. I swiped at my eyes. Eilahn held out a roll of toilet paper.

"You have nothing else that would serve for nose-blowing," she stated so matter-of-factly that I managed something that almost resembled a smile. I made use of the toilet paper, not caring that my nose-blowing was probably fairly disgusting. I'd already shamed myself enough. What was a little grossness at this point?

"What happened?" I heard Ryan say, anxiety deeply coloring his voice. I still couldn't bring myself to look at him, though I was aware that he was standing just beyond the open door. Eilahn had ordered him outside, and he was apparently abiding by her command.

"I don't know," I replied, eyes on my hands. "Ryan . . . I'm so sorry. I— " My voice caught, and I couldn't go on. I'd pretty much screwed up any chance of us remaining friends. A tiny part of me wondered if maybe that would be for the best, for my own safety, but the rest of me ached at the thought. I'd been alone for so much of my life that the thought of losing any of my newfound friends was agonizing.

"Oh, for fuck's sake, Kara," he said, anger in his voice. "Knock it off. Something happened to you that caused you to go temporarily nuts. Don't you fucking dare apologize."

I lifted my head to glare at him before I could remember that I was too ashamed for that sort of thing. He caught my gaze. "I guess that new cologne of mine that's guaranteed to drive women wild worked a little too well," he said with a reassuring smile that managed to ease a tiny bit of the horrible fear lingering inside me still.

I shook my head. "Nope. I think your geek show drove me over the edge."

He laughed, relief shining in his eyes, and I realized that he was just as afraid as I was that this would permanently mar our friendship. *Like there isn't enough going on already to affect that,* I thought. *It's a fucking miracle we can still even be in the same room.* And how would Rhyzkahl react if I ever did sleep with Ryan? Rhyzkahl had never batted an eyelash at the two of us being friends, and he'd never seemed the least bit possessive. *But even if they aren't enemies there's definitely some sort of conflict going on between those two. The last thing I want is to be caught in the middle.*

I snorted to myself. Who the fuck was I kidding? I was already hip-deep in the middle of whatever the hell it was. Best I could hope for at this point was to avoid being collateral damage.

I took a deep breath. "I'm inside the wards," I pointed out. "Could it have been some sort of attack—like the summoning attempts—that managed to get through?"

Eilahn's brows drew together in a frown. "I do not see how such would be possible. The wards I have placed on this house are as strong as I can possibly make them. Even if something were to get through, I would have felt it."

"But you knew something was wrong," Ryan stated.

Her gaze moved to him. "I felt your shock," she told him. She fell silent but her eyes remained on him. Unspoken—but as loud as if it had been shouted—was the assertion that if she hadn't felt that shock, or if she'd considered Ryan implicit in any way, she'd have attacked him first instead of simply pulling me away.

Ryan broke the gaze first, scrubbing a hand over his head. My hand seemed to tingle with the memory of running my fingers through his hair. Hey, at least I'd managed to do that. He had nice hair. Almost worth the total humiliation of the whole thing.

"Are you, um, better now?" he asked me.

"I don't feel an overwhelming urge to grab you and make you fuck me," I said, struggling to be cheeky. Hell, maybe being deliberately blunt would help desensitize the whole situation.

I could see that he was resisting making a joke. Not the right time, I could see clearly in his expression. "I guess you don't want to watch the rest of the show?"

"Not a chance," I replied, managing a smile. "At least not right now," I added. I gave a shrug. "It was actually . . . sort of cool."

His mouth twitched. "Only sort of?"

"Don't push your luck, nerd boy," I warned.

He smiled, though there was still tension in his eyes. "Fair enough. I'd better be going then. I get the feeling Eilahn wants to talk to you in private." His eyes met mine again. "I'm glad you're all right. And don't worry. Okay?"

I nodded. "Sure. Okay."

He closed the door, and I soon heard the crunch of gravel as his car headed down the driveway. I let out a ragged sigh and shoved both hands through my hair. "Fuuuuuuuuuucck. Eilahn. I . . . wanted him. I didn't care about any of the reasons why it was a mistake."

She stood, peered through the window briefly as if to assure herself that he was really gone, then turned back to me, worry on her face for the first time. "I did not wish to say anything while he was here since I knew it could be awkward, but it does seem to me that whatever affected you did so by removing your natural inhibitions and grossly enhancing your immediate desires."

Grimacing, I rubbed at my temples. There was a thought just out of reach but a slight headache was making it difficult to concentrate on anything. "I'm glad you were here," I said, then looked up. "I really mean that. Whether I want to have hot sex with Ryan or not"—I ignored the slight lifting of her eyebrow—"that's not how I would ever want the, uh, first time to be."

"Understandable," the demon replied. "I am pleased I was in a position to help."

My cell phone rang. My headache gave a throbbing jab as I stood to retrieve my bag, then settled back into a dull ache. I fumbled my phone from the outer pocket.

"Kara, you need to come over to my house," my aunt said as soon as I answered. Alarm spiked through me at the worry in her voice.

"What's going on?" I demanded. "Are you all right?"

"I'm fine," she said. "Someone died in my front yard. Police and ambulance are already here," she went on before I could say anything. "But you need to get over here."

My aunt wasn't the sort who needed me to hold her hand in a stressful situation. "I'm on my way, but can you tell me why?"

I heard her sigh. "Because I think he was trying to get into the house," she said.

That wasn't a good thing. My aunt's house was warded damn near as heavily as mine, mostly to guard the portal in her library.

"But there's more," she continued. "It's someone you know."

*Two is a coincidence. Three is a pattern.* My chest felt tight. "Who?"

"Your ex-boyfriend," she said.

A spasm shot through me. Roman? *No . . . please.* I'd

just seen him yesterday. I didn't have any reason to dislike him. We'd simply been a bad fit, and the breakup had been as amicable as such things could be.

I was so wrapped up in my thoughts I almost missed what she said. "Wait, what? Which ex-boyfriend?"

"Thomas," she repeated. "Thomas the Turd."

# Chapter 12

Tessa had made it clear from the first time she'd met my second boyfriend, Thomas Chartres, that she didn't care for him one tiny whit. Unfortunately, it had taken me almost two months to see what she'd seen—that he was a charming asshole, manipulative and controlling, and, I later learned, an abusive one as well. He never reached the point of physical violence with me, though, mostly because I discovered he was also a cheating jerk, and I told him to get lost. However, the breakup had been an ugly one—he slashed the tires on my car, stole one of my credit cards, and spread vicious and ugly rumors about me in an attempt to get me fired from the PD. Luckily I had a fairly solid reputation as a quiet homebody who kept to herself, so nobody—or at least, nobody who mattered—believed his stories wherein I supposedly had wild public sexcapades with strange men in exchange for drugs. Eventually, I had to resort to a restraining order. And when he broke into my car and stole one of my guns, I took a great and terrible pleasure in obtaining the surveillance video that clearly showed him doing so, and I made sure that he was arrested for it. Since the theft of the gun automatically made it an aggravated burglary—a felony—he went to jail, and the only lasting injury I sustained was the shredding of my self-esteem.

*So, can I blame him for the fact that I now have a demonic lord as a fuckbuddy?* I thought with a sour smile as I raced to my aunt's house.

I made it there in just over fifteen minutes, thanks to reckless disregard for speed limits, and not-so-judicious use of lights and siren to get through intersections and around cars. I slowed as I turned onto Tessa's street. There were several emergency vehicles clustered in the vicinity of her house, and a number of neighbors milled about in their front yards in an effort to see what was marring the normal calm of their neighborhood.

I parked as close as I could and jogged up to my aunt's house. Crime scene tape had been strung around the front yard and driveway. Low screens had been set up on her lawn to shield the body from the neighbors' too-curious eyes. Jill was on scene, taking measurements. Sergeant Crawford stood nearby, speaking to Detective Pellini, who, apparently, had been on call tonight. Sarge caught my eye and gave me a slight nod, then returned to his discussion with Pellini. He'd get up with me later to fill me in. That was fine with me.

I headed over to where my aunt stood. She was off to the side of her house and near the sidewalk—outside of her wards, I noticed. A neighbor stood with her, an older woman who had her arm slipped around my aunt in what was clearly meant to be a comforting gesture. For an instant I thought that having someone die in her yard had been more of a shock to Tessa than I'd expected, because she was sure as hell giving the impression of someone who was shaken and distraught. Then she looked up, caught my eye, and winked before slipping back into her role of slightly fragile, overwrought woman.

I hid a grin as I approached. "Oh, Aunt Tessa! You poor thing!" I exclaimed, pulling her away from the other woman's arm as I wrapped her in a dramatic hug of my own. "Such a terrible shock!"

"Don't oversell it, sweetling," she muttered, but I could hear the laughter in her voice.

I gave the neighbor a smile full of false gratitude, then steered Tessa away and closer to the crime scene tape— out of earshot. "Tell me everything," I demanded in a low voice.

"First, I must thank you for getting me away from that inane woman," Tessa replied tartly. "What a dingbat! She kept wanting me to pray with her 'for strength.'" She gave a slight shudder. "Anyway, I was in the front sitting room when I thought I felt a ping from the wards. I figured it was just a neighbor trying to drop by and visit, so I pretty much ignored it since the aversions would take care of that for me."

I nodded impatiently and resisted the urge to tell her to get to what happened.

"But they pinged again, which meant that whoever was trying to approach the house had more will to get to the house than the aversion could overcome. I looked out the window and saw someone in the front yard, so I turned on the lights. I didn't realize it was Thomas, otherwise I'd have called nine one one right then and told them to bring the K-9s and their Tasers." Her lips pressed together in distaste. "He was moving forward but fighting every step of the way." She shook her head, brow furrowed. "I figured the defensive wards would get the message across, but he didn't make it that far. Instead . . . he—"

"Grabbed his head, screamed, then keeled over?" I finished for her, a sick sensation building in my stomach that had nothing to do with the cuff on my wrist. At least, I didn't think so.

She gave a brisk nod, eyes on me. "The other two. They died the same way, I take it."

"I wasn't there when Barry Landrieu died, but Evelyn sure did. And she and Barry both had the same kind of strokes." My gaze slid to the shielded body. I had no doubt Doc would find signs of stroke in him too.

"I pulled the aversions back so that your people could work," she said, nose wrinkling in annoyance.

"I'm sure they appreciate it, even if they don't realize it," I said, frowning. Before I'd left the house I'd popped some painkillers that had successfully squashed my headache. I'd also taken a few minutes to pee on the pregnancy test stick—which had come up with a nice, lovely result of Not Preggers. Now, with less pain and stress, I could think again, and I didn't like what I was coming up with. "I think there's another connection between these three—not just the fact that I knew them all."

"And could conceivably have motive to want them dead?" she added.

I grimaced, nodded. Trust Tessa to get right to the point. "Yes. But Thomas was trying to get into your house. You have a portal in there." I rubbed the back of my neck. "Awhile back I found an old and buried portal in the detective's parking lot at the PD. There was a lightning strike, and it made a hole. . . . They covered it with asphalt so I didn't think about it."

Even in the dim light I could see that Tessa had gone pale. "And the first body?"

I hugged my coat closer around me, suddenly chilled. "I felt something off, but couldn't pin it down. But I'd be willing to bet one of my measly paychecks that there's a portal somewhere in that area as well." I eyed her. "What are they for? I thought the one in your library was random, but it's not, is it?"

"I'm not sure," she said, which surprised me. I'd somehow assumed she knew exactly what it was for and why it was there. "I only know that protecting it has always been of paramount importance. I inherited the place from my Great Aunt Nikki, even though I'd never met the woman, and she had children of her own. But she'd clearly been an arcane practitioner as well, because with the house came the contents of the library, along with a completely vague and rambling letter that maundered on and on about how vital it was that the portal be guarded and the wards maintained." Tessa gave a low snort. "She was ninety-eight when she died, and I think her mind had gone bye-bye several years before."

"Or maybe she didn't know why it needed to be protected either," I pointed out.

Tessa gave a quick bark of laughter. "Now that's a possibility as well! When I get the chance I'll have to look and see how she came into possession of this place." Squaring her shoulders, she said, "But for now I need you to stay here and make sure all this is taken care of." Tessa waved her hand at the goings-on in her front yard.

"And if I'm not back by the time they finish up, can you please reactivate the outer wards?"

"Sure thing. But where are you going to be?"

She gave me a hard smile. "I think that Carl and I are going to go on a nature walk."

After Tessa left, I waited for Sarge to get a free minute to talk to me. Since I had a personal involvement, I didn't want to go beyond the crime scene tape.

He came over to me as soon as the Coroner's Office van pulled up. "You all right?"

I briefly considered acting like I didn't know what he was talking about, but then I realized it would be pointless. The crap with Thomas had only been a couple of years ago and had been the talk of the department.

I gave him a nod. "You got a minute?"

"I got more than a minute if you need it," he said, looking at me with concern.

I took a deep breath. "There's a link between Thomas here, the death out at the Nature Center, and the lady who died after running into my car."

"You?"

I nodded.

He lit a cigarette, and I shifted upwind of him. "I knew about Thomas, of course," he said. "And Tracy Gordon told me about the Stark woman." He blew out smoke and didn't look at me. "What's the deal with Landrieu?"

"Gave me heroin when I was fourteen," I said, not looking at him either, but I could still see him twitch in surprise. "I overdosed. Nearly died."

"Damn," he muttered. He flicked ash onto the sidewalk. "Y'think someone's trying to set you up?"

"That, or someone thinks they're doing me a favor," I replied.

He made a sour noise in the back of his throat. "Well, it obviously doesn't look good that people you have plenty of reason to dislike are falling over dead. But I also don't believe for a second that you're doing it."

I inclined my head. "I appreciate your faith in me."

"Only because I know you'd find a way to hide the bodies." He snorted, smiled. "Well, if someone's trying to set you up, we need to beat whoever it is to the punch, and let the chief know what's going on."

A knot of tension in my chest began to unwind. "Yeah. Makes sense."

"Now, let me ask you a question," he said, peering at me.

I waited.

"These deaths. Are they part of all that magic woowoo crap you do?"

I bit back the urge to snicker at his reaction and kept my face sober. "Probably so," I replied.

"Fucking hell," he muttered. He dropped the cigarette to the sidewalk and ground it out under his heel. "I'll fill the chief in. I'll also need to reassign the Landrieu case."

"Understood."

"You need anything else from me?"

I shook my head. "I'm good. Thanks, Sarge."

"See you in the morning, then. Now get the fuck off my car."

I gave him a mock salute and stepped back from his car. After he drove off I looked around to see if Jill was finished up. She was leaning against her van with her hands stuffed into her pockets, which led me to assume she was done and was waiting for me.

"You okay?" I asked her as I approached and got a good look at her. She definitely wasn't her usual perky self.

She gave me a wan smile. "Stomach's been acting up lately."

"Ugh, I can sympathize." I shook my wrist with the cuff on it. "Eilahn just gave me this thing—blocks the arcane and keeps me from being summoned—but it makes me feel queasy all the time." Then I shot her a warning look. "But if you get me sick for real I'm going to be pissed."

A flash of her usual humor lit her eyes. "And what would you do then? I can outrun you."

"That's what cars are for, bitch," I retorted with a grin.

"So what's the deal with you and your ex-boyfriends?" She eyed me, slight frown puckering her forehead. Her tone was joking, but I saw worry in her eyes.

I muttered a curse. "I think someone's trying to set me up." I quickly recapped everything I knew, including the *graa* attack and my suspicion that a summoner was behind it all.

"Maybe someone thinks they're doing you a favor?" she suggested in an unconscious echo of my earlier remark, though it was clear that even she didn't really believe it could be true.

"Yeah, well if they think that, I sure wish they'd come forward so that I could thank them with a really hard punch in the neck," I said with a dark scowl.

Jill let out a peal of laughter. "Oh, good lord, you've been spending way too much time with that demon bodyguard of yours."

I grinned. "Careful. I'm sure she's around here somehow. She probably heard that."

"How does this killer know that all these people fucked with your life?" she asked, sobering.

I rubbed my eyes. "Dunno. Damn near everyone knows about my history with Thomas, and I guess it wouldn't be too hard to find out about my dad's death. But Barry Landrieu? Only a few people know about that."

Jill opened her mouth to speak then closed it as Pellini approached.

"Betcha it's a drug overdose," he said as he did his best to hoist his pants a little higher under his gut. "Fucking loser. What the fuck did you ever see in that dickhead, Gillian?"

Spreading my hands, I said, "Dude. I plead temporary insanity." I knew the answer, though. I was lonely and desperate, and Thomas acted like he understood the lifestyle of a cop. After all, he'd been a fireman. Of course, later I found out that he'd been fired for a laundry list of infractions—everything from insubordination to violations of safety protocols that put his coworkers at risk.

Pellini huffed out a breath under his mustache. "He was a fucking whiny bitch, too. I was booking a prisoner into the jail same time he got brought in, and he was crying like a little kid who'd lost his puppy. What a dumbfuck."

"You won't get any argument from me," I said.

He waddled off. Jill watched him go, then shot her attention back to me. "The jail," she said. "These people all went through the jail here."

I blinked. "That's right." I thought furiously for a moment. "And . . . my name would be in the records, in the victim impact statements."

"Which means that whoever the summoner is, he or she has access to the arrest reports!"

"But it's been long enough that those are public record now," I pointed out, wincing. "That could be anybody."

Jill frowned. "True. But what are the odds that whoever's doing this saw you listed as a victim somewhere and then decided to see if there were any other instances? Isn't it more likely that someone interested in finding people you didn't care for would check to see if you're listed as victim on any police reports?"

I considered her theory. It made sense. More sense than the theories I already had, which were nonexistent. "It's possible," I admitted, "but that's still an insanely large pool. Not just law enforcement, but anyone who works in records, the DA's office, the public defender's office. . . ."

"Okay, okay!" She held her hands up in surrender. "But we can rule out David the barista, right?" she said with a laugh.

I tapped my chin. "Fine. We can eliminate David the barista as a suspect. For now! But if he turns out to be our summoner, then I'll never let you live it down."

"Deal!"

My phone buzzed with a text message from Tessa.

*. . . portal just below surface. Pls put wards back after they scrape turd off the lawn.*

"Damn," I muttered, stomach sinking. I glanced over at Jill. "Portal at the Nature Center. There goes my last hope that all of this was one big happy coincidence."

She winced. "And still no clue what these portals are for?"

"Nothing solid."

"So what now?"

"First, I'll restore my aunt's wards," I said. "But after that . . . Well, three people are dead, I'm the most likely suspect, and I have no idea what direction to go next." I flashed her a tight smile. "Therefore, I'm going to go home and go to bed."

She gave my arm a light punch, smiled. "For once, you have your priorities in order."

# Chapter 13

I made my way down the broad corridor, the stone floor smooth and cold against my bare feet. Light filtered through tall, broad windows covered with grime. A few were broken, and through the gaps I could see clear blue sky and distant mountain peaks. Along the walls hung tapestries that had probably once been vibrant and colorful, filled with dynamic scenes. Now most were in tatters, and those few that remained were too faded and stained to make out more than the occasional figure. A man in armor. A woman reaching for a flower. A *reyza* perched on a stone. Lanterns hung between the tapestries, heavy iron things with wells at the bottom that had probably held oil at one time. But now they were cold and dark, smeared with soot.

The hem of my dress brushed the stone with a soft susurration, and I slowed, not wanting to make even that much noise, even though there was no one nearby. I knew that. No one in the entire structure.

Frowning, I looked down at what I was wearing. A dark blue gown, intricately embroidered in silver thread with a pattern that I had trouble focusing on. Some sort of ivy perhaps. Or birds. Or birds in ivy.

I took a deep breath, then let it out slowly. I could feel the rush of air through my lungs, taste the dust of the place, feel the warmth of my expelled breath on my lips.

But I knew without a doubt that I was dreaming.

I'd been here before in dreams—once, no, twice on the roof with Rhyzkahl, and other times somewhere nearby—though they'd never been as vivid, as real as this. I didn't know what exactly this place was—a keep, or fortress . . . something like that, nor did I have any idea where it was.

*Only this time I'm completely aware that I'm dreaming. That's a first.*

Maybe I'd been thinking of Rhyzkahl as I fell asleep? Had I unwittingly called him to my dreams? Considering the various revelations of the day, it would be understandable. Yet if that was the case, where was the demonic lord?

I put my hand out to the wall. *I am dreaming . . . right?* Frowning, I lightly scraped my knuckles against the stone—not enough to draw blood, but enough to scratch the skin and send a light twinge of pain through my hand. Fear tightened my chest. *Maybe I've been summoned . . . ?* But surely I'd be aware of that. *It's just a dream*, I fought to reassure myself. I'd been in other sendings from the demonic lord that were indistinguishable from reality.

*But why is this all so screamingly familiar?*

The silence seemed to press down on me, but I wasn't quite brave enough to shout, *Hello,* or anything like that.

Even though I felt a deep certainty that I was the only living creature in this keep, and that I wasn't really here, I'd seen enough horror movies to know that I could be quite wrong about both.

The corridor ended abruptly, opening into a vast hall lit only by dust-filled spears of sunlight coming from windows high on the walls. Surprised, I stood in the entrance to the corridor and took in the sight. Heavy tables and benches of dark wood filled the center of the hall. A higher table, that could easily seat forty, ran along a wall opposite an archway. Two chairs at the center of the table were intricately carved with scroll work and patterns I couldn't quite make out, though both bore harsh slashes that revealed the lighter wood beneath the varnish—deep gouges that had to have been made by an ax or a seriously heavy sword. I tasted mildew in the air, and a pungent scent of rodent droppings made my nose twitch.

*I've been here.* Through the archway on the right were the kitchens, and the entrance to the left led to a corridor that would take me to the great doors of the keep. And the stairs in front of me. . . . I balled my hands into fists as memory surged through me—this hall filled with people and scurrying servants. Laughter and song. Meat and wine. Fighting and blood.

Then it was gone, leaving only the echoes of shrieks and raucous calls skittering through my mind.

I breathed in shallow pants, turning slowly. If this was a dream, it had to be one sent by Rhyzkahl, since he had a link to my dreams. In which case he was . . . what? Wanting me to find something? Figure something out?

Screw horror movies. "Rhyzkahl?" I called out.

Goosebumps skimmed over my skin as the walls took my call and flung it around in scattered echoes. Gulping, I held my breath, waiting for the demonic lord to make an appearance.

Nothing. He wanted me to figure this out. Or I was completely wrong about this sending being from him. Either way, I had no idea what I was supposed to do or how to wake myself up.

Fine. I had some sort of inexplicable shadow memory of this place. Time to use it. Turning, I made my way back up the corridor at a jog. I stumbled once on the stupid skirts I was wearing, and I grabbed them with both hands, feeling absurdly like Cinderella running down the stairs at the stroke of midnight—if Cinderella had been in a weird abandoned castle-thing, sent here by a demonic lord with an agenda.

Snarling, I ran up a broad flight of stone stairs—or rather I ran about halfway up, then had to slow down and catch my breath. Great, even in my dreams I needed to be in better shape. *But I don't have far to go. I think.*

The stairs took me to another hallway. No windows here. Shadows swam along the floor and walls, but at the end of the hallway were a set of double doors, where whispers of light seeped from the cracks. I broke into a jog again, seized the handles and pulled. The doors were giant, heavy things of metal and black wood. They opened grudgingly, but once I had them moving they swung open wide.

"Holy shit," I breathed.

I thought at first that the room was round, then I realized it had about twenty sides—facets of polished grey stone that should have reflected my image back at me but didn't. Every other wall held a lit lantern, which made the room seem unusually bright after the gloom of the hallway. But I took that in almost as an afterthought.

It was a summoning chamber. There was no doubt about it. A diagram similar to the one I used had been precisely etched into the darker grey stone of the floor, though it was easily twice as large as mine, and it had certain differences that I couldn't quite make out. But the most remarkable thing about the room was the sculpture in the middle of the diagram—or rather what remained of it. On a broad circular base nearly three feet across was a statue carved out of a black stone with flecks within of something that sparkled. Like obsidian crossed with granite. I assumed it was a woman—though it was difficult to be certain, since it stopped at the waist. Long skirts swirled around her bare feet, and a hand clutched the fabric, broken off above the elbow.

The upper portion of the torso lay smashed and scattered about the room, no remaining piece bigger than my thumb. I let out a soft moan of grief for the loss of such incredible work. I bent to examine the intricacy of the sculpture that remained. I'd always been impressed by the statues from the Renaissance and the realism of the draped fabric in marble, but this totally kicked Michelangelo's ass. I peered at the design on her skirts. It was an intricate, twining pattern . . .

I heard a scrape of noise from behind me, and I whirled. I caught a fleeting image of someone standing in the doorway right before something hard struck me in the chest—

\*     \*     \*

I jerked awake, hands flying to my breastbone as I gasped in a ragged breath, absolutely certain I'd feel a crossbow bolt or a dagger sticking out. Nothing there except for a phantom tingling. I rubbed the heel of my palm against my chest and sat up, gulping for breath in the welcome crush of relief. *Just a dream. I wasn't summoned in my sleep.*

It was still dark outside, but the alarm clock on my nightstand showed that it was a few minutes before five a.m. Didn't matter. I knew I wouldn't be doing any more sleeping.

The house ticked with silence as I padded to the kitchen to make coffee. Maybe I should head into the office. Or the gym. Anything to distract myself right now. I was trying hard to go to the gym at least once a week. More often it ended up being every other week—just frequently enough for me to be sore all over again from working out. I needed to do *something* to keep myself from thinking about the dream and everything else that had been revealed to me. I'd wanted answers, and I was possibly getting them, but in horrible vague ways that only made things more confusing. What the fuck did any of it mean?

I actually got as far as pulling my gym bag out of the hall closet when the front door opened. I spun, holding the gym bag in front of me like a shield. Eilahn stepped in, then gave me and the bag an amused look.

"Are you planning to defend yourself with sweaty clothing?" she asked, closing the door behind her.

I lowered the bag, abruptly realizing that I *had* forgotten to take my yucky gym clothes out of the bag after the last time I'd worked out. Which had been about two weeks ago. Okay, might be safest just to throw the whole bag out at this point. "I thought you were still asleep," I said.

The demon suddenly grinned. "I have been busy. I have a surprise for you!" She darted forward and seized my hand, tugged me toward the living room. "Close your eyes!" she commanded.

"Um. Seriously?" I asked, eyeing her dubiously.

She stopped and frowned. "Yes. You must close your eyes. I am quite certain that this is how surprises are revealed."

Smiling weakly, I complied. The demon continued to lead me forward.

"Now, open them!"

I did so. And stared. "Wow." I didn't know what else to say.

The demon was practically vibrating in excitement. "Is it the correct sort of tree?" she asked. "Are the decorations appropriate? I perused many magazines and websites in an effort to determine what would be the best look for this space."

"Eilahn. It's . . . perfect!" And it was. She'd acquired a tree—the most symmetrical and perfect blue spruce I'd ever seen—and decorated it with white and blue lights, tiny gold stars, sparkly balls of dark blue and red, and silver ribbons. Pine garlands made graceful swoops along the wall near the ceiling, with delicate paper snowflakes hanging from them. Dark red ribbon had been painstakingly tucked around the door in exquisite swirls, topping the door with a perfect bow. On the desk, she'd placed ceramic figurines of angels, and red, green, and gold candles of every shape and size filled the mantel, gracefully accenting the pictures already there.

And in the corner by the fireplace, stood a brand new Kitty Kondo, with Fuzzykins perched on it as if to say, "Yes, I did all this."

"It's beautiful," I said. "I can't believe you did all this in one night!"

Her grin was ecstatic. "And there's more!" She took me by the hand, then stopped, fished the cuff out of my bag by the door, and snapped it around my wrist. "Close your eyes again!"

Laughing, I obeyed and allowed myself to be led outside and down the steps. About a dozen steps away from the house she turned me around and announced, "Now, open your eyes!"

It took everything I had to keep from bursting out laughing as I took in what she'd done to my house and the immediate surroundings. Where the inside decorations had been lovely, tasteful, and utterly beautiful, the outside was . . . well, I had a feeling my house could now be seen from orbit. The roof was barely visible beneath the carpet of lights, "icicles" of more lights streamed down the sides of the house, and a gigantic Santa—complete with waving arm—filled the porch. Surrounding the house were blow-up snowmen, enough reindeer to pull ten sleighs, giant candy canes, and several neon-green trees that flashed in chaotic patterns.

Eilahn looked at me expectantly. "It's the most awesome thing I've ever seen," I said, completely truthfully. "I love it," I said, and I even meant it. Sort of.

On impulse, I gave her a hug and was more than a little surprised when she hugged me right back.

"Now I need to ask you something of a more serious nature," I said after we finished with the hugging stuff.

In an instant she was back to being the serious demon bodyguard. "Let us return inside. You are barefoot, and it is chilly."

Demon bodyguard Mom. I hid a smile, returned inside, and continued on down the hallway to the kitchen. "It's pretty obvious that whoever's behind these murders is some sort of arcane practitioner," I said as I poured myself a cup of coffee. "And considering that I was attacked by that *graa*—"

"Yes," she interrupted. "I believe you were also dosed with something, though I do not believe it was exactly the same substance as the other victims."

I turned around. "Um. Yeah, I had this whole long explanation that I was going to use to convince you that the whole thing was related, but I guess I don't need to go into that now."

"You do not. I also believe that the cuff has been muting the effects."

"Right," I said. "Because, as far as I can tell, I've gone batshit at least three times—I threw my coffee at Roman, I attempted to molest Ryan, and I went off on Rhyzkahl." I grimaced. "And each time it's been when I wasn't wearing the cuff."

"Yes. And I do not believe that any of these were specific, directed attacks—merely episodes brought on by the loss of inhibitions that this drug apparently causes."

"In other words," I said, "you don't think I was drugged specifically to make me want to sleep with Ryan."

Her mouth twitched. "I think that, with the cuff off, your normal iron self-control was lowered."

I snorted softly and sat at the table. "The question now is, what the hell do we do about it?"

"We should go eat pancakes," the demon said.

"Pancakes?"

She nodded firmly. "Everything is better with pancakes."

"I'm not about to argue with you," I said. "You making?"

"No," she said with a smile. "You are buying."

# Chapter 14

Lake O' Butter pancake house was fairly well populated at seven a.m. on a Tuesday morning, though fortunately there still seemed to be a few available tables. Probably another hour before they really hit a rush, I figured. The welcoming scents of butter and coffee hugged us as we walked in, along with the clatter of plates and the clipped commands of the short order cook. Formica tables looked like they'd been salvaged from a fire sale, the vinyl chairs had more cracks than an old woman's heels, and the silverware was usually battered and bent, but the pancakes were fluffily sinful, the cooks used real butter, and the blueberry syrup was made from a patch in the owner's back yard. For breakfast it was nothing short of luscious. Lunch or dinner was another matter entirely. I'd only made the mistake of ordering a tuna salad sandwich here once.

A waitress grabbed menus, and gave us a thin-smiled order to follow her. I started to comply, then paused at the sight of Roman at a table in the corner. He had his back to me and papers spread out on the table in front of him. Guilt shuddered through me at my behavior the other day. "Eilahn, give me a minute, okay?"

She followed my gaze, gave a slow nod. "I will order coffee for you," she said.

She knew me too well.

Taking a deep breath, I walked to his table. "Hi, Roman."

He lifted his head, gave me an uncertain and cautious look. He looked tired and had a faint dusting of stubble on his chin. "Er, hi, Kara."

"I'm sorry," I said in a rush. "I don't know why the hell I did that to you yesterday."

Giving a self-conscious laugh, he rubbed the back of his neck. "Maybe because I deserved it?" He gestured toward the seat opposite him. I slid onto it, relieved, then shifted as a wayward crack of vinyl poked my backside.

"No, you really didn't," I said as I found a more comfortable spot. "People ask for that sort of thing all the time. And, to be honest, we do it all the time. Not fixing it, but it's not that tough to get tickets reduced, depending on your driving record. That sort of thing."

"It's all right," he said, meeting my eyes. Some of the fatigue seemed to have cleared from his expression. "I can afford it, and I *was* speeding."

"Okay, but still," I said, "last time I checked, the standard punishment for speeding didn't include getting scalded with hot coffee."

He cast his eyes upward, and pretended to consider. "Well, maybe when you factor in court costs . . . ." He chuckled and dropped his eyes back to me. "Seriously, though, apology accepted."

"Thanks." I skimmed my eyes over the papers in front of him without being too obviously intrusive. There was a stack of what looked like account statements, and some letters that looked like they were from law firms. "What's all this? One of your investments?"

"Something like that," he replied. "I'm part owner of an industrial park on the northeast side of town, and I'm trying to see if anything can be done with it that'll allow us to turn a profit." His eyes shadowed. "I don't know if you've heard, but I'm not with ESPN anymore."

I winced. "No, I hadn't heard. Um, was this your decision?"

His broad shoulders lifted in a shrug. "I was asked to 'voluntarily' resign earlier this spring. Personality conflicts." A scowl briefly crossed his face before being wiped away by a sardonic smile. "So now I'm looking for other opportunities for a beat-up ex-football player."

"You'll land on your feet," I assured him.

"I appreciate the vote of confidence," he said, smile turning warm. "But yeah, I'll be all right. I have money put away, and I've made some good investments that will keep me comfortable for a long time."

"Sounds like something I need to start doing," I said with a grin. "I need me some lifetime security."

He chuckled. "I'd be more than happy to set you up with my financial advisor."

Snorting, I shook my head. "Dude, I appreciate the thought, but right now I think I have an extra seventy-three dollars in my checking account that I could spare."

"All the more reason to talk to a professional," he said with a knowing tilt of his head.

"You have a point," I conceded. "Are you still leaving town tomorrow?"

He wrinkled his nose in annoyance. "One of the shareholders is dragging his feet on signing some paperwork. I'll probably be here another week." He glanced at his watch and winced. "Speaking of, I'm about to be late for a meeting about that project." He began gathering his papers up, but paused to give me another smile. "I'm glad to see you're doing so well, Kara."

"You too, Roman," I replied.

He slid his papers into a briefcase and stood, then leaned over to give me a kiss on the cheek before turning and walking on out. Mouth pursed in thought, I watched him go. He'd changed a lot in the years since we'd briefly dated. Silly of me to expect him to be the same person. I sure as hell wasn't.

I stood, made my way over to the table that Eilahn had staked out, dropped into a seat.

"All is well with your former paramour?" she asked.

I picked up the menu. "Seems to be." The waitress came over to fill my coffee cup. I gave her a grateful smile, then proceeded to add sugar and creamer. I waited until the waitress walked off, then looked back up at the demon.

She opened her mouth to speak, then paused and turned to look at the door. I followed her gaze to see Zack and Jill enter the restaurant. Zack hadn't changed in the weeks since I'd seen him. A bit less tan perhaps, but his hair was still as pale-blond as if he spent every day on a surfboard. Which, supposedly, he did during the warmer months, though now that I knew that he was a demon I had to wonder how much of that was true and how much was simply cover story.

The pair headed straight for our table without a second's hesitation, and I gave Eilahn a narrow-eyed glare. "You called the others?"

"I did," she answered serenely as she quickly inscribed the anti-eavesdropping sigil on the table. "You have many tribulations at the moment and require the assistance of those you call friend. And I knew you would not ask them for that assistance."

I frowned. She was right. It seemed more than a little selfish to call people up and say, "Hey, I have a problem, can you drop everything and help me?" *But that's what friends DO, moron*, I chided myself. I was still getting used to the whole dynamic, obviously.

"Hiya, chick," Jill said. Her tone was bright, but her expression was fierce.

"Hiya, yourself," I said. "I hear my roommate's been tattling on me."

Jill gave a shrug and a grin. "Nah, she just said you were buying breakfast."

"Sure. What the hell," I said with a laugh. "At least it's pancakes and not steaks. Is Ryan coming as well?"

"Right behind us," Zack said with a jerk of his head toward the door. True to his word, the man in question entered as if on cue.

Ryan paused as soon as he entered and did a scan of the interior. I could see him mentally cataloguing the occupants and exits—possibly not even aware he was doing so. Maybe that was why it was so hard for me to wrap my head around the "he's a demonic lord" idea. Other than a couple of rare breaks in the façade, he was every inch the federal agent. And his personal history was insanely complete as well. *Could I be wrong?*

No, I knew what I'd seen. And Eilahn had definitely shouted the name "Szerain." I also knew, logically, that I should be as wary of him as I was of Rhyzkahl. Maybe it was easier to trust him because he never—well, almost never—acted like a demonic lord? *Dear Santa*, I thought, *what I want for Christmas is for all this crap to make sense*.

Ryan headed to our table and slid into the empty chair beside me, positioning himself so that he still had a good view of the room and the entrance. "Morning," he said, almost as an afterthought.

"We should order," Eilahn instructed. "And then Kara can fill you all in."

Ryan gave me a questioning look. "Is it the usual? Life in danger, world ending, nasty magic creatures running around unchecked?"

Laughing, I nodded. "That about covers it!"

Breakfast was duly ordered and much coffee consumed, then I filled them in on everything I knew—the deaths, my connection to the victims, the portals, the *graa* attack, the cuff and what it was for, and the suspicion that I'd been drugged.

A silence fell after I finished.

"Goddamn, I'm glad we ate first," Zack finally said. A laugh swept the table, nicely breaking the tension.

Jill leaned her elbows on the table and propped her chin in her hands. "You suspect that the victims were given something that gave 'em temporary magic? Or whatever the fuck it is you do," she added with a wink at me.

Grimacing, I rubbed my temples. "I think their sensitivity is being increased, and somehow they're drawn to the resonance these portals have."

"And then when they actually find one it overloads their brains?" she asked.

"That's the working hypothesis," I said. "As far as I know, none of those people had any sort of arcane skill, or if so, only a trickle."

"Is there a drug that can do that?" Ryan asked. To my surprise he looked over to Eilahn for an answer.

The demon pursed her lips, frowning. "I have heard of such—compounds that can open the channels used for manipulating and detecting power flows."

Zack tensed, and alarm flashed quickly across his face. He quickly schooled his features, but his eyes flicked toward Ryan then away. I had the impression he had something to say but didn't dare.

*Ryan doesn't know Zack is a demon,* I reminded myself. *If Zack revealed knowledge of that world it would give him away.* In other words, I needed to find a way to get him to spill what he knew. Not an easy task since Zack was oathbound against talking about much demon stuff.

"Use of these compounds is generally proscribed," Eilahn continued, "due to the unpredictable and dangerous side effects."

"Would stuff like that show up on a tox screen?" Jill asked.

"Doubtful," Eilahn said, forehead puckering. "Most of the ingredients used can only be found in the demon realm."

"Yeah, Doc's in a tizzy," I said. "He can't figure out what's causing these strokes."

"Poor guy." Jill grimaced. "It's not like you can clue him in that it's something out of this world."

"No kidding!" I said. "He already thinks I'm weird enough."

"Is Kara in danger of having a stroke?" Ryan asked Eilahn, face dark and serious.

"It is my suspicion that Kara is being affected by a different substance than the others," Eilahn stated. "She already has extensive arcane skills."

I noticed that Eilahn didn't answer Ryan's question. "Well, that's cheery," I said. "But if the others were used to find portals, that means I was tagged to find something as well. Plus," I lifted my arm and shoved my sleeve back, "I'm only experiencing side effects when I'm not wearing this thing."

Jill leaned forward to snag the maple syrup. "And you think this *graa* attacked these other victims as well? Wouldn't they have freaked the hell out?"

"Demons are fast," Eilahn answered. "All it had to do was scratch them. It's quite possible they never saw it, especially if it was dark."

"Hang on." I yanked my phone out of my bag, then thumbed in a text to my aunt. *Can you pls ask Carl if stroke vics had any weird scratches on bodies?*

"Let's make sure there's really a connection before we get too confused," I explained to the others. "If the *graa* is the common vector, then we know our main focus is finding the summoner who called it." A few seconds later my phone dinged. *Yes.*

Frowning, I texted a reply: *is that yes they had scratches or yes you can ask him?*

I scowled at the phone as I waited.

*yes to both. Vics had deep scratches. I'll have Carl let me into morgue so I can check if from demon.*

I related the exchange to the others.

"Your aunt rocks," Jill said. "She's weird and scary, but she rocks." She tilted her head. "Kinda like you."

"Thanks," I said drily.

Jill grinned then tapped the table. "But I don't understand something. Why would someone set Kara up to make her look like a possible killer and then also drug or poison her?"

I sat back. "Right. That doesn't make sense to me either."

"Someone who wants to fuck with her," Ryan said. "Get her off balance. Maybe someone with an ax to grind."

Jill let out a bark of laughter. "Oh, god, if we have to track down everyone Kara has ever pissed off, we're screwed."

"Bitch," I said and stuck my tongue out at her for good measure.

"You know it!" she said, eyes sparkling with humor.

"I have to say, though, it really is the perfect setup." I grimaced. "Drug me with something that makes me do irrational shit, right when people around me start dying."

Eilahn pursed her lips. "And it would have appeared far worse if not for the fact that most of your 'irrational shit' has been controlled by the cuff."

I nodded. "But still, if they're going after me—another summoner," I said, musing, "—they have to figure the payoff is worth the risk."

"Or they're desperate enough to risk it," Ryan added.

I tugged my hands through my hair as an uncomfortable thought occurred to me. I slid my eyes to Eilahn. "Are you able to assess for summoning ability?"

"That is not one of my skills," she said, spreading her hands in apology.

Zack eyed me. "You have a suspect?"

I shifted in my chair, uncertain. "I'll be shocked if he turns out to be a summoner, but . . . well, this ex-boyfriend of mine, Roman Hatch, lost his job at ESPN earlier this spring. He arrived here in town shortly before the first murder. In fact he found the body."

Zack raised an eyebrow. "I think that qualifies him as a person of interest."

"Right." I cast my memory back over the conversation. "He also said he was staying in town a few extra days because one of his projects was taking longer than expected."

Jill gave a smirk. "I think that's what we in the biz call 'a clue.'"

I nodded, smiled tightly. "I guess I'll be summoning a demon to check him out tonight."

"Cool!" Jill said, mischievous smile on her face. "We can have a demon summoning party!"

"Like hell!" I said, giving her a dark glower. She merely chuckled. My phone dinged and I dropped my eyes to it, expecting it to be from my aunt.

It wasn't. "Shit," I muttered as I read the text.

"What's wrong?" Ryan asked.

"Chief wants to see me, ASAP." I sighed. "Somehow I have a feeling he's not calling me in to offer me a promotion."

# Chapter 15

Despite joking, my nerves were a frayed mess about being called in to talk to the chief. I had no doubt as to the reason, and I could only be deeply glad that I'd already spilled the beans to my sergeant.

I flashed a relaxed smile to the secretary in the chief's outer office—even though I felt anything but relaxed—and tapped on his door frame. "You wanted to see me, sir?"

Chief Robert Turnham gave me a smile as he waved me in, but there was a tightness around his eyes that did nothing to ease the knot of worry in my gut. He'd recently decided to give in to his ever-retreating hairline and shave his head, but the combination of that with his dark skin, his height, and his gangly, thin limbs had him resembling one of the creatures from the movie *Aliens*. Though without the slavering teeth and poison blood and all that. He and I had always gotten along fairly well. He had a tendency to be dour and anal retentive, but he was a damn good cop with tons of experience, and he'd always treated me with respect.

But right now it was pretty obvious he was stressed and worried. Obviously something more was going on.

"Have a seat, Kara," he said. I complied, doing my best to keep my expression even and calm. He'd had the walls painted in here, I noticed—a warm blue that matched the tones in the Beaulac PD seal on the wall behind his desk. The carpet had been updated too—a dark gray that that was a huge improvement over the bilious tan of its predecessor. The desk, chairs, and bookshelves were real wood now instead of metal, but nothing that looked like it cost and arm and a leg. Not much else had changed, though. The books and various awards were still aligned neatly, and I doubted I'd find any dust on the shelves. The overall effect was "serviceable and classy," which pretty much fit the chief to a T.

He leaned forward and interlaced his fingers together on the desk in front of him. His face fell into lines of concern that I knew weren't fake. "I'm not going to waste time with bullshit small talk, Kara. I received a tip this morning, from an anonymous person, stating that the deaths of Barry Landrieu, Evelyn Stark, and Thomas Chartres are connected. And that we should be looking at you as a murder suspect."

I took an unsteady breath. "As I told Sergeant Crawford, yes, I knew all three. And no, I sure as hell didn't murder any of them." I gave him a terse explanation of who each person was—everything I'd told Sarge. Okay, maybe not everything. I could probably safely leave out the bit about the demons and portals and whatnot.

He blew out his breath and leaned back in his chair. "So there are two possibilities that leap to mind. First is that you're being set up, and second is that you're a serial killer." He cocked an eyebrow at me.

"Or both," I replied with a weak laugh.

"Or both," he acknowledged, barest hint of a smile playing on his mouth, but the tension around his eyes hadn't left.

"Sir, I'd like to point out that that there's nothing to suggest any of these people were murdered."

"True enough. However, I've spoken to Dr. Lanza and he's concerned that all of them had similar causes of death, though right now he's more worried that it could be something contagious, and he's currently going back and forth with the CDC."

That was a troubling thought, but I had a tough time believing it. If it was contagious then more people would be affected than just the ones on my not-invited-to-my-birthday-party list. The tox didn't show anything because it wasn't the sort of thing a tox screen could detect. At least that was *my* theory.

He cocked his head. "Do you think it's all a giant co-incidence?"

"Fuck no," I said. "What's that saying? 'Once is chance, twice is coincidence, three times is a pattern.'"

He steepled his fingers in front of him. "There's a variation of that phrase that says 'three times is enemy action.'"

Scowling, I nodded. "Can you tell me how this tip came in?" Because if that wasn't sent by my mystery summoner or someone working with him, I'd eat my demon's cat.

"Phone call, from a prepaid cell phone. Cash."

Crap. There'd be no chance of tracing that.

"It's a damn good thing that you told your sergeant about your connection to these victims," he said. "But until we—"

He was cut off by the opening of the door. I glanced back to see who it was, deeply unsettled to see Mayor Peter Fussell enter and close the door behind him. I fought to keep any of it from showing on my face. The mayor gave me a tight smirk of a smile, which didn't do a damn thing to relax me. He didn't like me, and the feeling was completely mutual. Not long ago he'd attempted to coerce and threaten me into revealing confidential information on an active murder investigation. With the help of my sergeant, I'd recorded the conversation and had threatened him right back. Yeah, he didn't love me.

"She's still here, Robert?" he said as he pulled his overcoat off. "I'd have thought you'd have her gun and badge by now at the very least. And maybe have her in jail for good measure."

My stomach dove into my toes. I was fully aware that the Chief of Police was appointed by the mayor. It didn't matter how much Chief Turnham admired, respected, or even tolerated me—if it came down to a choice between me and his job, I knew which way it would fall.

Annoyance swept over Chief Turnham's face. "I have nothing to arrest her *for*, Peter."

The mayor dropped into the other chair and eyed me. "Three people dead. And you hated them all, didn't you?"

I eyed him right back. "Is this an interrogation?" I asked, then looked over at my chief. "Because, if so, I want a lawyer." I shifted my arm to reassure myself the cuff was still there, relieved that I'd been so stressed about being called in that I'd forgotten to slip it off. Yeah, the white hot rage I was feeling right now was all my own.

"It's not an interrogation, Kara," the chief replied. "However, until we can get this whole mess cleared up, I think it's best if you go on administrative leave."

Even though I was half-expecting it, the news was still a punch in the gut. "I haven't done anything wrong, sir," I managed.

"That we know of," Fussell said with a dubious sniff.

Chief Turnham shot him a quelling glance, then gave me a more reassuring look. "It'll be with pay, and it's in your best interest. This way there can be no question of impropriety in the investigation."

"Yes, sir." I understood it. I really did. But I didn't have to like it one bit.

"Stop coddling her, Turnham," the mayor sneered. "Get a search warrant for her house, and get the evidence you need."

I leveled a black glare at the mayor. "You don't have the probable cause for a search warrant."

He sat forward. "Then sign a consent-to-search and prove you're innocent."

"Not in this lifetime," I shot back.

He laughed and looked over to the chief. "See? She's obviously hiding something. You could fire her for insubordination for refusing to follow an order."

"Oh, for God's sakes, Peter," the chief muttered.

"Mayor Fussell," I said as I fought to remain calm, "with all due respect, just because I'm a city employee doesn't mean that you or anyone else has leave to trample all over my civil rights. And if you insist on having me fired for refusing to consent to a search of my private residence, you and this city can most certainly brace yourselves for a lawsuit."

"It won't come to that," Chief Turnham said, voice sharp and firm. My respect for my chief soared.

I gave him a polite nod. "And I appreciate that. Am I to assume that my leave is effective immediately?"

He sighed, deep regret in his eyes. "I think that would be for the best."

I stood and gave him a grateful smile, then gave the mayor a slight, mocking bow. "Y'all have a Merry Christmas!" I turned and left, and even resisted the desire to slam the door behind me.

But once I was out, the smile slid off my face as I strode quickly down the hall to my office. True, it could have been worse. Administrative leave was a shitload better than a suspension. Basically I'd just been given a paid vacation. But I still felt as if I'd been hamstrung.

No one else was around, which was a relief. I didn't feel like going into an explanation of the whole thing for anyone right now. I ducked into my office and quickly gathered up the few personal items I gave a damn about, just in case this whole situation turned to even more shit, and I couldn't get back here for a while.

On my way home I called Jill. "Guess who's a murder suspect!"

She groaned. "Please tell me you're not in jail."

I laughed. "Not yet. But I am on administrative leave. Paid!"

"Woohoo! Vay-cay!"

"Yeah, under any other circumstance it would rock. Anyway, I'm headed to the house. The mayor was in there with the chief when I was given the lovely news, and he's seriously gunning for me. Wanted me to sign a consent-to-search form to let them rummage through my house."

I heard her suck her breath in. "Yikes. I'm assuming you told them to get stuffed?"

"Pretty much. But I have a bad feeling that the mayor's gonna be pressuring Chief Turnham to scrape up enough probable cause to get a warrant."

She made an unpleasant sound. We both knew that there were ways to get around the strict legalities of search and seizure. All they had to do was come up with a "confidential informant" to attest that I was hiding evidence of my dark deeds in my house. "You're still planning to summon tonight?"

"Hell, no," I said. "I'm summoning as soon as I get home."

"Good plan. You need something to cart your demon around in once you get him here?"

"Crap. I might, depending on which demon I summon. I'll need to go rent an SUV—"

"No, you won't," she interrupted. "We can put him in the back of the van."

It took me a couple of seconds to process what she meant. "Wait. Your crime scene van?"

"That's the one!"

I burst out laughing. "This is yet another reason why you're my best friend."

After I hung up with her I called Roman, spun him a fiction about needing his signature on a witness statement so that I could close out the Barry Landrieu case, and could he possibly meet me at *Grounds For Arrest* in say, two hours?

He agreed without hesitation. I breathed a sigh of relief. I still figured it was a long shot, but even eliminating him as a suspect would be progress. And since my progress thus far had been zilch, I'd take what I could get.

Eilahn was waiting for me on the porch with the cat on her lap when I pulled up. I had absolutely no idea how the demon managed to be everywhere I was, but I wasn't going to complain.

Fuzzykins eyed me balefully as I climbed the steps. I reached to give her ears a scratch, and she gave me a dubious sniff. Well, at least it was an improvement over the usual hiss/snarl/claw reaction.

"I'm on administrative leave," I told Eilahn.

"I know," she said. "I listened in on your meeting."

Again—no idea how she managed that. Did she hide in the air ducts or something?

"Any suggestions for demons to summon who can do a discreet assessment of Roman?" I glanced at the sky and scowled. "In broad daylight?"

She thought for a moment. "A *nyssor* would be the most prudent choice."

I bit back a groan. She was likely right. But a *nyssor* ... ugh. "They can assess for summoning ability?" I asked, hoping she'd respond with something like, *Oh, wait, my mistake, you don't need a* nyssor *after all.*

"Yes," she said, dashing my brief hopes. "And it would only need a heartbeat or two of contact." Her lips twitched. "You do not care for the fifth-level demons?"

"They creep me the fuck out," I confessed, adding a shudder for emphasis.

She laughed, a crystalline sound. "You are not the first summoner to say so."

"There's a reason for that," I said sourly. "Do we have any bacon in the house?"

"Second drawer in the fridge," she replied as she stroked her fingers through the cat's fur.

I stood and headed inside, shedding the cuff and pulling my cell phone out as soon as I was through the door. While I walked to the kitchen I typed a text to Jill, then retrieved the bacon from the fridge, kicked the door closed, and walked back down the hallway to the basement door.

*Yes, you really do need to summon this demon*, I told myself firmly as I hesitated. I didn't really like summoning during the day, but the use of the storage diagram made it easier. Muttering something nasty, I set the package of bacon down, stripped off my clothes, retrieved the bacon, then headed down the stairs to get garbed up for the summoning. The sooner I got this over with, the sooner I could dismiss it.

# Chapter 16

I'd just finished changing back into jeans and a long-sleeved shirt when Jill entered the front door. She flashed a smile at me, then stopped dead at the sight of the demon waiting patiently in the living room.

"Good, you brought the stuff," I said, moving forward to take the bag from her hand. "I appreciate it."

"Sure thing," she replied unsteadily. She swallowed, frowned. "Is, um, this the demon . . . ?" She wrenched her gaze over to me, and I couldn't tell if the pleading in her eyes wanted me to say yes or no.

Exhaling, I nodded. I totally understood her reaction. *Nyssor* looked almost exactly like human children. This particular one looked like a little boy, perhaps four years old, and utterly beautiful, with flaxen curls and an angelic face. The "almost" part came in when you looked at their eyes, which were a little too large and had sideways-slit pupils. And the features were a little *too* perfect. They definitely fell into that "uncanny valley" territory. *Creepy.*

I crouched by the demon and pulled clothing out of the bag. "Jill, this is Votevha. He's a *nyssor*—a fifth-level demon. Votevha, this is Jill. She is my friend."

The demon's eyes shifted to Jill. "Friend," he repeated in a high treble. It bared its teeth in a vulpine smile full of hundreds of sharp teeth.

Jill paled. "Jesus," she muttered, but she managed to pull together a smile of her own. "So nice to meet you."

"I have clothing for you," I told the demon. "Do you require assistance?"

He shook his head and took the pants and shirt from me, examined them briefly, then slipped them on easily. He gave me a questioning look. "Good?" he said.

"Good," I said with a nod. "There are shoes, too."

He pulled them on while I straightened and turned to Jill. "Did you bring the booster seat?"

"Yeah, borrowed it from my next door neighbor. Told her I was babysitting for a friend." She gave a mock shudder. "I hope she doesn't think I'm available to baby-sit *her* little darlings." She paused, looked at the demon with a slight frown pulling at her lips. "Does, um, he really need one?"

"Nope," I said, "but if by some chance I get stopped, I don't want to get a ticket for not having my demon properly secured."

Part of my text to Jill had been to ask her to bring her personal car instead of her crime scene van. Since I didn't have an overly large demon to tote around, I figured it was better if we went with something a little less obvious. In theory we could have used my departmental vehicle, but since I was on administrative leave, I didn't want to be seen driving it around too much, just in case someone remembered that, technically, I should have been asked to turn my keys in for the duration of my leave. And I didn't currently have a personal vehicle. About a year and a half ago, the engine of the ancient Honda Civic I'd been driving since college had finally gone into a spectacular meltdown after two hundred and forty thousand miles. Buying another car—even a crummy used one—had been beyond my budget and relegated into the category of "things I really should do one of these days."

Luckily Jill had a nearly new Nissan X-Terra. It took a few minutes to figure out how to belt the demon into the booster seat, and then we were on our way.

Jill glanced over at me after we were both in the car, and gave me a wink. "Look at us being all domestic and mom-like and shit."

I let out a snort of laughter. "Take a picture. This is the closest I'm likely to get."

The drive into town was uneventful, though I discovered that Votevha had a preference for National Public Radio. We parked about a block down the street from the coffee shop and walked, the demon trotting along between us. I couldn't help but be amazed at how much he resembled a human child—not just in looks, but in demeanor as well. He paused to tug on a fluttering piece of tinsel, darted forward to peer at a bug crawling along the sidewalk, pointed and laughed at a battered snowman decoration.

Apparently he looked convincingly child-like to others as well. A middle-aged woman dressed in a full-length leather coat and a fur hat paused in her cell phone conversation as we approached. She frowned as her gaze came to rest on the demon.

"That child needs a coat!" she informed us with an imperious sniff as we passed her.

I gritted my teeth and kept going. "Pushy bitch," I muttered. I'd even asked the demon if he was cold. What, I was supposed to make him wear a coat he would be uncomfortable in?

"Maybe Votevha can go smile at her," Jill said, eyes glinting wickedly.

The demon stopped, looked back at the woman. His eyes narrowed, and then he looked back up at me. "Free."

I blinked, then shook my head, fighting back a smile. "I am grateful for the offer, but it is best that we remain discreet."

He nodded once, and continued walking. Jill and I fell into step on either side of him again.

Jill gave me a baffled look. "What was that about?"

My lips twitched. "Votevha was offering to, ah, smile at that woman as a free service. Apparently he thought she was a pushy bitch too."

The demon gave a firm nod. "Bitch."

Jill grinned broadly. "Eloquent and no doubt accurate."

We slowed as we neared the shop. "Okay, I see his car here," I said, nodding toward the BMW parked across the street. "You two sure you can handle this?" I shot Jill a concerned look.

"Oh, please," Jill said. "We walk in, we walk by his table, Votevha here grabs his hand and assesses him, we walk out." She looked down at the angelic-looking demon. "Did I miss anything?"

He shook his head. "Perfect."

"All righty, then," Jill said. She gave me a reassuring look and took the demon's little hand. "Let's roll!"

I waited until they entered then followed. Despite the demon's confidence, there was still plenty that could go wrong. If Roman *was* a summoner and got a good look at Votevha's eyes, he'd instantly recognize a *nyssor* and know that we were on to him. *Maybe I should have found sunglasses for the demon*, I fretted as I walked into the coffee shop.

Roman was at a table against the far wall. He'd apparently been watching for me, and he lifted his hand in greeting when he saw me. I gave him a nod in response, but I was also trying to keep an eye on Jill and Votevha without actually looking their way and drawing attention to them.

I started moving toward Roman as Jill and the demon went past his table. In a smooth, effortless move, Votevha set his hand on Roman's without even looking at him, without even a hitch in his stride, then pulled his little hand away as he walked beyond the reach of his arm. It looked like nothing but a curious kid who wanted to touch everything around him.

Fucking hells, I hoped the contact was long enough.

"Oh, darn," I heard Jill mutter. "C'mon, sweetie, Auntie Jill forgot her purse." The pair turned around, retraced their steps through the tables, and a few seconds later were out the door.

I gave Roman a broad smile, and pulled a report out of my bag. "Hi, Roman. I'm so sorry to call you down here, but I really need to get this sewn up. My sergeant's on my ass, and I'm in a huge rush." I handed him a pen and plopped the report down in front of him, positioning it so that he could only see the last page which, conveniently, had nothing case-related on it. Important, since this report was for a completely different case, due to the inconvenient fact that I had yet to write anything up on the Landrieu death.

He chuckled, lifted the pen, signed where I was pointing. "Not a problem. Anything else you need?"

"That's it," I said with a cheery smile. "Thanks a million!" I quickly scurried out before I could be drawn into any conversation. Less than a minute later I was climbing into the car where Jill and Votevha were already waiting.

"Well?" I twisted around to look at the demon. "Is he a summoner?"

He shook his head. "No."

I sagged back in my seat. "Damn." Then I jumped in shock at a tap on the window. I turned, half expecting to see Roman, but instead it was Eilahn, expression grim.

I hit the button to lower the window while trying to get my pulse back under control.

"We have a problem," she said.

"You mean, besides the fact that Roman isn't the summoner, and we're back to square one?"

"Yes. Someone is trying to get to the house." Her eyes narrowed. "Several someones. I think they are there to search it."

"Shit!" I gripped the steering wheel as my mind whirled. "The basement. Fuck. My implements. The summoning circle and the storage diagram. It needs to be cleaned. I can't let anyone see that storage diagram."

Her expression grew dark. She understood my concern. I'd created that diagram with a generous boost from Lord Rhyzkahl. He'd seemed very pleased when I discovered the way to store potency, which made me be-

lieve that it had been his intent to point the way. But as
corny as it sounded, such a diagram in the wrong hands
could be pretty damn dangerous. With a sufficient quan-
tity of stored power, a summoner would have little problem calling and binding a demonic lord. Even Zack had
posited that the reason I was a target was because I
knew how to store potency. I wasn't completely convinced of that, since I had yet to figure out how to increase the capacity, but then again, someone else might
be able to work that out. At any rate, for now, it was
surely best to keep the details of the diagram secret.

She placed a hand on my arm. "I will go there at speed
and remove all evidence of your arcane activities." Her
eyes went to the demon sitting in a booster seat in the
back of my car. "Protect her if the need arises. I will pay."

"Done," came the treble reply. Then I blinked and Eilahn was gone.

"That's so hard core," Jill said under her breath. I
gave her a questioning look, and she grinned. "The way
she does that gone in a flash thing. I wonder if she practices it?"

"Yes," Votevha piped up.

Jill and I stared at each other for a second, then burst
out laughing.

There were three cars parked in front of my house when
I made it home. A St. Long Sheriff's Office vehicle, a
Beaulac PD vehicle, and an unmarked black Crown Victoria that I recognized as Sergeant Cory Crawford's. Actually, they were parked about fifty feet from my house,
at the outer edge of the open area in front of my house.

I took a ridiculous amount of pleasure in telling Jill to

go around them. She obliged with a grim smile and parked right smack up by my porch, next to my departmental vehicle and a different Crown Vic—a familiar dark blue one. I couldn't help but smile. Eilahn had recruited reinforcements again.

"Why are they parked way back there?" Jill asked as we got out. She looked back at the cars in my driveway.

"They're held up by the aversions," I said, and quickly explained how they worked. She hadn't had to experience them, since I'd made sure to adjust the wards to allow her access before she'd come over. "They probably aren't even aware they're being delayed," I said with a lift of my chin toward the cars out in the driveway. "Most likely they all suddenly had the urge to make a phone call or check their email. That sort of thing."

"That's a relief," she said, a satisfied smile curving her mouth. "Is Eilahn finished with the basement?" Jill asked as she gave the *nyssor* a hand out of the car.

"Hope so," I said. "It'd be bad enough if people saw the diagram and all the other stuff in my basement, but that would simply brand me as a weirdo." I snorted. "I think I have that designation pretty well sewn up right now anyway. It's the storage diagram I'm most worried about. I can't risk pictures of it leaking out." I glanced over at the Crown Vic. "Looks like Ryan might be helping her as well." I had to grin at the image of those two working together.

"Safe," Votevha said abruptly.

I gave him a nod. "Thanks. Jill, why don't you take Votevha around back. There's no need for them to talk to either of y'all."

She nodded and complied, mouth tight as she and the

demon headed around the house. About half a minute later it was clear that Eilahn had deactivated the protections, because the men seemed to remember why they were there. They continued up the driveway, and parked about twenty feet from the house. I fought to keep a neutral expression on my face. Despite my preparations and the support of my friends, my stomach was a churning mess, and only a fraction of it was due to the cuff on my arm.

I didn't recognize the deputy who stepped out of the St. Long Parish Sheriff's Office vehicle. Ruddy complexion, stout build with a slight pot belly, and bright red hair cut in a flat top. His duty belt held a Sig Sauer .45 on one side and a Taser on the other. He gave me a nod and a thin, polite smile. "Miz Gillian?" he asked.

I didn't bother correcting him with "detective" since it didn't matter right now. "That's me. They dug up probable cause for a search warrant? Or are y'all here to sing Christmas carols?"

He gave me a wider smile that revealed a number of gaps in his teeth. "I love me some carols, ma'am, but these folks have a warrant to serve." It was a Beaulac PD case, but since I inconveniently lived outside of city limits they needed an observer and representative of the St. Long Parish Sheriff's Office.

Tracy Gordon climbed out of the Beaulac PD car, looking deeply uncomfortable at the whole situation.

"You know I have to do this, right, Kara?" he said, apology etched into his dark features.

"It's cool, Tracy," I said. "It's bullshit, but the sooner this is over with, the sooner I can get back to figuring out who the fuck is behind all this."

Cory walked up to join Tracy. "It is bullshit," he muttered. Then he swept his gaze over the exterior of my house and the decorations. "Holy shit, Gillian. You have the whole fucking north pole here."

I pressed my lips together to keep from laughing. "My, ah, roommate was expressing herself."

My front door opened, and Ryan stepped out. He gave the various cops a polite nod, closed the door behind him, and came down the steps to join me. I gave him a grateful smile. "Thanks," I murmured.

"Anytime," he said, warm affection in his eyes.

A fourth car came down the driveway and parked next to Sarge's. "Who's that?" Ryan asked.

"That's my chief," I told him. "He's cool. He'll make sure this doesn't become . . ." I trailed off as both doors opened, and the chief *and* Mayor Fussell exited the car.

"Oh, hell no." I strode forward. "With all due respect to both of you, Chief Turnham, he—" I jabbed a finger at the mayor "—is not allowed into my house."

Chief Turnham gave me a pained look. "Detective Gillian—"

"No," I stated as firmly as I could. I planted myself in my driveway between them and my house. "He's not law enforcement. He has zero jurisdiction or authorization to enter my residence. I absolutely do not give consent for him to enter."

I swung around to the deputy who was watching the proceedings with thinly veiled amusement. "If he sets foot anywhere inside my residence or any of the outbuildings, I intend to press charges for trespassing."

The deputy grinned, spat a stream of brown onto my gravel. "Works for me."

The mayor narrowed his eyes, then turned to the chief. "Robert, are you going to put up with this?"

Chief Turnham looked from me to the mayor and spread his hands. "Not much I can do. She's right."

Mayor Fussell's face flushed red as he rounded on the deputy. "This woman is suspected of serial murder. Do you seriously intend to keep me from assisting in the search for evidence?"

The deputy spat another stream of tobacco juice then hiked his belt up. "With all due respect, yer mayorness, you ain't a cop," he drawled in his thick country accent, "and Louisiana Revised Statute title fourteen section sixty-two point three says that if she says yer ass can't go in there and you do, then I can arrest yer ass." He folded his arms over his broad chest and smiled a gap-toothed smile at the mayor.

Mayor Fussell's face went cold, and he turned and stalked back to the car without another word. The chief sighed heavily. "Gillian, I respect that you have the right to ban him from your house, but was that really necessary?"

I met his gaze. "I wouldn't have done it if it wasn't, sir." *And why the hell is Mayor Fussell so keen to get inside my house?*

I leaned against my car, crossed my arms over my chest. Ryan came beside me and crossed his arms in an echo of my stance. I couldn't match his dark glower, though. I needed to work on that.

I saw that Jill and Votevha had retreated to the back of the house and were sitting on a bench, observing with a careful disinterest. There was no way to know where Eilahn had gone, but I knew she'd stay out of sight. I continued to give the mayor the stink eye while the others entered my house. Tracy gave me another look full of regret as he followed the rest in, a camera slung about his neck. Usually someone from the crime lab came along on search warrants to photograph and record the scene.

"I hope Jill doesn't get in trouble for being here," I murmured, suddenly worried.

"Relax," Ryan replied softly. "She'll be fine."

I wasn't convinced. The mayor was definitely the sort to carry a grudge. Maybe he wouldn't even realize she was a Beaulac PD employee.

"By the way," I said, "Roman's not our guy."

Ryan grimaced. "I know. Eilahn filled me in. When she wasn't ordering me to scrub, that is."

I bit back a laugh. "Is it wrong if I say, I wish I could have seen that?"

"You're a mean woman, Kara Gillian."

I hugged my arms around me as I listened to footsteps in my house. I'd conducted any number of search warrants in my years in law enforcement, and I'd always done my best to try and ignore the looks on the people's faces as we violated their privacy and rummaged through their personal belongings. It was horrible and intrusive, but I could try to take solace in the fact that I'd done my best to make sure it was done with the goal of preventing or solving a crime.

But this was complete fucking bullshit. This was someone fucking with my life just to fuck with it. I resisted the urge to shoot a death glare at the mayor. "Is it just me," I muttered to Ryan, "or does the mayor seem hell-bent on getting into my house?"

Ryan flicked me a glance. "You think *he* could be the summoner?"

I cast a sideways look at Peter Fussell. "Fuck, I don't know, but he sure is acting weird. I mean, I know he hates me, but what if all this is just because he wants a look at my summoning chamber? Or the storage diagram?"

A grimace passed over Ryan's face. "If so, he's tipping his hand pretty heavily. And how would he know about it anyway?"

"He could have learned of it from a demon," I said after some brief thought. "I've used it to summon quite a few demons, so I would imagine that word has spread a bit." I jammed my hands into my pockets and hunched my shoulders. "This sucks." I didn't mind them sifting through my not-so-delicates, but the thought of them rooting around my basement made my stomach hurt.

"Can you get the demon you just summoned to check him out?" Ryan asked.

"That would be ideal," I replied, "I'll need to renegotiate terms with him." I glanced at my watch. "Shit. Maybe not. He's been here for a long time." At Ryan's questioning look I explained, "The lower-level demons can only stay a couple of hours. Not like *reyza* who can stay most of a day or longer." In fact I really needed to dismiss the *nyssor* soon, but I couldn't do that until all the searchers had left. Crap. I didn't want to draw attention to the demon by going to check on him. Instead I pulled my phone out and thumbed in a quick text to Jill. *How is he doing?*

A few seconds later the reply came: *he says he's tired.* Yep, I'd have to find another way to check out the mayor.

It was nearly twenty minutes later when Chief Turnham emerged, followed by my sergeant and Tracy.

The mayor straightened and lifted his chin as the chief walked down my steps. "Well? Did you find the evidence you need?"

I was thrilled to see the Chief Turnham give the mayor a withering look. "No, we didn't find any evidence. I told you this was a waste of time."

Well, that confirmed my suspicion that Mayor Fussell had been the supreme driving force behind this crap.

Fussell's face twisted into a scowl. "You didn't look hard enough. Get back in there and tear the place apart! She has drugs hidden in there somewhere. You know she had to have poisoned those people!"

Chief Turnham's eyes narrowed, but I didn't give him a chance to speak. "Hey, asshole!" I shouted as I stalked over toward him. "You got a problem with me, that's fine, but while you're dicking around with this shit, the real killer's sitting back laughing at us." *Unless it's you*, I added in a silent death glare.

He drew himself up. "What did you call me?"

I stopped, thought back to my words. "I'm pretty sure I called you an asshole. But that was wrong of me to do. I meant to call you a *complete blithering fucking asshole idiot.*"

"Gillian!" The chief's voice snapped out. "That's enough."

I struggled to hold onto my anger. I had the cuff on — this was my own very righteous fury. "Really? He won't be happy until he tears my house to the ground to look for evidence that doesn't fucking exist! I want him off my property. Now!"

"Detective Gillian, dial it down," he said through gritted teeth.

I took a ragged breath. "Certainly, sir. But as a *citizen*, I respectfully state that this man is not welcome on my property.

Fussell sneered. "I'm an elected official. I'm on official business."

The deputy cleared his throat. "Nope. Yer out of yer jurisdiction, and yer not law enforcement. Under title fourteen section sixty-three, if she forbids you to stay on her property, and you don't leave, then I'm obliged to carry out my duty as an officer of the law." He spat, then added. "Y'ain't *my* boss, Mister Mayor."

Fussell stared at the deputy, then spun and marched back to the chief's car, got in, and slammed the door.

The chief gave me a dark glare. "Gillian, the only reason you didn't just earn yourself a suspension for insubordination is because, as you said, you were acting as a citizen and not as an officer of the law, and these were most assuredly extenuating and trying circumstances. But, from here on out, if you so much as look sideways at the mayor, or fail to calm your shit down when I tell you to, you'll be out of a job so fast your head will spin. Am I clear?"

I'd never seen the chief so angry. And especially not at me. "Yes, sir," I replied, as meekly as I could.

He turned, stalked to his car, and drove off. I let out an unsteady breath and then turned to the deputy. "Thank you. Seriously, you have no idea how grateful I am."

He chuckled. "No problem. Fussell's my brother-in-law. He's a complete dickweed. This was the most fun I've had in months." Giving me a wink, he climbed into his car then headed off down my driveway.

Smiling weakly, I walked back to my house. Sarge stood on the bottom step.

"Did y'all take anything?" I asked. By law if anything was seized, they had to provide a receipt.

"Just pictures," he said. "Probably would have seized your computer, except apparently you don't have one." He cocked an eyebrow at me. I replied with an innocent shrug. "Anyway," he continued, "sorry about all this."

"Not your fault." I glanced back at Tracy. "Just, please make sure those pics don't get out. I don't trust the mayor. He's up to something."

"They won't," Tracy assured me gravely. "Promise."

"Thanks, y'all," I said, suddenly insanely weary.

"But, Kara?" Tracy said. I turned back and gave him a questioning look. "You might want to do something about that bag of old gym clothes in your closet." He gave a comic shudder. "Next time warn a brother!"

"Damn," I said. "I should have given those to the mayor!"

# Chapter 17

The first thing I did after everyone left was to go to where Jill and Votevha were waiting. The demon sat with his legs pulled to his chest, face pale. Jill shot me a worried look. "I don't think he feels good."

"He's been here for several hours," I said as I crouched in front of Votevha. "Forgive me for the delay, honored one. I am deeply grateful for your service. Are you ready to go back?"

Votevha nodded, then bared his teeth in a razor-tipped smile. "Fun."

I grinned. "I'm glad you enjoyed it."

Standing, I gave Jill a nod. She scrambled back while I began the dismissal chant, but then I stopped and scowled. Hard to pull potency when you're blocked from the arcane. "I'm sorry, Votevha. We need to get onto the back porch so that I can be inside the wards."

The demon nodded and trotted to the porch. I joined him there, pulled the cuff off. I had absolutely no doubt that Eilahn had restored the wards the instant the interlopers had left. Once again I began the dismissal chant, exhaling in pleasure as the power came into my control.

Pulling potency, I focused on the bindings that held the demon in this world, shaping the portal that would pull him back to his own. A wind rose, bringing with it the stench of sulfur as a light-filled slit widened behind Vote-vha. A few seconds later a ripping *crack* split the quiet of my backyard, and the demon was gone.

I sank to sit on the back steps until the spots could fade from my vision. Dismissals were like sprinting while holding your breath. A rustle from the woods grabbed my attention, but before I could even think to find a weapon Zack emerged from the woods, carrying a large cardboard box. Grinning, he came up to the steps and set it down in front of me.

"We figured you didn't want anyone seeing this stuff," he explained.

Puzzled, I looked down into the box then laughed at the sight of the knife and candles and various implements I used for my summonings, as well as half a dozen books with titles that would likely raise eyebrows.

"I have the best friends in the world," I announced as Ryan and Eilahn came out to join us.

"Anytime, babe," Jill said. "At least that's over."

"For now," I replied. I went inside and did a quick prowl through my house and basement to be absolutely certain nothing had been unduly disturbed. Other than the clothing in my drawers being a bit mussed, everything seemed to be all right. I headed to the living room where the others had gathered, and flopped onto the couch. Eilahn was looking out the window with a troubled look on her face.

"Is something wrong, Eilahn?"

She glanced my way. "I am troubled that it was necessary to destroy your storage diagram."

I grimaced and ran both hands through my hair. "Yeah, well at least I was able to use it to get Votevha here to check Roman." Then I made a disparaging noise. "Not that it mattered." I heaved a sigh. "And at least I kept Mayor Asshole out of here. But now *he's* my number one suspect for being the mystery summoner, and it would have been damn nice to be able to get a demon to verify that for me."

"He did seem most eager to enter." Her mouth pursed in a frown. "But I thought perhaps it had more to do with this." She extended her hand to show me a baggie of white powder. "Am I correct in assuming it is contraband of some sort?"

"Yowza," Jill said, eyes going wide.

I took a careful breath. "Where did you get that?"

Eilahn tilted her head. "It was in his right coat pocket." A whisper of satisfied amusement lit her eyes. "I noticed that he kept his hand very near that pocket, and would often dip his hand into it as if to make certain that something was there. I was curious to see what he was so concerned about."

I took the baggie from her and peered at the contents. "Well, I have a good feeling it is contraband, but unlike on TV, one does *not* taste the drug to find out what it is. I don't happen to have a field test on me, but it doesn't matter. I'm quite sure this is either cocaine or heroin, and it's about to get flushed." Renewed anger suffused me. "He was going to plant it. What a cocksucker!" I shot her a grateful look. "Nice job picking his pocket."

"I replaced it with a similar substance," she said. "I have hopes he will not notice the exchange."

"You seriously rock," I said fervently. "What'd you use?"

"Powdered sugar." Vicious amusement lit her eyes. "Though I admit I was tempted to replace it with the ant killer in your shed."

I laughed. "And that, boys and girls, is why you never taste the drugs!"

The cat stalked in and rubbed against Eilahn, then walked across Jill's lap and onto Zack's lap to thrust her head into his face. He gave a surprised laugh, then obediently scratched Fuzzykins behind her ears.

Jill smiled and reached over to give her a pet. "What a sweetie kitty!" Bemused, I watched as Fuzzykins bumped her head briefly against Jill's hand in cursory appreciation of the adoration, then returned to her passion fit on Zack's lap.

"That's a bizarre cat," Ryan muttered.

"Yeah, she hates me and Ryan, but she seems to go nuts for, um," I stopped myself and quickly fumbled for something to say besides *demons*. "Um, Zack and Eilahn. Do y'all use the same kind of soap or something?" I forced out a laugh while Zack gave me a *Seriously?* look.

"Maybe she's mellowed," Ryan said. He leaned forward and reached a hand out, then quickly pulled it back as the cat turned on him with a snarl and hiss. "Or not."

We lapsed into silence, broken only by the cat's insane purring. My thoughts continued to rampage madly. Too much I needed to be doing. I needed to rebuild my storage diagram and start channeling power back into it. I needed to figure out who the fuck was killing these people and why, so that I could get my job back.

"Perhaps I could make waffles," Eilahn said. "Is it too late in the day for waffles?"

"It's never too late for waffles," I told her, relieved at any excuse for a distraction. She smiled in satisfaction and headed to the kitchen.

"Your computer and the map are out in my car," Ryan told me. "I'll go and get them now."

Zack gently removed Fuzzykins from his lap. "I'll help," he said.

The two men left. I looked over at Jill. She had a smile on her face, but it seemed strained and I could see lines of worry around her eyes. I gave myself a mental kick. I'd been so preoccupied with my own crap that I hadn't even paid attention to how she was doing.

"How are things with Zack?" I watched her face as I asked. I didn't like it, but I had a horrible sneaking hope the two of them would break up. Not because I wished ether of them ill, but more because I really didn't like that Zack wasn't being honest with her. Or was he? Had he finally come clean to her?

"Well," she said, spreading her hands. "Things are great."

I narrowed my eyes. "I sense a 'but' coming."

She shrugged and smiled, but it was unsteady. "I like him. Hell, I'm crazy about him. He treats me like a goddamn queen, we have a lot of fun together, the sex is great, we seem to be really compatible . . ."

"But?" I prompted, biting back the urge to say "But he's a demon." *Let her say it,* I thought, relieved. Zack had finally told her. At least that was one stress off me.

She took a deep breath. "But things are suddenly moving really . . . fast."

I waited.

"I'm pregnant."

I had no doubt that the expression on my face was a combination of shock, horror, disbelief, and nothing else that could make her think I was possibly happy for her. I fought to put a smile on my face, but it wasn't happening.

"It's Zack's?" I asked, somehow keeping my voice in a mostly normal register.

A scowl flashed across her face. "No, it's Pellini's! We've been doing the nasty in the back of the van after every crime scene. Of course it's Zack's."

"Sorry," I muttered. "Um, are you okay with this?" *Don't you know he's a demon?* I wanted to shriek. "And does he know?"

She was silent for several seconds. "Yeah, he knows, and yeah . . . I think I'm okay with this. It was a shock, to be sure. I use protection, but nothing's foolproof, I guess. But if I have to get knocked up by accident, at least it's with a guy who's pretty damn awesome."

I reached out and squeezed her hand, since it seemed like the right thing to do. "That's great, then." And because I couldn't hold the question in any longer, I blurted, "How much do you know about Zack?"

She opened her mouth, then closed it and gave me a penetrating frown. "Why? You have that look on your face."

"What look on my face?"

"The one that you get when you're—" She broke off as the door opened and the two men entered, laden with my stuff. We both leaped up to help them, and the next several minutes were occupied with getting my computer hooked back up, and the map on which I'd marked the portal locations up in the hallway by the kitchen.

By that time Eilahn announced that waffles were coming off the iron, and so we trooped into the kitchen. Ryan gave me an odd look as I sat in the chair that faced the back door.

"I thought you hated that chair," he said as he took a seat.

I blinked, frowning. "Yeah. I do." So why did it feel right to be facing this way?

Then Eilahn plopped a waffle onto my plate, and I forgot all about where I was sitting. Ryan even got up to help Eilahn with the cooking, giving her a chance to sit and eat as well.

I caught Zack's eye. "I hear congratulations are in order,"

His smile faded. I had no idea if he had any ability to read thoughts, but I had no doubt that mine were pretty clear on my face. I made a quick flick of my eyes toward where Ryan stood at the counter with the clear message, *If he wasn't right here I'd spill the beans because I'm not going to let you fuck with my friend, and holy fuck how can a demon get a human woman pregnant anyway?*

Okay, maybe that was a lot to read in my face, but he seemed to manage it. He gave me the slightest of nods, acknowledging. But now I couldn't help but wonder—why was I so shocked that Zack had knocked up Jill when only a little while ago I'd been worried that Rhyzkahl had done the same to me? *But the demonic lords aren't demons,* I reminded myself. *Yeah, great, so what are they?*

Ryan turned. "Who are we congratulating for what?" he asked, gaze flicking from me to Zack and Jill.

Zack spoke up first. "Jill's pregnant."

Ryan inhaled sharply and gave a cautious smile. "Surfer boy's going to settle down now?"

"Looks that way," he said. Zack gave Jill's hand a squeeze along with a look of such fondness that I almost felt guilty for being so angry at him. Almost. I was still plenty pissed. I wasn't an expert on relationships by any stretch, but it didn't seem like starting off with a big whopping lie—like the fact that he wasn't *human*—was a good way to go about it.

"He's stuck with me now," Jill said after giving him a return squeeze and an equally fond look.

Ryan finished up at the counter and slid into his seat. He lifted his chin toward the map hanging in the hallway. "I get that the red marks are where bodies were found. But what are the blue marks?"

"Well . . ." How to explain this? Crap. Nothing to do but just say it. "Not long ago Rhyzkahl went onto my computer," I told him. "Did some sort of internet search on a bunch of locations in this area." I waved a hand at the map. "That's the blue marks."

Ryan's brows drew together. "Well what are they?"

I shrugged. "No clue."

His frown deepened. "You didn't ask him what he was doing?"

I poked my fork into a waffle. "I wasn't there when he was doing it." I jammed a piece of waffle into my mouth. "I fas sweep."

Jill's eyes were dancing in amusement, but Ryan's narrowed even farther. "You were what? Asleep?"

Jill piped up to save me. "Maybe they're places where people are *going* to die. Have you checked out those sites?"

"Only a couple of them are nearby," I said, giving her a grateful look. "There are a few more that aren't even on this map. But no, I haven't gone and checked them out yet." I sighed and ran my fingers through my hair. "I've been a bit preoccupied."

Ryan's scowl hadn't abated. "Hang on, did he go up and use your computer without you knowing about it?"

I set my fork down. "Ryan, let it go. I've already dealt with it."

"Dealt with it?" Ryan said, anger in his voice palpable. "He's sneaking around, and you're acting like it's nothing!"

"Would you stop treating me like a goddamn child?" I exploded. "I don't need you looking out for me! Yes, I confronted him. We've established boundaries. I fucking dealt with it. Like the grownup that I am! Could you please get off the 'I hate Rhyzkahl' horse for just a few minutes and try and work with me?"

Hurt and pain seared across his face, and I immediately regretted my outburst. "Shit. Ryan, I'm sorry. I just can't take any more sniping right now. It doesn't help anything."

"I understand," he said quietly. "I'm sorry." A horrible silence fell, and after about a dozen heartbeats Ryan pushed back his chair. "Excuse me. I need some air."

My chest constricted as I watched him exit out the back door. Zack began to stand to go after him, but Eilahn put a hand on his shoulder. "I will see to him," she said. "You three need a moment anyway." The two demons exchanged a long look, then Zack gave a soft sigh, nodded, and sat back down. To my surprise Zack looked at me expectantly as Eilahn left and quietly closed the back door behind her.

I frowned. "What?"

He took Jill's hand in his, gave her a fond look, then returned his attention to me. "I am in need of your assistance."

"Sure thing," I said. "What do you need?"

He took a deep breath. "You are wroth with me for failing to disclose information that you feel your friend and my lovemate deserves to know."

I narrowed my eyes a touch, gave a cautious nod. I didn't miss the fact that he was talking like a demon and not like Zack Garner. Jill merely looked baffled.

"Information?" Her eyes went from him to me and back again. "What are you talking about?"

Zack gave her hand a light squeeze but kept his eyes on me. "I do not deny her right and need for full disclosure. I dishonor her by failing to provide it. Yet I am bound by oaths that counter my ability to be fully truthful."

The light bulb went off over my head. My anger at him evaporated. "Ohhhhhh. Wow. Gotcha." He wanted to tell her and couldn't. Apparently there were hierarchies of honor, where some oaths outweighed others. Poor guy. No wonder he looked so frazzled. "You, uh, want me to help explain things?"

Jill frowned. "You guys are weirding me out. What the hell is going on?"

I looked at her. "Zack has something that he wants and needs to tell you because you totally deserve to know it, especially now that you're all pregnant and shit—"

"Even were that not the case," Zack interrupted, expression painfully earnest, "I still dishonor her by—"

I waved him silent. "Yes, we know. You're a good guy." I gave Jill a reassuring smile. "He really is. But he's not allowed to come right out and tell you this thing."

"Kara," Jill said. "I swear to god I'm about to throttle both of you. Just tell me." Her mouth twisted in annoyance, but I could see a touch of fear in her eyes. Fucking hells, I hoped this wasn't a dealbreaker for her.

"You can't tell anyone," I said. "Even Ryan."

"Especially Ryan," Zack added, face a mask of worry.

"Fine!" she said, bafflement and worry warring on her face.

"Zack's a demon," I announced.

I half expected her to yank her hand from his and storm out. But instead she pursed her lips, fell silent for a moment, then gave a short nod. She cocked her head and looked at Zack. "You're like Eilahn?"

He shot me a pained look.

"He can't confirm it directly," I explained, more than a little surprised that she took it so well. Then again she'd also accepted pretty easily the presence of demons and my ability to summon them. *And she and Votevha hit it off pretty damn easily, too. What's up with that?* But I didn't have time to wonder about that right now. "Apparently he's under some pretty serious oaths," I said. "But as far as I've been able to determine, yes, he's a *syraza*, and he's protecting Ryan."

She frowned and looked down at their intertwined hands. I watched as she absently ran her thumb over his.

"Okay. So, hypothetically speaking, if a human woman and a demon were to have a kid together, what would the kid . . . be?"

Zack cleared his throat. "First off, I wish to state that if, hypothetically, I *were* a demon, I would never purposely get a child upon a human woman without her informed knowledge and consent." The look he gave her was agonized and earnest. "And truly, if I *were* a demon, I would likely have had utter faith in contraceptive methods in place." Then he winced. "Although, if I *were* a demon, I should have remembered that we are quite . . . virile."

Jill's lips twitched ever so slightly at that.

"But a child," Zack hurried on, "would appear human in every way, though as the babe matured it might show an aptitude for handling arcane power." He fell silent and looked at her miserably. "Jill, I care for you deeply, and I already love this babe beyond measure. But if you wish me to leave and cease to bother you, I will abide by your wishes. I do not wish to cause you to suffer."

She let out a snort of laughter. "You ass," she said and leaned in to kiss him. "Stop talking like that. You're freaking me out. Don't you fucking dare leave me."

I excused myself as the two started shamelessly snogging, though I don't think they noticed me leaving.

I headed out to the front porch, surprised to see Eilahn and Ryan sitting on the steps, the cat on the side of Eilahn away from Ryan, who glanced back and gave me an uncertain smile.

I gave him a reassuring one back, then crouched and tried to pet the cat. To my annoyance it hissed and swiped a claw at me, then ran off in a streak of calico fur.

I watched it go. "That cat is psychotic."

"It hates me too," Ryan offered, shrugging.

"Yeah, but . . ." I trailed off as a realization smacked into me. "She didn't hate me when I was wearing the cuff." I turned to Eilahn. "Can you go get her?" I asked.

Eilahn stood, nodded. "Interesting theory. You think she dislikes non-demons with arcane ability?"

"Exactly!" Maybe I didn't need to worry about summoning another demon after all. Grinning, I dashed back inside and grabbed up the cuff. Jill and Zack gave me a curious look, but I simply winked at them and hurried back outside, just as Eilahn was returning to the porch with the cat snuggled in her arms. I snapped the cuff on and did my best to ignore the rush of queasiness that came with it.

Eilahn held the cat loosely as I reached out to pet her. Fuzzykins gave a mild *mrowr* and bumped against my hand. Grinning, I pulled the cuff off, nearly chortling in delight as the cat's mood instantly shifted to hostile.

"Do all cats act this way around arcane practitioners?" Ryan asked, peering doubtfully at the cat. "Or is this one more than just a regular cat?"

Eilahn picked Fuzzykins up and nuzzled her. "She is simply a cat. Not a demon in disguise." She shot Ryan an amused look. "Which is what you were thinking, yes?"

He chuckled, shrugged. "Do you blame me?"

"You know," I said, thinking, "I had a cat when I was a little girl, but when I asked Tessa if we could have one she said she was allergic. And then after she introduced me to summoning she explained that cats didn't like the smell of demons on us. I'd forgotten about that."

Eilahn rubbed her nose against the cat's. "She *loves* the smell of demons!"

I laughed. "Clearly so. I doubt Tessa ever conducted this sort of experiment. But either way, it's nice to know we have a summoner-detector."

"Time to pay a visit to the mayor?" Ryan asked.

"Damn straight," I replied, then I glanced at my watch. "Well, first thing in the morning, that is. And with any luck he'll also be violently allergic to cats."

# Chapter 18

After the others departed, I headed down to the basement and looked forlornly at the pristine floor. Even though I'd semi-promised myself earlier this year that I'd be better about concealing all signs of my summonings between rituals, my resolve to do so hadn't lasted long. It was one thing when I'd only been summoning once a month, but when I started doing so more often it was tough to convince myself to scrub everything down when I'd only need to redraw it the next day or so. Plus, the power storage diagram kind of worked better when it wasn't erased.

With a sigh I dug through my implements and found the tourniquet and syringe. The "traditional" way to get the blood necessary for the creation of a diagram involved a sharp knife and any of the veins in the forearm. Screw that. This summer I'd trained myself to use the same sort of equipment that phlebotomists used when taking blood. Helluva lot easier, hurt less, and I didn't end up with scars all up and down my arms.

Luckily I only needed a couple of syringe-fulls to mix with the chalk. It took nearly an hour, but by the end of it I had both my summoning circle and my storage diagram rebuilt—and even had a bit of power channeled into the latter.

Then I went upstairs and slept like the dead.

The next morning I returned to the basement. I focused on gathering in as much available potency as I could, and carefully fed it right back into the storage diagram. Since it was only a few days after the full moon the power came to me fairly smoothly but still with enough hiccups and unsteadiness to remind me of why I used the storage diagram. I could feed potency in as unevenly as I wanted, but when it came time to use that stored power, I'd be able to draw it out in a smooth and steady flow. Glitches in the flow of power during a summoning tended to make for a dead summoner. I had enough threats to my person as it was. No need to take any unnecessary risks.

I was sweating with the effort after about thirty minutes, but it pleased me to see that I was already probably quite close to having enough for a summoning. After moving on to a quick shower and fresh clothing, I was ready to go meet the rest of our fine posse at Grounds For Arrest for a discussion of strategy.

Despite my thoroughly reasonable suggestion to test my theory by shoving the mayor into a small closet and then throwing the cat in there with him, the others overruled me and decided that it might be more prudent to simply approach him with cat in hand and watch Fuzzykins's reaction. It was also decided that it'd be best if I wasn't anywhere around, and that Eilahn should be the one to approach him, since, as far as we knew, he'd never encountered her.

Fine. But I still intended to watch from a distance. With binoculars. If there was any chance that I'd get to see the mayor's face get clawed off, I didn't want to miss it.

The plan was simple. Eilahn would have Fuzzykins in her arms and would wait for the mayor to come out of the City Administration building. She would "accidentally" walk into him, and we could then see how well my arcane-ability-detecting cat worked. Hopefully, with lots of blood. Then, once we confirmed that he was our bad guy summoner, Eilahn could somehow subdue him, we'd load him into the car, and then proceed to dig out every detail of this arcane-enhancing, multiple-stroke-inducing drug and his plan for tracking down the portals.

Really, it was a perfectly sensible plan.

Ryan and I were in his car, parked just down the street from the admin building. Zack had already done some recon and assured us that the mayor was, indeed, in his office.

I glanced at my watch. Nine a.m. Eilahn was in position, leaning against a bench with the cat draped over her shoulders like a stole. The cat didn't seem to mind the position one bit. The demon scratched her under the chin while the cat kneaded her upper chest in ecstasy. "When the hell is he going to come out?" I muttered, impatient.

"Jill should be calling him now," he assured me. The mayor would be getting a call from an 'informant' with information about the murders and my supposed part in them, with instructions to meet in the parking lot of the coffee shop. I didn't think he'd be able to resist that.

"There he is," Ryan said, unnecessarily since I had my

binoculars locked onto the front door. I watched as the mayor tugged his coat around him and looked up and down the street, a cautious smirk on his face.

*Smirk all you want, asshole*, I thought with a smirk of my own as I watched through the binoculars. He started walking down the street towards the coffee shop, and a few seconds later Eilahn stepped out from between two cars and bumped into him. I smiled as I watched. It was beautifully done, and the demon shifted the cat to her arms smoothly as she flashed a dazzling smile at the mayor. He gave her a winning smile in return and reached to give Fuzzykins a scratch behind the ears . . .

. . . and Fuzzykins acted like a completely ordinary cat and calmly accepted the proffered affection.

"Fuck," I muttered. No blood. No claws. No screaming.

"Either he's not the summoner," Ryan said, "or the cat has completely mellowed."

I lowered the binoculars as Eilahn and the mayor parted ways and continued in their respective directions—Eilahn to the corner and the mayor to a nonexistent meeting. Ryan started the car as I slumped in the seat, annoyed and disappointed. He drove around the corner and stopped, and a few seconds later Eilahn climbed in and put Fuzzykins back into her carrier.

"I am sorry, Kara," the demon said. "She did not react adversely at all."

"I saw," I said, sighing. "Maybe I was wrong about the cat." I grimaced and rubbed at my eyes. "Though it's more likely I was wrong about the mayor."

Ryan slid me a sympathetic look. "It's possible he's simply a dick."

"I already knew he was a dick," I replied, then sighed again. "Oh well, thanks for all y'all's help." I suddenly felt insanely weary and nauseated. "I guess I need to hit the books or something and see if I can shake anything loose."

I had a feeling Ryan wanted to suggest some course of action that he could help out with or participate in, but as much as I enjoyed his company, I also desperately needed to not be around him for a while. Too much craziness going on, and unfortunately the mysteries surrounding him made up a big chunk of it. Maybe he could sense that, because after a few heartbeats Ryan gave a reluctant nod. He drove us back in silence to where my car was parked, put the car in park. Eilahn got out of the car, murmuring softly to the cat in her carrier.

"Thanks for all the help," I said to Ryan. I gave him a smile, but it felt brittle and forced.

It must have looked it too, because his eyes seemed to darken with a tired worry. "I'll check with you later, all right?" I thought he was going to give me a hug, but he seemed to check himself at the last second and instead merely gave my arm an awkward pat.

I nodded, then climbed out of the car. As soon as Ryan pulled away I turned to Eilahn. "Do you know anything about the locations that Rhyzkahl pulled up on my computer."

"I do not," she replied. "You wish to investigate them?"

"The local ones, at the very least."

The demon gave a slight nod. "I am curious as well. You remember where they are?"

"I do."

"Then let's rock."

I blinked at her, then grinned. "'Let's rock'? Where did you pick that up?"

"There was a movie about humans fighting aliens on your television the other night," she said. "And one of the female warriors shouted it right before she unleashed her mayhem upon the creatures." A smile curved her lips. "I rather liked it."

"Well," I said, "if there's anyone who knows about the proper format for unleashing mayhem, it's you."

Unfortunately, there was no mayhem to be had, at least on this particular expedition. The first location we checked was Leelan Park, however I had zero idea where, in the park, we were supposed to look for whatever it was we were looking for. I was going on the theory that these locations had something to do with portals, but it was equally possible that Rhyzkahl had looked them up for some other reason entirely. Hell, maybe they were places where he'd shagged a previous girlfriend. But I couldn't shake the feeling that he'd meant for me to figure out what he'd been searching for. If he was oathbound against telling me something that he wanted me to know, he was certainly devious enough to find a loophole.

Leelan Park was a sprawling mix of sports fields, playgrounds, and picnic areas that took up nearly a mile of lakefront on the eastern end of Lake Pearl. There weren't too many people out and about, even though it was around lunchtime and the sky was fairly clear. But school was still in session for another couple of weeks, plus the temps were probably in the low forties—a bit too brisk for most southerners to want to sit and eat their lunch outside.

I stood by the boat launch and zipped the collar of my coat higher. Now *there* was an impulse decision I was happy about. I couldn't be sure if the purchase of the coat had been affected at all by the influence of the let's-make-Kara-nuts drug, but I was fine with it, either way. Here by the water the wind did its best to find a way beyond this black leather armor, but my coat held its ground beautifully and kept me comfortable and warm. The wind had to be satisfied with whipping my hair into my face and mouth while I fidgeted and watched Eilahn scan the surroundings for any sort of arcane signs or residue. We'd already tried several other random locations within the park and came up empty, and I had little reason to believe that was going to change now.

As expected, after a few moments Eilahn sighed and shook her head. "I cannot detect anything untoward," she said, "but that does not mean nothing is here. If there is a concealed portal, I would need to be nearly atop it in order to sense its resonance."

I gave a thoughtful nod. "Which is likely why our bad guy is using people to pinpoint it."

I already knew about the portal underneath the Beaulac PD parking lot, so I didn't bother wasting my time going there. The only other site within reasonable driving distance was east, near the parish line, which was also in the middle of the swamp. We went ahead and drove out there, but soon realized that without a boat there'd be no way to get within a mile of where Rhyzkahl had indicated.

I stood on the side of the road and hugged my coat

around me, frowning out at the swamp. "Bodies are found out here all the time," I said, as much to Eilahn as to myself. "I mean, not *all* the time," I corrected, "but it's not unusual at all for people to die out here. Hunters or hikers who get lost or have accidents. And the occasional murder victim gets dumped as well, of course."

Eilahn hiked herself up to sit on the hood of my car, crossing her legs tailor-style beneath her. "Tell me your thoughts."

A low breeze ruffled the grasses by the edge of the road, bringing with it a moist scent of algae and mud. "I'm aware of these last three victims, mostly because I was on call. But what if there've been others?"

"But would not those have been mentioned by whoever is seeking to frame you?"

Pursing my lips, I considered that for a moment. "I guess so. If they were connected to me." Then I sighed, rubbed my eyes. "I dunno. I'm stuck. Let's go see my aunt. Maybe she has some ideas."

The demon hopped nimbly off the car. "And I think you should contact the others and have them meet you there. At this point you need as much input as possible, as well as people around you in whom you trust."

My spirits lifted slightly at this reminder that I did have people around who I could trust—which was most likely Eilahn's intent.

"Sounds good. Let's rock."

She paused with her hand on the passenger door, gave me a quizzical smile. "You are teasing me?"

"A little," I said.

She chuckled. "Now we unleash mayhem."

\*　　\*　　\*

I wasn't terribly surprised to see two Crown Vics and a Beaulac PD Crime Scene van parked in front of my aunt's house. I made the appropriate greetings and expressions of thanks—which earned responses that were variations of, "Don't be stupid. You need help. Of course we'd come."

With that out of the way, our posse trudged up the steps of the house. I gave a desultory knock, waited for the answering yell, then pushed in, with the others following behind.

Tessa was in the front room in practically the same position she'd been in when I last saw her, though today she was dressed in a bright red caftan and the book in her hand was *Guns, Germs, and Steel: The Fates of Human Societies*. She took in the sight of us, eyes finally resting on the carrier in Eilahn's hand. "You're bringing me a cat?"

Shaking my head, I flopped into a chair and pulled the cuff off. "It's my cat. Well, technically it's Eilahn's since the cat hates me." The others took seats as Tessa moved to crouch by the carrier. It was small consolation to my mood that the cat snarled and tried to claw her.

"Lovely creature," she said with an arched eyebrow as she resumed her seat.

I stood up from the chair and shifted to sit on the floor on the other side of the room. "She seems to hate people who have arcane ability," I told her. "I thought that the mayor might be my big bad summoner since he seems to have such a hard-on for me, but the cat loves him." I glared at the cat.

"Kara," Ryan said, frowning, "why did you just get up and move?"

I opened my mouth to answer, then closed it. "I'm not sure," I replied, abruptly unsettled. There were seats available on the other side of the room. Jill and Zack had taken up the loveseat on that side, while Ryan, Tessa, and Eilahn occupied the available seats on the side that faced away from the lake. But there were two armchairs facing the other way that stood empty.

My throat felt oddly dry. "It feels more right to face this way," I said.

"And you sat in the chair you don't like at your house," he pointed out.

"Moreover, you changed seats after you removed the cuff," Eilahn added.

Tessa set her book down and tilted her head. "Perhaps this summoner wants you to find something for him," she said.

I got to my feet. "I need a map!"

"I have one in the kitchen," Tessa said, and scurried off.

Closing my eyes, I pivoted very slowly, trying to feel which direction felt the most right. "There," I said, opening my eyes. "It's super faint, but now that I'm looking for it, there's definitely a . . . pull, so to speak."

Jill stood and handed me her smartphone. "Compass app," she said. "Point where you think you need to go. You can't actually go look for whatever it is, but we can triangulate. Right?"

"Jill, you're a fucking genius." I took the phone from her and allowed her to note down the bearing. "My house, the PD, and here are all places where I either tried to rearrange the furniture or I changed my seating preference. And, in some welcome good news, they're all warded."

Zack frowned. "Can you get into the PD?"

"Sure," I said with a breezy assurance I wasn't sure I felt. "I'm on leave, not fired."

Jill carefully marked the points on the map where the three bodies were found, and then took a pencil and drew a line from my aunt's house with the bearing she'd just taken. "All right, saddle up, folks. Time to do some triangulatin'."

Zack, Jill, and Fuzzykins stayed behind at my aunt's house while Ryan, Eilahn, and I sped back to my house to take a bearing. It felt weird to close my eyes and let myself feel which way was "best" but when I opened my eyes I was once again facing my back door. Ryan took note of the bearing and texted it to Zack.

"Next, the PD," he said as we all piled into his car again.

Even though I knew I was allowed back into my office, I still felt a silly fluttering of nerves as I stepped through the door marked Investigations Division. With Ryan by my side I walked down the hall to my office, breezing past my sergeant's door without glancing in. I didn't want to put him in an uncomfortable situation, plus, the sooner we got these bearings, the sooner we could figure out what all this was about. At least I sure as shit hoped so.

I slipped into my office and closed the door as soon as Ryan was all the way in, then moved behind my desk—mostly since that was the largest "clear" area in my tiny office, and that was only if you defined "clear space" as about two feet by two feet. I pulled off the cuff, closed my eyes and slowly turned, relaxing and allowing myself to feel which direction felt right.

I finally opened my eyes, took the phone from Ryan and told him the bearing. I put the cuff back on and waited for him to send the text to Zack. At least now I knew why I'd been struck by the urge to rearrange furniture in here.

"Okay, done," Ryan said. "Jill's factoring in some margin for error, so even with three readings we'll still probably have a good sized area to search."

Grimacing, I nodded. Even one or two degrees would probably make a big difference over such a large area. "All right. Well, let's head back and see what we have."

We left the office to make our escape, but my sergeant was standing in the hallway by his door, a cup of coffee in his hand.

"Hi, Sarge," I said brightly. "Forgot a couple of things in my office. Just came by to collect them."

He gave me a slight nod that told me he wasn't fooled one bit. "Everything all right?"

"Sure," I said. "It's been a perfectly *lovely* day. How's everything going here?"

He snorted. "Well, gee, my best detective is on leave, and somehow Pellini and Boudreaux haven't been able to pick up the slack."

"You know I'd help you if I could," I said.

He took a sip of his coffee. "I figure whatever it is y'all are up to will help out. Then he gave me a sour look. "Please tell me that you're close to figuring all this shit out?"

I shoved my hand through my hair. "I don't know if we're close, but I think we're on the right track."

"Well, hurry the fuck up," he grumbled. Then a whisper of a smile crossed his face. "Oh, by the way, you might be interested to know that the mayor went to the emergency room a little while ago."

I gave him a guarded look. "Um. Why?"

"Somehow, the mayor accidentally ingested a substance he thought might be poisonous." His eyes lit with a fierce amusement. "And when I say 'ingested' I mean 'inhaled through his nose.'"

I allowed my eyes to widen. "How awful. How on earth did he accidentally snort what he thought might be poison?"

He shrugged. "It's a mystery. I'm sure that the fact that the alleged poison was a white powder is completely beside the point."

"Gosh! That's so odd!" I started to grin, then sobered. "Is he going to be all right?" That was actually a serious question. As much as disliked the man, I didn't want to see him hurt. Would snorting powdered sugar be dangerous?

"He's completely healthy," Sarge assured me. "But I'm not sure his tenure as mayor will be doing as well. Twitchy fucker. I'm not surprised he's a cokehead."

"I'll be sure to send him a get-well card," I said. "Maybe even a Christmas fruitcake."

"Remind me to stay on your good side," he said with a wink, then he stepped back into his office and we continued on out.

# Chapter 19

We raced back to my aunt's house, ready to finally figure out what the deal was with the portals, but the triangulation hadn't been as miraculous as we'd hoped, mostly due to the margin of error that Ryan had mentioned.

"The problem is that each location you triangulated from is fairly far apart," Jill explained as she showed us the map. "And there's no way to know if you were holding the compass *exactly* in the direction where you felt the pull. Therefore, I went ahead and charted it for the bearings you gave us, then with a two-degree margin for error, and also a five-degree margin." She grimaced. "Even with only a plus or minus of a couple of degrees, it still gives us a pretty large area."

She'd drawn colored cones extending from each triangulation point, giving us an intersection of what looked like a diamond several blocks long, located on the northeast end of town in what looked like a mix of homes and businesses. "Crap," I said. "There's something in there that I'm supposed to open or activate or find or whatever."

"I'm betting it's more than just a portal," my aunt said as she peered at the map.

"I concur," Eilahn said. "This summoner made the effort to have you drugged, most likely because whatever is in this location requires someone with extensive aptitude or innate talent in utilizing potency."

"Great," I muttered. "So what could it be?"

"I would imagine it's something that uses the portals," Tessa said, lifting her shoulders in a light shrug. She straightened. "But no matter what it is, I think it's best if you don't go anywhere near it."

"Again," Eilahn said, "I concur."

"Look, I'm cool with that," I said, then fell silent. Something about the whole thing was bugging me, and I needed a minute to tease it out. "This drug," I said finally, "it's not just making me point in a particular direction. My impulse control seems to be shot to hell. And I think it might have been the same with the victims as well." I thought back to what Pellini had said about Barry getting into his face. Maybe his impulse control had been slipping? Why else would an ex-con take a chance on antagonizing a cop?

Zack cleared his throat. "I have a theory about that, actually."

I looked over at him, suddenly realizing with a stab of embarrassment that he'd surely been aware of what had happened between Ryan and me the other day. I didn't know the precise dynamic between those two, and I had a feeling it wasn't quite the same as the arrangement Eilahn and I had—wherein she was always within touching distance of me—but still, I had no doubt he knew what was going on with Ryan at all times.

But more importantly, I remembered that he'd reacted when we first mentioned the drugs. If he had any information, putting forth a "theory" would certainly be the best and easiest way to share any knowledge he might have.

"The reduction of impulse control is probably as vital as the enhancement of sensitivity to the arcane," Zack explained. "What good is it if the recipients become more attuned to portals—or whatever it is you're being drawn to—if they can simply resist the desire to go see for themselves?"

Ryan frowned. "Shouldn't this drug wear off at some point?"

"I do not know," Eilahn confessed. "Theoretically, yes, but the cuff is shielding its effects, and also possibly increasing the time it takes to degrade."

"It's also possible," Zack added, "that there's a link between you and the portals, since you had a strong emotional connection to the victims."

Damn. Now that made a hideous amount of sense. "So this summoner might not even need me to find whatever this is?"

Zack shifted uncertainly. "It's only a theory," he qualified. "But I would imagine he already knows where the, um, focal point is."

I shot him a look of pure gratitude. From the look of tension on his face it was clear he was skating hard and fast over the thin ice of breaking the oaths that bound him to secrecy.

"I'd love to know what the hell this thing is that I'm supposed to go find," I said, "but I'm well aware that finding out would probably involve bad things happening to me. However, I do wish we could pinpoint the location a little better. Maybe we could find some locations closer to this area and get them warded so that I could take the cuff off and take new bearings."

Jill nodded. "That would work, but," she looked over at Eilahn, "how long would that take to do?"

The syraza pursed her lips. "Wards of that design and strength are not simple. Even if the chosen locations were small, it would likely take much of a day."

Did we even have that long? I rather doubted this summoner intended to blithely sit back and wait for the drug to wear off. He or she surely had a backup plan in mind. "Okay, so we can try to narrow the location down. In the meantime, we need to figure out how to track down this other summoner." I stood and began to pace the length of the sitting room. "I swear, if I ever get loads of free time, I'm going to create a directory. Or a social network."

Jill snickered. "What, like MagicSpace?"

Tessa's lips twitched. "Somehow I doubt that the ones engaged in illicit activities will be eager to sign up."

I waved my hands. "Details! But I can't help but wonder how the hell Peter Cerise was able to get six summoners together for his summoning of Szerain."

"Perhaps they had the same mentor," Tessa suggested.

"Maybe," I said. "But . . ." I stopped pacing. "Wait. That's six summoners we haven't checked out."

"Aren't they all, yanno, dead?" Jill put in.

"True," I said. "But if any of them had kids, maybe they became summoners as well." I turned to my aunt. "I mean, you did. We know there's a genetic component."

Tessa's expression was shadowed as she nodded, and guilt swam through me for making her relive painful memories. However, when she looked up at me she had a smile on her face. *She has my back*, I reminded myself.

"You really only need to check out four of them," she said, "since you already know about Peter Cerise and your grandmother. Your best bet will probably be the married couple. I'm blanking on their name, but I seem to remember something in the news about them being survived by a son."

"I'll head back to the office and pull up the report. . . ." I trailed off, frowning as Jill grinned and pulled a ridiculously small laptop out of her purse.

"The lab gets all the cool new toys first," she said as she opened it and set it on the coffee table. "Remote access to the database. I can pull up the report from the fire here."

"That's not fair," I pouted. "Why can't the detectives get some of the nice shit?"

"Because you don't know how to use it," she retorted.

I *hmmfed* and plopped into a chair. It didn't help that she was right.

"Okay, according to the report the victims were Robert Lamothe, Frank McCreary, Cherie and Keveen Bergeron, Peter Cerise, and Gracie Pazhel." At my grandmother's name she glanced up at me with a slight grimace before returning her attention to the screen. "Now I'll run a check on them through my various people search functions."

I felt a bit silly just watching her work, but Ryan and Zack watched her just as intently.

"Got something!" Jill crowed. "The married couple did indeed have a son. Gerald Bergeron. He lives in Baton Rouge at—" She grimaced. "Nope, scratch that. He died several years ago." She continued to click the touchpad and finally exhaled. "Ah, but *he* had a kid.

He'd be in his late twenties now." She looked at me. "Could be?'

"It's our only lead so far," I said with an answering shrug. "Gimme everything you have on him."

Her brow puckered in concentration as she worked the search. "Well, I have a name—Raymond Bergeron." Her forehead puckered. "But no DL, no passport. No pics that I can find anywhere." She clicked a few more keys. "Oh, here we go. Raymond was reported as a runaway when he was fourteen."

The back of my neck prickled, and I sat up. "This sounds promising. Maybe he changed his name."

"What about the parents?" Ryan asked. "What else do you have on them?"

"Lemme get back to that screen," she said. "Plenty of stuff on them." She fell silent, her eyes flicking across the screen. "The mom died about two years before Raymond ran away." Jill winced. "Suicide. Shut herself in the garage, stuffed blankets under the doors, and left the car running." Pursing her lips, she clicked through some more screens. "And the dad, Gerald Bergeron, passed away from a heart attack about five years ago."

"Crap," I muttered, frustrated. "This kid, Raymond, has to be our guy. I just know it. There are no pictures of him anywhere?"

"Not on any databases I have access to, but . . ," she trailed off and tilted her head, frowned. "Oh, wow. . . ."

"What?" I demanded, fighting an urge to rip the laptop away from her.

She exhaled. "Well, no pics of Raymond. But I do have a DL pic of his dad." She turned the laptop toward me.

I stared. I couldn't have been more shocked if she'd shown me a picture of the Pope. "There's no way," I said.

Jill shrugged. "It might not be," she said. "This is a picture of the father, after all, so any similarity in appearance could be nothing more than coincidence."

"I don't understand," Ryan said, frowning. "Who do you think it is?"

"Well," I said, "unless this guy has a double running around, this is the father of one Officer Tracy Gordon."

# Chapter 20

"He was in my house. In my basement." I kicked at the carpet and scowled. "He took pictures of my summoning chamber!"

"The basement was clean," Eilahn reassured me for about the tenth time. "He saw nothing."

*But surely he could sense the arcane residue from the diagrams. Would he be able to figure out the configuration?* No, I decided after a moment's thought. Without knowing the structure of the sigils it would be impossible. I'd been able to figure a lot of it out on my own, but it had been that one particular sigil that Rhyzkahl gave me that jump-started my whole thought process.

"Is he working today?" Ryan asked. "Maybe we can get into his house while he's not there and see what we can find. Do you know where he lives?"

In answer I looked to Jill. She was the one doing the fancy computer work. "Hang on," she said as she slid her finger on the touchpad. "Got his address—lives in Lakewood Heights subdivision. And according to the shift schedule, no, he's not working," she said, mouth tight. Ryan grimaced.

Yeah, that would have been way too easy. "Okay, so we don't have shit for info on Raymond," I said, "but what do we have on Tracy Gordon? He had to go through a background check to get hired."

Jill bent her head to the screen again. "Good point." She chewed her lower lip as she did her computery stuff. "Hmm. Well, according to this, Tracy Gordon is about two years older than Raymond, and ran away from a foster home in Colorado about a year before Raymond took off."

"They met as runaways," Ryan murmured. "Something must have happened to the real Tracy—died or was killed, and Raymond took over his identity."

A terrible chill walked up my back. *Is that why Ryan and Zack's backgrounds are so perfect? Did they replace real people?* I tasted bile in the back of my throat. Somehow I knew that was the truth. Nothing else made sense. *Whoever exiled Ryan...did they kill the original Ryan and Zack? Or were their deaths fortuitous and convenient?*

"It gets better, folks," Jill said, frowning at the screen. I forced myself to pay attention. "Tracy went to a shelter for runaways when he was sixteen, got his GED, and was accepted to LSU—possibly because his standardized test scores were through the roof."

"He's definitely not stupid," I said.

"Uh huh, and then he proceeded to graduate with a degree in chemistry, and went on to—ta-da—pharmacy school, though it looks like he dropped out after three years." She cocked an eyebrow at me. "I think any doubt that he's our man is gone gone gone."

"And then for some reason he decided to become a cop," Ryan murmured. "When did he get hired?"

Jill clicked some more keys. "Early summer of this year."

I met Ryan's eyes. "Right after we stopped the Symbol Man."

"He read between the lines of the news reports and figured it out," Ryan said, eyes narrowed. "Figured out you were a summoner. Maybe had you assessed to be sure."

"And whatever his plan is," I said, pinching the bridge of my nose, "he needs a summoner or someone with a decent level of arcane ability."

Jill looked up from her keyboard. "So, is he also behind these attempts to summon you to the demon realm?"

"No," I said with a shake of my head. "Or rather, if so, certainly not directly. Whoever's doing that is actually *in* the demon realm. A summoning is just that—a summons, or call. It's not possible for someone to push or send me through from this end." I glanced at Tessa and Eilahn for confirmation.

"Correct," Eilahn answered as Tessa gave a nod. "The summoning attempts must be considered a completely separate threat."

I sat down on the fainting couch and dropped my head back to stare up at the ceiling. "Right, because one threat simply isn't enough for my boring ol' life." I sighed as another realization came to me. "Y'all do realize that there's no way we can prove Tracy killed those people, right?"

The answering silence told me that if they hadn't realized it before, they sure as hell did now. I lifted my head to look around at them. "Seriously. I doubt he conveniently left behind a To Do list that says, 'Murder Kara's enemies' on it."

"Maybe not," Ryan said, "but he seems pretty hell-bent on fucking with you. There isn't enough evidence to have you arrested right now, but what if that's his next step?"

"But if I'm in jail, how can I go do whatever it is he wants me to do with whatever's in that hot zone?" I shook my head. "No, I don't think that's part of his plan. He has something else in mind." Sitting up, I shot a hard look over at my aunt. "You need to stay tight within these wards, y'hear me? If he's gunning for revenge for his grandparents, you'd be a target."

Tessa pursed her lips. "I doubt there's any way for him to know of my role in what happened the night his grandparents died, but I agree that caution is called for until he can be contained. He's been going after your enemies so far, but that doesn't mean he won't start in on people close to you." She eyed me with a fierce glare. "But I think we can all agree that you're his primary target."

"But why?" I said, but even as the words left my mouth I knew. "Crap. Nevermind. Probably because I'm getting it on with the demonic lord who killed his grandparents." Damn. Probably shouldn't have blurted it out like that with Ryan in the room. But when I slid a cautious glance his way he didn't seem to be fazed by the comment. Maybe he really was getting a better handle on how he felt about the whole thing.

Or at least better about hiding how he felt about it.

"Well, I was thinking more of the fact that you're Rhyzkahl's sworn summoner," my aunt said. "But the sex thing probably doesn't help."

Jill closed her laptop. "How would he know?"

"He could have learned it from any of the demons he summoned," Eilahn spoke up.

"Well, either way, he's shit out of luck," I said, "because I have no intention of going to wherever it is this drug is wanting me to go until he's out of the way, and I can take care of whatever's there safely." Standing, I reached for my coat. "I'm going to go home and summon a *kehza*. They can assess, right?" I asked with a glance to Eilahn. At her nod I continued, "Then I say we go to his house, sic the demon on him—which will have the combined effect of neutralizing him and making sure he's our guy. Then we take it from there."

Ryan cocked an eyebrow at me. "And what if he's not a summoner? We're oh-for-two right now."

"Then we'll get to figure out a way to convince him that the big scary creature that grabbed him wasn't real," I said.

Jill let out a snort of laughter. "Has anyone ever told you that your plans suck?"

"Constantly!" I grinned. "It's either this, or Eilahn and I go in, throw the cat on him, and then take him down ourselves."

"I think I prefer plan A," Ryan said, his voice dry. He eyed me. "And what would the rest of us be doing in this oh-so-complex plan of yours?"

"You'd be standing by to snag him if he rabbits, or for when things go to shit."

"When?" Zack asked.

I gave Zack a look. "How long have you known me? Do you really expect any of this to work the way we want it to?"

Zack blew out his breath. "True." His gaze swept the room, taking in our meager army. "Good thing we have the cat."

While the others set up a command center in my aunt's living room, Eilahn and I returned to my house.

My thoughts raced as I trotted up my steps and entered. A *kehza* would work, right? I probably didn't have quite enough power for a *reyza* or even a *zhurn*. A *kehza* would be the perfect combo of muscle and ability to assess, even though they had a tendency to be slightly twitchy and unpredictable. One had to be *very* clear in instructions with the seventh-level demons.

Pulling the basement door open I flicked on the light switch. Two steps down the stairs I paused. *What's wrong with the floor?*

"Oh no . . . ."

My heart slammed as I skittered down the rest of the stairs. The sound of trickling water came from one corner of the basement, and a thin sheen of water covered over two thirds of the floor, including nearly half of my carefully reconstructed summoning circle. But that wasn't the most disastrous part. My gaze fell on the swirls of chalk in the water beside my summoning circle — what remained of the storage diagram.

I heard Eilahn's cat-like footfalls on the stairs behind me. "This is not good," she breathed.

"I have no power for a summoning," I said grimly. "Or hot water, for that matter." I sank to sit on the stairs and looked glumly at Lake Basement. I knew I needed to go back upstairs and turn off the water, then find a shop vac or some other way to get all the damn water out of here, but I couldn't muster up the energy. *Damn.* I was looking at a full day's work ahead of me simply to get the basement into any sort of condition where I could do a summoning. Then another day or so for the floor to dry. And then a couple more to recreate the storage diagram and load it with power.

I dropped my head into my hands. "This. Sucks." I could conceivably use my aunt's summoning chamber, but I was still looking at a delay of at least a day to create and "charge" a storage circle.

Eilahn sat down beside me. "I cannot argue with you. But take heart, we are not completely without strength or options."

I cocked a glance at her, gave her a sour smile. "Yeah, but this means we're back to the 'throw the cat at him' plan."

A pained expression flashed across her face, and I nearly laughed. "I will call the others," she said. "Best to get this over with before we lose our nerve."

# Chapter 21

Our plan wasn't *quite* as reckless as "storm Tracy's house and throw a cat at him." First Ryan, Eilahn, and I did a drive-by of his address to get a sense of what protections he had in place. But to everyone's surprise, there was nothing—no wards or arcane protections of any sort that we could see. Or rather, that Eilahn could see. I was still effectively blind due to the cuff. I had no trouble seeing the physical, though: a single-story house with brick façade and beige vinyl siding on the other three sides. Well-groomed lawn with a minimum of high-maintenance landscaping. Some very basic plastic patio furniture in the back. Two vehicles in the driveway—his Beaulac Police Department cruiser, and a Dodge Charger. And blinds in all the windows that kept us from seeing any of the interior.

"No wards here simply means that he does his summonings somewhere else," I told the others, but I couldn't completely keep the sliver of doubt from creeping into my voice.

"You're starting to think he's not the summoner, aren't you," Ryan said.

"I've been wrong twice now. I don't know what to think," I confessed as I eyed the house. Even if he did summon elsewhere, surely he'd have some sort of protections on his house? "Of course, if he's wanting to hide the fact that he has arcane skills, then it would be pretty pointless to have glowy sigils visible to anyone with othersight."

"So Fuzzykins is our way in?" he asked with a wry twist of his mouth.

"Looks like it. I have a bad feeling we're going to tip our hand no matter what we do." I glanced into the back seat where Eilahn sat with the carrier. "Sorry, Fuzzykins. Looks like it's all up to you." I pursed my lips. "Maybe we should change the cat's name."

Eilahn gave me a puzzled look. "What is wrong with her current name?"

"Well, it's not very tough-sounding," I said. "And she's turning out to be a pretty kick-ass cat. Even if she does hate me."

Eilahn shook her head as she nuzzled the cat. "Her name suits her," she stated firmly. "It sounds like *fahs kehln* which means *whirling knives of justice*."

Yep, that name definitely suited the cat.

Ryan gave me a troubled look. "And you're just going to go knock on his door?"

I grimaced. "I don't exactly have a SWAT team at my disposal. I think bluffing him is the best scenario we have. Right now he has no reason to think we're on to him. If I call him and ask him to meet me somewhere, he's going to know something hinky is going on. Hopefully this way we'll catch him off guard."

"I will be with her," Eilahn told Ryan. "I agree this is

not a perfect plan, but we are running out of time and options."

Scowling, he nodded. "Fine. But you're going to wear a wire. And at the first hint of trouble, I'm coming in."

I gave him a smile. "I would expect no less."

Before we approached the house Ryan pulled into a parking lot, retrieved a case out of the trunk of his car, and quickly rigged me up with a tiny little button-mike and a discreet earpiece. Once we tested it and adjusted things accordingly, we climbed back into the car, and continued to the house, while I fought the urge to touch the mike to reassure myself it was still there.

Ryan parked and let us out directly in front of the house—a thoroughly non-tactical position, but we wanted to give Tracy the impression we were clueless about him. Meanwhile, Zack was parked around the corner, with a good view of Tracy's back yard in case he made a run for it in that direction. Jill was still at Tessa's—after she and Zack nearly got into a knock-down drag-out fight over the fact that she was pregnant and didn't need to be in the midst of the action.

Taking a deep breath to settle my raging nerves, I walked up to the house and knocked on the door. A few seconds later I heard footsteps, and then Tracy Gordon pulled the door open.

I watched as he took note of us as well as the car out front. Then his eyes crinkled in a smile. "Two beautiful women on my doorstep. My lucky day."

I flashed a grin. "I sure hope you think so after I ask you the big favor that I want to ask you."

He gave a deep chuckle and stepped back. "Come on in. I'll at least let you get warm before I dash your hopes."

I caught a glimpse of Ryan's frowning visage before Tracy closed the door. Eilahn set the carrier down and crouched by it. Fuzzykins hadn't reacted yet. *And if it turns out she loves him, does this mean he's not a summoner or does it mean that she's simply an ornery beast?*

I did a quick scan of the house. Neat as the proverbial pin, and no weapons out in plain sight. The place was simple and ridiculously tasteful—somehow perfectly suiting a single man living alone. The walls of the living room were painted in a dark rust, but the hallway that led to the kitchen was a light tan, which helped keep the room from looking gloomy. A few bookcases lined one wall, and décor pieces like fossils and agates were interspersed with books, mostly non-fiction and classics. Though I did see one shelf of science fiction—Isaac Asimov, Robert Heinlein, Larry Niven, James S.A. Corey, to name a few. On the opposite wall a widescreen TV was mounted above a gas fireplace, though both were off now. A dark oak coffee table with a dish full of decorative stones of assorted colors was centered in front of a brown leather sofa. No pictures of any sort that I could see. If there was any possible way that this could turn out so that he was *not* our bad guy, I was totally going to invite him over to my house to help me decorate.

"Well, Eilahn and I are going out of town for a few days, and I was wondering if there's any possible way you could cat-sit for me?" I flashed him a pleading grin as the demon pulled the cat out of the carrier.

Wary curiosity flickered in his expression. "Seriously?"

"Seriously!" I cheerfully lied. "Here, meet our cat!" I said as Eilahn thrust the feline into his face.

To my utter delight, Fuzzykins reacted as if she'd been confronted with a slavering Doberman. With a snarling yowl, she lashed out with all claws. Tracy yelped and backpedaled, only barely avoiding losing an eye.

Eilahn stooped and stuffed the cat back into the carrier in a swift and smooth move, while I pulled my gun from the holster in the small of my back and trained it on Tracy. He went still, eyes on the gun.

"Kara? What's going on?"

"Cut the bullshit, Tracy," I said. I wasn't smiling now. "I know what you are."

His eyes flicked from Eilahn to the cat and then back to me. "What I am?" he echoed. "What the hell are you talking about?"

"I'm talking about Raymond Bergeron," I said, oddly pleased when he jerked in surprise at the name. "You're not going to deny you're a summoner, are you?"

He wilted and sank to the couch. "No," he replied, voice unsteady. "I won't deny that." Then he buried his head in his hands. "You don't understand."

"I understand plenty," I said, scowling. "Cuff him, Eilahn."

The demon was grim-faced as she moved to him, handcuffs in hand. Tracy lifted his head and dropped his hands to the table, fingers closing on one of the rocks—

Eilahn realized it before I did. She dropped the handcuffs and shifted to dive at me, tackling me to the floor as Tracy flicked the rock in our direction. I fired, but the shot went wild. The rock hit the carpet and flared brightly, and even with the cuff I could feel the shock wave of power. Nausea slammed into me. I instantly lost what little food I had in my stomach, dimly aware that the *syraza* was beside me, pale and shaking as she struggled to get to her hands and knees. Whatever that rock had been, the cuff seemed to have shielded me from the worst of its effect, even if it had made me puke in reaction. I struggled to get control of my stomach as my hand curled tight around my gun.

I froze at the feel of a gun barrel against the side of my head. "Don't, Kara," Tracy said, voice utterly calm. "Let the gun go."

My pulse slammed as I loosened my grip and pulled my hand back. I still had my backup piece in my ankle holster, but I knew I'd lose several precious seconds getting to it, and Tracy only needed to tighten his finger.

He kicked my gun under the couch. "I don't know how you're fighting the drug," he said. "But it's pissing me off. I want to finish this shit up."

Where the hell were Ryan and Zack? Surely they'd heard the gunfire? "What shit?" I managed, fighting to get enough control of my gut that I could function.

He chuckled. "No, not playing that game. Just stop fucking around. Otherwise I'll have to provide some extra incentive."

"You need me alive to find it," I said, lifting my head to stare down the barrel of his gun. Holy fuck, but pointed at me that thing looked big enough to crawl inside and take a nap in.

"I already know where it is," he said, mouth curving into something resembling a smile. "But yes, I need you alive to make it work." Then before I could even twitch, he shifted his aim to Eilahn. "But not her." He fired twice, and I jerked in shock as the sound slammed through the room.

My ears rang as I scrabbled for my backup gun, but he turned and ran, and was out of the room before my gun even cleared the holster. I spun to Eilahn. Her eyes were wide as blood tracked down her chest from two neat little holes.

"Hang on, Eilahn." I grabbed the couch throw and pressed it to her chest to try and stop the bleeding. "You're gonna be fine. I'll call an ambulance, and you're gonna be fine!" I fumbled my phone out of my pocket but her hand seized my wrist.

"No. No time for that," she rasped, and my gut clenched at the bubbles of blood in her mouth.

"No, no, no, it's just blood," I gabbled. "If it was fatal you'd be . . . you'd be leaving."

She gave me a wavering smile. "It is coming. I can sense it. I am sorry I cannot protect you in what is to come."

"I'll summon you back," I said fiercely. "You can't get out of this that easily!"

She gave a small nod. "It will take time before I return to my world. But when I do, I will find you. You will not get rid of me so easily, my friend." Her grip loosened on my wrist, and her arm dropped to her side.

"Stand back, Kara," Eilahn whispered, then her head sagged to the floor. I looked down to see that the bleeding had stopped, and light was beginning to stream from the two punctures. I retreated a couple of feet, breathing raggedly as the light increased to near-blinding levels. A few seconds later a ripping *crack* filled the room, and she was gone—even the blood. Nothing left but a smell of sulfur and ozone and a faintly discolored patch on the carpet.

I don't know how long I stood there, staring at that dark patch, but it was probably only seconds later that Ryan burst in, gun at the ready, gaze sweeping the room.

"He's gone," I said. I swallowed. "Eilahn's gone too."

A heartbeat later I heard the sound of splintering wood from the back door, and then Zack was there as well. His eyes went to the stain then widened. "Fucking hell."

"What happened, Kara?" Ryan asked. "Are you all right?"

"What happened to *you*?" I demanded, rounding on him. "Didn't you hear us? What happened? He shot her! She's gone!" I was shouting, and the next thing I knew he'd holstered his gun and had grabbed me by the shoulders.

"We didn't hear anything," he said, face twisted in pain. "The signal grew garbled as soon as you went inside. Zack and I were coming up to the house to abort the mission when suddenly there was some kind of . . . surge that knocked us flat." His hands squeezed my shoulders. "I'm sorry. We got here as soon as we could."

I let out a shuddering breath. "He threw a rock . . . some kind of . . . fuck, like an arcane grenade. Made me puke, but she could barely move. He said he needed me alive, but not her." I fell silent, and when I spoke again my voice shook with anger. "He shot her. Didn't even hesitate."

I pulled away from him. "And now we're going to tear this fucking house apart."

I took out my rage on the walls, smashing through the drywall in the living room with a sledgehammer I'd found in the garage. As much as I wanted to gut the house into a pile of rubble, my strength gave out before my fury did, and after about ten minutes I let the sledge-hammer drop while I panted for breath and swiped at my eyes with the back of my hand.

Ryan leaned the sledge against the wall then drew me into a hug. "I'm sorry," he said, voice low and rough.

"For what?" I muttered, petulant and depressed. I leaned my head against his chest, listened to the steady thump of his heart.

He let out a soft sigh. "I'm sorry you lost Eilahn. I'm sorry you have to go through all this. I'm sorry you seem to be in constant peril. And I'm sorry I can't fix it all."

"It's okay," I said, then pulled back and swiped at my eyes again. "Thing is, all that shit sucks, but y'know what the worst part is?" I didn't wait for him to say anything. "The worst part is that I don't trust my judgment any-more. I've been wrong over and over, and I've been wasting time and energy chasing down hunches and sus-picions. I even thought *Roman* was a summoner." And I'd *liked* Tracy. Jill was wrong—I wasn't a hunk magnet. I was a men-who-would-fuck-my-life-up magnet. "And now my stupidity got Eilahn shot."

"You did what you thought was best," he said, giving me a chiding scowl. "And you've made progress. You found out that Tracy was the summoner, yes? Now, are we going to simply tear this place apart, or do we have some sort of idea of what we might be looking for?"

Straightening my shoulders, I did my best to throw off the cloud of despair. "Anything that might give me an edge in finding him and figuring out what this is all about," I said, gaze sweeping the living room. "I figure that when he ran away he took his grandparents' notes or books and stuff."

"Or maybe he came back for all of that after his dad died," Zack suggested.

I nodded. "Either way, I want to find any notes or papers or anything that we can. If I know what we're up against, we might stand a chance of being able to stop it."

"And you don't think this unknown thing we're facing is something nice and tame, I assume." Ryan's mouth twisted in a sardonic smile.

"Call me a cynic," I replied.

We started searching again, this time with a touch less rage. First was a quick search through drawers and closets, but, as I'd expected, Tracy hadn't left any useful information out where anyone could easily find it. But I'd been on enough search warrants to know that there were a lot of places to hide stuff, especially if the stuff was only papers or a notebook. I let the guys bash walls in, and I focused on pulling every one of his books out of the bookshelf and riffling through the pages.

Two hours later there were holes in all the walls, the books were all over the floors, the mattresses had been slashed, and we were still completely empty-handed. And exhausted.

Ryan looked around as we slouched on what remained of the couch, a slight frown pulling at his mouth. "Sure hope he's not renting this place. If so, I don't think he's getting his deposit back."

I burst out laughing. "Sucks to be him!" Then I stopped and frowned. "He's not doing his summonings here. So where the hell is he doing them?" I straightened and looked to Zack. "Ask Jill if she can check the property tax rolls to see if Tracy owns any property in the area."

The blond agent grinned and pulled out his phone. Impatient, I stood and began pacing, though it proved to be difficult with all the crap we'd strewn all over the place.

"Jill says there's nothing in that name," Zack said after a brief moment.

I chewed my lower lip as I stepped over detritus. "Have her try Raymond Bergeron, just for giggles."

"And his dad's name too," Ryan suggested.

"Right!" I turned to Zack. "His parents and his grandparents. See if there's anything current."

Zack relayed the info, then said, "How about I just put her on speaker phone?" He pushed a button on the phone and set it on the coffee table."

"I feel like I've become the Oracle," Jill complained.

I gave Zack a puzzled look as he burst out laughing. "It's from the Batman comics," he explained to me. "Barbara Gordon—the first Batgirl—was shot by The Joker and paralyzed, and so she became The Oracle, a computer expert and information hacker who provided intelligence to other superheroes."

"There was more than one Batgirl?" I asked weakly.

Zack heaved a sigh. "You have so much to learn."

I snorted. "No, I think I'm perfectly fine not knowing how many Batgirls there were."

"No results for any of those names," Jill's voice piped up. "What next?"

"Okay, so who owns *this* house?" I said. I waited impatiently as the sound of clicking keys came through the speaker.

"Company named Imperium LLC," she said after a few seconds. "And before you ask, yes, I'm searching the Secretary of State records to see who's behind that." A few more seconds. "Oh, good grief," she muttered. "Corporate name, Posterula Inc. Searching on that now." A pause. "Crap, it may take a while to dig through all these layers."

I stopped my semblance of pacing. "Don't worry about that right now. Are there any other properties in this area owned by Imperium?"

"Hang on. Yeah, two others. A residence in Clearwater Estates and a strip mall on the east end of town on Oakwood Street. I'll text you the addresses."

"Any chance either of those are in our 'hot zone?'" I asked.

"Nope. Sorry."

Nothing about this was going to be easy, obviously. "Okay, thanks a million, Jill. We're going to go check those two spots out. If you find out anything else, give us a shout."

"Will do!" came the cheery reply, then she clicked off.

"Okay, kiddos," I said, "We don't have much time. I can't sense wards as long as I have this on, so I'm going to be relying on y'all to point them out to me."

"You mean Ryan," Zack said with an easy smile, but there was a glint in his eye. "I can't see wards."

"Oh, right," I said with a laugh. "My mistake." I held his gaze for another heartbeat. *Find a way to warn me if you see something dangerous,* I thought, hoping it would come through somehow. I knew perfectly well Zack was capable of seeing and manipulating wards, and with far more skill than Ryan seemed to currently possess. Ryan would *hopefully* be able to tell if any protections were in place, but I had no way of knowing just how far his demonic lord powers had been throttled back. With the loss of Eilahn, I was relying on Zack's skill more than ever.

He broke the gaze, but not before giving me an infinitesimal nod. He understood.

"Let's ditch this joint," I said, "and hope to hell that we find something useful in one of the other places."

# Chapter 22

Traffic was a fucking bitch, adding to the mounting frustration already plaguing us. Tracy's threat about finding a way to motivate me haunted me, and I knew I needed to be prepared. I knew without a doubt that he needed me alive only because he intended for me to end up dead or drained or something worse. Personally, I wanted to avoid that sort of fate.

The strip mall ended up being a complete bust, but luckily not one that took too much time to check out. It helped that it stood completely empty, and through all the window fronts we could easily see that there was nothing nefarious going on there. Moreover, Zack gave me the slight shake of his head that told me he couldn't detect arcane residue of any kind—which would surely be there if Tracy had been summoning anywhere around there.

But the residence was a different matter. It was a small single-story house in the middle of the block in a neighborhood that had probably been decently middle-class a couple of decades ago. Now shriveled grass pushed up between cracks in the sidewalk. Several of the mailboxes had dents in them, testimony to someone's game of mailbox baseball. Few of the yards were maintained beyond a sporadic mowing, and there were several driveways with cars in them that looked like they hadn't been moved in a while, to judge from the amount of leaves and pine needles caught in piles against tires. A house further down the street looked like it had been broken into and vandalized a number of times—probably a foreclosure. Several windows were smashed and the door had been tagged with spray paint and other unknown substances. The house we were looking at had no cars in the driveway, and a dried brown lawn that probably hadn't been cut in six months, but even though it looked and felt like an empty house, it remained untouched by any vandalism.

"This is it," Ryan murmured. "There are definitely protections around this place." I flicked my eyes to Zack, and he dipped his head in the barest of nods.

Elation surged through me, quickly followed by frustration. We were on the right track, but now what were we supposed to do? "I can't do anything about the wards with the cuff on," I said. Not that I was sure I'd be able to do anything even if I didn't have it on. There was a reason I called demons to do my heavy ward work. I flicked a glance to Zack. He answered with a faint grimace and shrug, then tapped his watch. In other words, Sure, he could probably get through them, but it would take time. And he would need to do it where Ryan couldn't see what was going on.

I could get Ryan out of the way, but I didn't think we had much time.

Ryan scowled. "Do you think he's in there?"

I considered this. "No," I finally said. "I think he's wherever he wants me to go. He said he was going to provide incentive for me." I rubbed my arms through the coat, then I pushed my sleeve back and narrowed my eyes at the cuff.

"When that arcane grenade-thing went off," I asked, "what did it feel like? What did it do?"

"Hurt like hell," Ryan admitted. "And left me super-dizzy for a couple of minutes. Could barely focus my eyes."

I glanced over to Zack, and he nodded. "Same. Pain, dizzy, disoriented."

I pursed my lips. "And I didn't feel any of that. I only puked." A smile slowly spread across my face. "Holy shit. Duh. This cuff not only blocks my own arcane, but blocks arcane shit from affecting me—which is why the drug hasn't done much to me yet. I'm a moron. Of *course* that would make me immune to arcane protections as well. "

"You can cross the wards," Zack breathed, beginning to grin.

Ryan still frowned. "Won't it still make you sick?"

"It passes. At the worst I'll puke, but I'll be able to get through without getting hurt." *I hope*, I added silently.

"And what if he is in there?" Ryan asked, clearly still less than thrilled with this plan of mine.

"Then I shoot him," I said bluntly. "He needs me alive. I have no such need of him."

Ryan considered this for a few heartbeats, then gave a firm nod. "Okay. As long as we're agreed on that." He handed me the transmitter. "Just in case he doesn't have a ward blocking the signal." I nodded and obediently tucked it inside my collar.

Despite my confident words, my heart pounded as I approached the house. A mild queasiness washed over me as I stepped onto the walkway that led to the front door. *Those were probably aversions*, I thought as I moved forward, gun in hand though tucked inside my coat. No sense freaking out any neighbors who might be watching from behind their curtains. About five feet away from the door, a stronger wave hit me, and I had to pause and take deep, gulping breaths to get it under control. *Okay, and those are some of the actual protections.* But I was making it through. So far at least. Puking was better then being fried. Still, I hesitated before I tried the door. That's where the strongest protections would be. Taking a deep breath, I seized the door handle.

Nothing. I exhaled in relief, then frowned in annoyance as I tried to turn it. Locked. *Great, a zillion levels of arcane protection, and he still feels the need to use a mundane lock.* Shielding the view with my body as much as I could, I broke the decorative window beside the door with the butt of my gun.

And that's when the nausea slammed into me like a truck. I dropped to my hands and knees and lost breakfast, yesterday's dinner, and even a few meals I didn't eat yet, or so it seemed. After what felt like forever it finally faded but I stayed there, gasping for breath as I slowly regained control of my body. *Okay, whatever that ward was, it was definitely meant to be a lethal one.*

Legs shaking, I pulled myself upright then reached through the broken window and unlocked the door. I braced myself for another layer of protections as I entered, but thankfully I seemed to have already triggered everything that was there. I glanced back. "I'm in, and

I'm cool so far," I said. I gave a thumbs up toward the Crown Vic in case he couldn't hear me, then closed the door behind me.

There were no furnishings or décor. Nothing on the walls. Only a tired beige carpet with obvious traffic stains. I listened carefully for any sign of life, but silence held the house in a strong grip. Breathing shallowly, I edged forward with my gun at the ready. Clearing a house of possible suspects was best done with backup—preferably *lots* of backup but since I didn't have that option I went slowly and methodically as I searched from room to room. Though I did pause in the kitchen to rinse my mouth out. Bile was never a fun aftertaste.

I hit pay dirt in the master bedroom. The floor had been stripped to bare concrete and painted black, and on it a complex diagram had been carefully inscribed in white and red chalk. Black bookshelves lined two wall, and a long low chest made of a lighter wood rested against a third. Books and scrolls and papers filled every shelf, but unlike my aunt's library these were all placed with nearly pathological precision.

But all that was nothing compared to the sight of the *reyza* crouched against the far wall, casually paging through a book in his wickedly clawed hands. The twelfth-level demon looked like a living gargoyle made of burnished copper, with a bestial face, massive leathery wings, and a sinuous tail that coiled around his feet. I knew that if he were to stand he'd tower over me by several feet, and even crouched as he was he seemed to fill the room.

He lifted his head, and I dared to smile. "Greetings,

Kehlirik," I said as I holstered my gun. It would be useless against him if he wanted to attack me.

He bared his teeth in his version of a smile and lowered his book. "Greetings to you, Kara Gillian," he rumbled.

I didn't move into the room, merely stayed just beyond the doorway. "Does your current bargain prevent you from answering questions regarding the reasons you have been summoned and the circumstances regarding said summoning?"

The demon tilted his head as if considering the question. "There is nothing in my current bargain that prevents or precludes me from answering questions."

I thought for a moment. I could ask questions until the cows came home, but unless I offered him something in return, I wouldn't get any useful answers. "I have no suitable offerings on my person," I said, "but would you be willing to accept my promise of a jar of popcorn kernels— payable the next time I summon you—in exchange for information about the reasons you are here?"

He snorted, nostrils flaring. "I would."

I grinned. He'd developed a fondness for *papcahn* the last time I'd summoned him. "Who summoned you?"

"The summoner who names himself Raymond Bergeron."

"What have you been tasked with?"

The demon lifted his head and settled his wings. "I am to guard this focus point." He dipped his head toward the diagram on the floor.

I frowned as I peered at it. At first glance it looked like a fairly normal summoning diagram, but then I realized that there were several crucial differences—at least a half dozen sigils coming off the center portion that flowed into each other with exquisite and intricate beauty. "If I enter this room, are you honor bound to attack me?"

"I am."

Well, that was pretty much what I figured. Damn. I had no doubt that all his grandparents' notes were in this room. Once this whole thing was over I intended to come back and take every last scrap of paper in here. "This focus . . . is it connected to the other portals?"

The reyza gave a low rumble. "Not at this time."

Perfect. "Is it intended to be?"

"Yes." His eyes seemed to glow, and I had the unerring feeling he was enjoying this tremendously.

I skimmed my gaze over the diagram, annoyed that I didn't dare enter to get a closer look. Each of the sigils no doubt referenced a portal, which meant there were some that he'd either already known about or had found by some means other than killing people on my Do Not Like list. The detective in me itched to call Doc and find out if there'd been any other stroke deaths in the past year where the body had been found in a seemingly random location. But the summoner in me knew that would be a waste of time. I wasn't going to be able to pin these deaths on Tracy/Raymond anyway.

"What is Raymond Bergeron's plan?"

The *reyza* set the book down. I saw with amusement it was one of the Harry Potter titles. "He wishes to open a gate that will allow him to summon at will, without need to store potency."

"Holy shit," I breathed. That was a summoner's wet dream. I loved and cherished my storage diagram—

which I intended to rebuild as soon as possible—but even that had its limits. At the most I could summon every few days, unless I wanted to wear myself out, constantly channeling power into the diagram. But to have unlimited access to the demon realm. . . . Anyone who had that would end up pretty damn powerful. "How did he learn about this?"

"From papers left behind by his grandsire and granddam—instructions given to them by the demonic lord to whom they were sworn."

A cold chill of foreboding went through me. "You mean Szerain, right?"

Kehlirik nodded.

"What were Szerain's plans?"

"I am oathbound. I cannot answer that question."

I tucked my thumbs into my pockets and nodded. I was getting used to this sort of questioning. "Would his plans be detrimental to this world?"

"That is subjective," he replied. "But I would conjecture that one such as yourself would not be pleased with the possibility of widespread destruction and upheaval of the current society."

I swallowed. "Yeah, good conjecture there," I muttered. "Why does Raymond Bergeron need a summoner?"

"Because the abilities of a summoner are required for the initial opening of a gate," he answered. He tilted his head. "And if that summoner is bound into the gate by another summoner, it can then be opened and closed at the second summoner's will."

Figured. "And is he doing this with the goal of impressing Szerain and perhaps calling him?" I eyed the

demon with a knowing smile and he gave a soft hiss of
approval.

"I do not know his mind," the *reyza* answered. "But
there are other lords, and I'm certain you are able to
conjecture the benefits of owning a gate."

I shoved my hand through my hair. I could definitely
conjecture what would happen if a sociopath like Tracy
ended up with it. "If I destroy this," I lifted my chin
toward the diagram in front of me, "will it make it impossible for the gate to form?"

"No," Kehlirik replied. "This merely refines and con-
centrates the power drawn from the portals."

I frowned, disappointed.

"However," he continued, "destroying it will cause
the power flows to be weaker. It is far more likely that a
skilled summoner could dismantle an unfocused gate."

That was better. A lot better. "Did Raymond Bergeron
screw up by not telling you to keep quiet about all this?"

The demon stood and spread his wings, baring his
teeth in an unmistakable grin. "He did."

I had the feeling the demon didn't care much for
Tracy/Raymond. Laughing, I retreated to the kitchen
and found an empty plastic pitcher. After filling it to the
brim with water, I returned to the door of the bedroom.
"Just so we're clear," I asked, "you'll only attack me if I
enter the room, right?"

"That is correct, little summoner." Clearly he knew
what I was up to, because he shifted to the far corner of
the room and shielded his book with one wing.

"Awesome." I let fly with the pitcher of water toward
the diagram, smiling in vicious satisfaction as the chalk
lines blurred and melted into each other. I couldn't feel

the arcane, but I knew there was no way that diagram was still active.

I set the pitcher down and gave the demon a respectful bow. "My thanks, Kehlirik."

"It was my honor, Kara Gillian," he replied, bowing his head in response.

I started to leave, but then paused and turned back. "One more thing . . . would the wards surrounding this house prevent me from being summoned?"

The demon shook his head. "Those protections are far more specialized."

Oh well, that was probably too much to hope for. "Okay, then, are you prohibited from altering the wards protecting this house?"

A deep rumbling came from the demon. "I am not."

I flicked a glance to the book he was reading. "There's this TV show that I think you'd really like." I said, thinking of the space cowboy thing Ryan had strong-armed me into watching. I looked back to the demon. "If you could deactivate the wards, I'll summon you as soon as is possible so that you can watch it."

"These are terms I can and will abide by," he answered, to my delight and relief.

I could tolerate watching the show again if it meant I wouldn't have to puke on my way back out.

I headed to the front door. "Ryan, did you hear all that?"

"I did," he said through the earpiece. "Tell Kehlirik I love him."

"Like hell," I replied. "I'd rather not piss him off."

                    *      *      *

As soon as I got back in the car—without having to stop and puke, thankfully—I called Jill and put her on speakerphone to give her the rundown. "My next job is to figure out if there's some way to block the portals so he can't pull power from them," I said after I caught her up. "Problem now is that I don't know if that's possible. Plus there are probably some other portals in play that he knew about before he started using enemies of mine to find these latest three portals."

"I was thinking there might be other portals too," Jill said. "I put this focus you just found on the map to see if we could maybe figure out where other portals might be, but it still isn't all that clear. I mean, it's not forming some recognizable pattern."

I considered that for a moment while I absently toyed with the cuff. My eyes dropped to the mark on the inside of my left forearm. Without othersight it was practically invisible, like a faint and faded henna tattoo. "Well, unfortunately it might be part of a pattern that we don't recognize. A sigil or a mark."

"Sort of like constellations, right?" she replied. "If you only have half the stars of the big dipper, you'd never realize that's what it is."

"Exactly."

Ryan rubbed his chin. "But do we need to know what the whole constellation is?"

I exhaled. "Well, without knowing the whole pattern we don't stand much chance of figuring out how to disable it—which would be a whole lot nicer and neater to do instead of having some big fucking showdown or confrontation. He can't start this shit without me, and as long as I'm wearing the cuff, I'm not going to be feeling compelled to head there."

Zack grinned. "No confrontation? Is that even allowed?"

"Well, if not," I said, "I plan on being a bad girl."

Jill gave a snort. "So what else is new?"

I ran a thumb over the mark on my forearm. "Jill, if I give you some general locations, can you look in your database and see if there've been any deaths there in the last, say, forty years or so?"

"I *think* so," she said. "The records department supposedly just finished putting the last fifty years of reords online."

I gave her the locations that Rhyzkahl had looked up on my computer. "Look for deaths that would have occurred right before the summoning of Szerain, or within a year or so."

Ryan narrowed his eyes. "You think that they might have tried to open this gate-thing once before?"

"Right," I said. I didn't look up at him, since I wasn't sure I could keep my face totally neutral. "Szerain was up to something, and I think that he needed an easier way to be summoned." But would that have been enough to get him punished? There had to be more to his crime than that.

Out of nowhere the memory of my dream swam up. For an instant I could smell the dust of the place on my tongue, feel the stone against my feet.

*. . . smooth marble cool against my cheek as I struggled for breath, the taste of blood thick in my mouth . . .*

"Kara. Kara?"

I blinked and jerked my gaze up to Ryan. *What the hell just happened? That wasn't part of the dream.*

"You okay?" he asked. "You just went pale."

I forced a smile. "I'm fine. Just hungry, most likely. We should go grab a bite to eat soon."

"Sounds like a good plan," he said.

Jill cleared her throat on the phone. "You were right, Kara. Three deaths. All looked to be natural."

"And I'll bet anything that all three were linked somehow to one of the summoners," I said. "Then that summoner was killed by Rhyzkahl in the summoning-of-Szerain that went wrong, and so now Tracy's picking up where he or she left off." I fought the urge to slide a look toward Ryan. *I wonder how Tracy would react if he knew that Ryan was Szerain.* I bit back an inappropriate giggle. With as many oaths and secrets and whatnot going on around Ryan, I had no doubt that Tracy was completely clueless as to that little detail.

My phone beeped to indicate another call was coming in—one with an out-of-state area code. Something about the number tickled at my memory, but I couldn't immediately pin it down. "Lemme get this call, Jill. If it's a telemarketer I'll just hang up on them."

I took it off speakerphone and clicked on the new call. "Detective Gillian," I answered.

"Kara? It's Roman."

Something about the tone of his voice sent a warning zing through my body. "Hiya, Roman. What's up?" I replied, keeping my own tone light.

"There's a man here with a gun pointed at my head," he said, and now I could hear the slight shake in his voice. "He says if you don't come to the . . . the gate he's going to shoot me."

I couldn't breathe for several seconds. When I finally

could I said, "It's going to be all right, Roman. Let me talk to him, please."

Ryan's eyes narrowed. I upped the volume on the phone and motioned him closer so that he could listen in.

"Hello, Kara," Tracy said after a few seconds. "I figured you needed some incentive to move you along."

"You're a cocksucker. Where is this gate? I haven't been able to pinpoint it."

"That's because you're being stubborn and resisting it, but it doesn't matter now. Come to three five two Garden Street. Oh, and the usual 'no weapons' and 'come alone' rules apply. I have a *zhurn* helping keep a lookout. If it catches a whiff of any of your FBI friends—or any other cops for that matter—your ex here will get splattered, and the cops will get torn apart." He said it easily, with a laugh in his voice. "Speaking of, I'm intrigued by the fact that there's been no traffic on the PD radio about a shooting victim at my house. I know I didn't miss. How'd you manage to cover that one up?"

"She was wearing a vest," I managed through the white-hot rage sweeping through me. *He had no clue she was a demon. He meant to kill her.*

"Ah, smart of her. Anyway, your ex here is *not* wearing a vest. So please do get your ass down here. I have shit to do. You have half an hour." And with that he hung up.

I slowly lowered the phone. "Guess we're going to have a confrontation after all."

# Chapter 23

The first confrontation turned out to be an argument with Ryan about whether I should go there alone or not. Obviously, Ryan was in the "or not" camp. So was I, to be honest, but at the same time I didn't want to risk anyone else getting hurt or killed.

"Yes, it's a hostage situation," I finally said after he tried to convince me to call in the SWAT team. "But I'm not about to risk other cops if there really is a *zhurn* acting as lookout and guard. Plus, the fact that our suspect is a cop is going to raise all sorts of issues." I checked my watch. Ten minutes left. We were parked about a block away from the address Roman had given us. I'd retrieved my ballistic vest from the trunk and put it on beneath my shirt and coat. I also wore the wire and earpiece.

"You don't sound sure about the *zhurn*," Zack said, frowning. He wasn't any happier about our limited options or our time frame. But I had no doubt Tracy would pull the trigger. He'd killed plenty of others already.

"I'm not, but only because of Kehlirik. If Tracy summoned a *reyza*, would he be able to summon a *zhurn* as well? That's two major summonings—tough for anybody to do, even if done on two different days." Plus it was several days after the full moon. The summoning of Kehlirik would have already been insanely difficult.

"Tough, but not impossible," Ryan pointed out.

"Right. And Tracy's a smart guy. It's quite possible he has the chops to do it, so I'd rather act on the assumption that there *is* another demon in play. Or something else he hasn't told us about."

Ryan's mouth tightened. "Fine. No SWAT, but Zack and I are going to be watching the perimeter and listening in."

I took a deep breath, trying to settle the churning of my gut. "He needs me alive. And as long as I'm wearing the cuff, he can't use me to activate the gate. That's our big advantage. I'll go in, get him to release Roman, and then fuck up his world."

"I hate this plan," he muttered.

I forced a grin. "I would expect no less." I glanced at my watch. "Okay, we're not going to get any readier. Let's get this shit over with."

Garden Street was anything but garden-y. It was probably intended to be a high-tech industrial park, but whoever had built it failed to consider the fact that Beaulac's industry tended more to tourism and general suburbia. Sprawling warehouses had been built, but the expected flock of high-tech industry failed to materialize. Now it housed run-of-the-mill businesses such as a carpet store and a plumbing supply place. Although most of the warehouses actually had tenants, I had a feeling the owners found it necessary to drop the rent far below what they'd initially expected to get.

The warehouse I was going to was not one of the occupied ones. It looked like it had been at one time—there was a faded patch on the front façade that looked as if a sign had once been there. But when we drove by to see if we could make any sort of security assessment, we couldn't see any lights beyond the glass doors in front. And there were no cars parked anywhere nearby.

Ryan stopped the car a few hundred yards away from my destination. I half-expected him to come up with another argument against me walking in there, but thankfully he simply gave me an encouraging smile and silently handed me the mike and earpiece.

I clipped the mike inside my jacket, stuck the earpiece into my ear. "Here goes," I said, then got out of the car before I could lose my nerve.

The brief walk should have given me a chance to try and calm my jangled nerves, but I couldn't stop the worries from crowding in. Could Tracy sense that I'd destroyed his focus diagram? Or would he only know that when he tried to fire the gate up? Surely he would have said something on the phone if he knew. And how much would that affect the gate? Kehlirik had said it would still work but not as well. How much was "not as well?"

"Can you hear me?" Ryan's voice came in through my earpiece.

"Loud and clear," I murmured under my breath as I approached the double glass doors. The previous tenants had apparently been in some sort of stucco business, to judge by the faint imprint of painted letters that still remained on the doors.

"And you're coming in strong too. I'm worried about how it's going to work in the metal building though."

"Guess we'll find out the hard way," I replied, pausing before I entered. *Here goes. Let's not fuck this up, 'kay?*

I stepped into a foyer area that looked like it might have once held a number of cubicles. Horribly ugly wood paneling covered the walls, and a dust-covered metal desk squatted against a far wall. I could see my breath in the musty air. The air didn't feel any warmer than the outdoors, but at least I was out of the wind.

A set of metal doors in front of me probably led to the warehouse proper. My earpiece popped and hissed with static as I moved forward, and I grimaced. So much for staying in contact. I took hold of the door handle in front of me, then paused and peered into the corner.

"Greetings, honored *zhurn*," I said, taking a chance that my hunch was correct.

I waited several heartbeats and was rewarded by the sight of two red eyes. "Greetings to you, summoner," it responded in its distinctive crackling voice.

Okay, so at least my over-caution had been warranted. I didn't bother trying to find out what this demon's terms were with Tracy. The tenth-level demons were insanely reticent even under the best of circumstances. I had no doubt that if it was here, it was tasked with guarding the place. And since *zhurn* were able to communicate mind-to-mind with the one who summoned them, I was sure he was currently reporting to Tracy that I was here.

No sense in keeping them waiting. I yanked the door open and barged on in.

Inside was simply a vast open area. The ceiling above me rose at least thirty feet. There were no furnishings or interior walls. The only thing to look at was in the middle of the warehouse floor. That's where Roman was sitting in a chair with his hands behind him—I assumed tied or cuffed. He looked shaken as all hell but didn't seem to be injured or beaten up. Behind him stood Tracy, holding a gun to Roman's head.

Tracy gave me a broad smile. "Look who finally decided to join the party!"

My earpiece crackled again as I walked forward. "Jill . . . owners . . . corporation." Shit. I had no idea what Ryan was trying to tell me.

"Let's not waste time, shall we?" Tracy said. "If you'd be so kind as to step into that diagram, we can get on with this whole thing."

I opened my mouth to tell him to release Roman, then paused as Ryan repeated what he'd said. I could hear him this time. *Well, now . . . that changes everything.* "You're sure?" I said.

"Quite sure," Tracy replied.

"One hundred percent," Ryan said in my ear. "As soon as we deal with the *zhurn*, we're coming in."

"Excellent." I stopped and crossed my arms over my chest. Tilted my head. "And what happens if I don't do as you ask?"

Tracy gave a bark of laughter. "I shoot your ex. Do you really think I won't? You know I won't hesitate."

"Okay. Shoot him," I said. "And no, this isn't some stupid bluff. Why the fuck should I care if you shoot your partner?" I locked eyes with Roman. "Isn't that right, Posterula Inc?" I snorted. "You're listed as the CEO, right? Posterula . . . secondary door or gate. Very imaginative." I resisted the urge to pump my fist in the air and give an exuberant shout. *Damn straight! My instincts weren't off!*

Roman shot to his feet—not bound after all. He rounded on Tracy, scowling. "You said no one would figure it out!"

Tracy's mouth pressed into a thin line. "I said the chances were low. It doesn't matter now. Grab her and put her into the goddamn diagram."

I spread my hands as Roman stalked toward me. "Oh, you don't have to manhandle me into the diagram. I'll walk there on my own, but first I want to know why the hell you tried to get me busted for murder." Then I winced, shook my head. "Never mind. I know why." Fucking hell, I could be dense sometimes. I looked at Tracy. "You wanted into my summoning chamber, didn't you? You set me up just enough to get them to do a search warrant."

"You did a good job cleaning up your diagrams," he said. "But like all good summoners, you use blood as a component when tracing them out."

Shit. "Luminol. You sprayed the floor with luminol." It would have glowed like the Christmas decorations on my house. And since the glow usually faded after about thirty seconds, all he'd needed was a few minutes alone in the basement to spray the floor down and take a long-exposure picture. Then he could go back and build his own storage diagram. No wonder he was able to summon two major demons back to back.

I shifted my attention back to Roman. "Okay, I get why Tracy—or Raymond—would want to get some revenge against me. But why the fuck are you helping him with all this? What the hell did I ever do to you?"

Roman shrugged. "Not a damn thing. You were convenient. You're the only summoner I know, and it helped that you had plenty of people who could serve as victims to link the portals."

"Are you fucking kidding me?" I said before I could censor myself. "I was convenient? What kind of sociopath are you? Dude, you need serious therapy."

I barely had time to throw up a block before he closed the distance between us and clocked me hard in the side of the head. My arm took the brunt of it but he still hit me hard enough to drop me to my knees and make me see stars. I sent up a silent thanks to Eilahn for her attempts to teach me self-defense. I'd be out cold if not for her relentless drills.

"Cut it out, Roman," Tracy snapped. "She needs to be alive *and* conscious."

Roman grabbed my arm and jerked me to my feet, frog-marched me to the center of the diagram and then dumped me in the middle. "I financed this whole thing because with this gate I can be a summoner as well. Then I won't need those fuckers at ESPN or anyone else." He backed out of the diagram and folded his arms across his chest.

I gave a dry laugh and shifted my attention to Tracy. "Is that what you told him? That's hysterical."

Roman's eyes narrowed but Tracy just shook his head. "Don't listen to her, Roman. You'll see for yourself in just a few minutes." He holstered his gun and then lifted his hands, eyes unfocusing briefly. Queasiness hit me, and I had no doubt he was activating the diagram. I couldn't see the energies, but I was quite sure that he was getting things started.

Roman smiled. "I'm not a summoner, Kara. But I do have sensitivity to the arcane—enough to allow me to work the gate. That sensitivity is one of the reasons I was drawn to you, though I didn't realize it at the time. It wasn't until I met Tracy, and we became friends, that I figured it out. He's the one who told me I didn't have to sit on the sidelines. And after the Symbol Man murders he knew you were a summoner." He gave an ugly laugh. "You were an obvious choice."

The queasiness grew a fraction, and Tracy's forehead furrowed in concentration. Clearly he was expecting something to happen, and it wasn't. "But he was wrong, Roman," I said, shrugging. "I'm not a summoner." I gestured around me at the diagram. "The gate would be open if I was, right?"

"Don't listen to her!" Tracy snarled. A bead of sweat trickled down the side of his face despite the chill in the building. "She *is* a summoner. You know she is! It's just taking longer to open than I expected." His eyes snapped to mine. "The focus. You destroyed the focus." His lip curled. "Doesn't matter. I can still do this without it."

"But you still need a summoner," I said, acting a hell of a lot more casual than I felt.

Roman shifted, frowned. "Are you sure about this, Tracy?"

"She's a goddamn summoner!" he shouted, fury suffusing his face. "Now shut the fuck up and let me do this!"

I took a deep breath. This was going to suck. Hard. "If I was a summoner, I wouldn't be able to walk out of this diagram."

Tracy's eyes widened. "You're bluffing," he said. Then he sneered. "Badly, too. You'd be torn apart. You wouldn't risk that."

"You're right," I said. "I wouldn't." *Come on cuff, don't fail me now*, I thought as I walked out of the circle.

Okay, the first step was walking, the second and third were stumbling as the nausea slammed into me. It was gone as soon as I was past the outer perimeter, but I fell to my hands and knees in front of Tracy and puked on his shoes anyway.

He gave a shout of horror and dismay as he leaped back, then he looked to the diagram. "I don't understand," he said, utterly flabbergasted. "I *know* you're a summoner." He shook his head as if trying to get his thoughts to fall properly into place. "And even if you're not, the wards should have dropped you."

Shakily, I wiped my mouth and got back to my feet. "Yeah, well, I'm clever that way. Now why don't you be a good boy and shut this thing down before someone gets hurt." As if to underscore my point the sound of gunshots came to us from the foyer.

"This is bullshit!" Roman seethed, rounding on Tracy. "You promised me!"

Tracy held up a hand, still staring at me. "It's impossible. I had you assessed. There's no way you can simply stop being a summoner." He shook his head. "We don't have a choice. They make sure we become summoners."

A weird chill ran down my spine. "What are you talking about? Who's 'they?'"

He gave a dry and tortured laugh. "The lords. Come on, now. You haven't figured this out? If your dad hadn't died, do you think you'd have ever become a summoner? You wouldn't have been mentored by your aunt—who conveniently left Japan and returned here in order to raise poor, orphaned you."

The breath froze in my chest. "My dad was killed by a drunk driver."

Tracy snorted. He was beginning to recover his composure now. "Right. Have you ever looked at the accident report? I have. He shouldn't have died in that wreck."

I swallowed hard. Of course I'd never read the report. Why the hell would I torture myself like that? "Why . . . why would they do that?"

His eyes grew dark with unshielded agony. I suddenly wondered if the death of his mother had truly been a suicide. "Because without us they have no way to return."

"Return? What—"

"Fuck this!" Roman snarled, cutting me off. "Show me how to work the goddamn gate, and then these lords can have one more summoner on their payroll."

"No, shut up, Roman!" I said, eyes on Tracy. "What are you talking about?"

"Don't tell me to shut up, bitch!" Roman shouted. "Tracy, hurry up and make me a goddamn summoner!"

Tracy leveled a glare at him. "Don't be stupid. You can't be a summoner." His hand dropped to his gun, and I had zero doubt that Roman was about to die.

But I'd forgotten that Roman was strong and fast as hell. Before any of us could blink he'd knocked the gun aside and tackled Tracy. Roman wrenched the gun from Tracy's hand with the accompanying sound of breaking bones, wrenching a scream of pain from Tracy. "Doesn't matter," Roman said through gritted teeth. "You *are* a summoner, and I'm going to get my fucking gate no matter what!" With that he stood, holding Tracy in a bear hug from behind and headed to the diagram.

"No!" I shouted, leaping toward Roman to yank him back from the circle. "It's active!" I grabbed onto his arm to try to stop him, but I might as well have been a mosquito on an elephant.

Tracy kicked and twisted, but Roman was still one strong son of a bitch. He flung Tracy into the diagram just as the doors burst open behind us. I turned away and ducked as Tracy let out a spiraling scream of horror and agony. The scream abruptly cut off, and I quickly covered my head to shield myself from the spatter of gore as the energies of the gate shredded Tracy as effectively as if Roman had thrown him into a jet engine intake.

A silence fell, broken only by my ragged breathing and the sick, wet plop of stuff I didn't want to look at. I cautiously looked up as Ryan and Zack ran forward, then got back to my feet, and reluctantly turned to look back at the carnage. The diagram itself looked untouched, but surrounding it was a corona of blood and flesh, no piece bigger than a fingernail. I fought back a surge of nausea, abruptly thankful that there was nothing left in my stomach to throw up. I'd seen grisly scenes before, but this was beyond horrific. I'd never quite grasped just how much gore one human body could make.

Seeking to distract myself, I grimaced down at my coat—now covered with blood and bits of Tracy. Shuddering, I yanked the zipper down and shrugged it off. Not sure if I could bear to wear it again, even if I could get the gore cleaned off. I resisted the urge to run my fingers through my hair. I wasn't ready to face Tracy-parts mingled with my split ends.

"Take him into custody," I told Ryan, jerking my chin

toward Roman. "I'll find a way to pin these murders on him if it's the last fucking thing I do."

Roman didn't resist. He too was spattered in gore, and he seemed to be frozen in shock. "You might want to hose him off first," I added. *And me as well.* Though a brief assessment seemed to indicate that my coat had taken the worst of it. My poor, beautiful coat. *Yes, I'm worrying about my coat. Better than thinking about what just happened.*

I started to inspect the coat to see if it was salvageable, but I froze as a tremor shook the floor.

"Kara," Zack said, standing a few feet from the diagram. "We have a problem."

"The gate," I breathed, cold clenching my gut. I couldn't see the energies of the portal, but I could imagine what they looked like. Under normal circumstances the gate could have held steady until a summoner closed it down properly, but when Roman threw Tracy into it, the whole structure had unbalanced. *Like an uneven load of laundry in a washing machine.* "How bad is it?" I asked. "Won't it just collapse in on itself?"

Zack shook his head, face stricken as he turned back to me. "No. I mean, yes, but the backlash of the power...." He swallowed visibly. "Kara, it could wipe out everything in a mile radius."

My mouth went dry. There was a school only a couple of blocks away. Subdivisions, businesses. "A summoner needs to shut it down," I said, barely hearing myself over the pounding of my heart. "How long do we have?"

"Only a few minutes," he replied, voice cracking.

I nodded. Not enough time to get Tessa here.

"Wait," Ryan demanded. "Zack, how can you be sure?

Kara, I know what you're thinking. If you take the cuff off, you'll be summoned! Have you forgotten that someone in the demon realm is still after you?"

"I haven't forgotten. But would that stop *you*?" I challenged.

"Fuck." He closed his eyes, shook his head. "No."

"If I work quickly, I might be able to get this shut down before a summoning gets a lock on me." I moved to the edge of the diagram, glanced back at the two agents. "Here goes."

I slipped off the cuff and dropped it behind me, then nearly staggered at the force of the energies raging around the diagram. Damn good thing I'd destroyed the focus. I didn't even want to think how bad it would be if I hadn't. But as bad as it was, this was—first and foremost—a portal, and all I needed to do was ground it and release the power safely. And that was one of the first things I'd had Rhyzkahl teach me.

Working as quickly as I dared, I set up the power sinks, tied the arcane strands into them, then shunted the energy away from the gate and into the earth where it would dissipate harmlessly. Within heartbeats the raging tempest had wound down to a mild whirlpool, and I could release the breath I was holding.

I spun to retrieve the cuff, but a blast of cold air stopped me as my fingers were millimeters from the cuff. I froze, mind racing. *Run. I need to run!* I thought in flailing panic. But even as I thought it, I knew there was nowhere I could run *to*. There were no wards nearby that would shield me from this summoning. And if I put the cuff on now—after the summoning had locked onto me—it would alter the forming of the portal and tear me to shreds. I'd be effectively committing suicide. Mouth dry, I straightened, leaving the cuff on the floor. *I guess this is it.*

"What are you doing?" Ryan shouted. "Put the cuff back on before it's too late!"

"It's already too late," Zack said, agonized. His eyes met mine. "I'm sorry."

"It's all right," I said, even though it wasn't all right. Not at all. I was scared shitless, but I couldn't let them see it. "I knew it was a long shot. But at least I saved the world, right? At least a little piece of it." I gave a weak laugh, then took a shaking breath. "Take care of my aunt and Jill. And Fuzzykins."

"We will," Zack said. "You have my oath."

The wind swirled around us, and I felt the first cold touch as the tendrils of the portal began to wrap around me. Ryan shot a look at the swirling energies, then stepped to me and seized my face in his hands.

"God damn it. You'd better come back to me. You hear? You fucking come back to me!"

I tried to nod, but it was tough with him holding my head like that. And the big lump in my throat made it tough to speak. He didn't seem to care, because in the next instant his lips were on mine. This wasn't some friends-kissing-friends kiss either—this was a full-blown, passion-filled, hungry as hell kiss as if there would never be any more kisses after this one. This was a kiss to tell each other everything we'd danced around for so long, full of fervor and heartache and grief and joy and longing. I clutched him to me, returning it with just as much passion, not breaking it until the arcane tendrils began to tighten and pull. I quickly released him and pushed him away from me. "You ... you need to stand back now," I gasped.

He stepped back reluctantly. "I love you," he said.

The pull on me was increasing to the point of pain, but I managed a weak smile. "If I say 'I know' will you laugh?"

He chuckled. "Nerd."

The power swirled higher as the portal widened. "I love you too," I said.

And then the world disappeared.

# Chapter 24

I'd been to the demon realm once before. The last time I was here I'd been close to death. I remembered lying on a white marble floor. I remembered it was full of light and wonder. I'd been in the throne room of Rhyzkahl, and it was beautiful. A throne of white and gold. Marble walls and open archways. A turquoise sea and demons in flight.

Even without looking up, I could tell this was different.

I was on my hands and knees on a dark stone floor. Blood dripped from my nose with thick plops, marring the grey of the stone. Razor coils of pain wound around my limbs, slowly fading as I struggled to catch my breath through the burning in my lungs. Holy shit, but that hurt. Did it hurt the demons like that when I summoned them? If so, why would they ever agree to go through that? Because that sucked *ass*.

I slowly pushed myself back to sit on my heels, blinking to focus. I wasn't surprised to see that I was inside a summoning circle. Even without shifting into othersight I had no trouble seeing the bindings and protections wound around the perimeter. I didn't make any attempt to move from the center. I was already hurting enough.

A young man stood a few feet from the edge of the circle, looking almost absurdly pleased with himself. He had a slim, athletic build—easy to see since he was naked from the waist up. Below the waist he wore black jeans and boots with silver buckles—the kind one could find in a goth shop. Pale grey eyes met mine. Curly blond hair stood out in a halo around his head. I pegged him at eighteen or nineteen, at the most.

I frowned at him. "Aren't you a little young to be a demonic lord?"

His smug smile flickered into a scowl. "You will not speak until I give you leave."

"Oh, fuck off, blondie," I said, levering myself carefully to my feet. "I've had tougher people than you try to shut me up."

Anger suffused his face. Good. I wanted him riled up. Kill me quickly so that I could get out of this place. I crossed my arms over my chest and regarded him sourly. I could feel the blood still trickling from my nose, and I wiped it away simply to keep it out of my mouth.

"You're not a demonic lord," I stated. He didn't have the feel about him, the aura of power. So what was he? Just a summoner on this side of the portal?

He puffed up again in anger, but before he could speak a deep laugh sounded from the darkness behind him. "You didn't really think you'd be able to fool her, did you?"

A man in a dark business suit stepped forward into the light. He didn't have to say anything. *This* was the demonic lord. The aura announced him more than anything else could have.

He stopped at the edge of the circle. For several heartbeats we regarded each other. He was not quite as tall as Rhyzkahl, but only by an inch or two. The suit he wore was clearly expensive—Armani perhaps—and so exquisitely tailored that it didn't feel the least bit odd to see a demonic lord dressed in such a way. His features looked faintly oriental, though his eyes were a piercing silver grey. Jet black hair was bound back by gold cord in an intricate braid that hung to the small of his back.

And power shimmered from him in pulsing waves. A year ago I'd have most likely been curled into a mewling ball on the floor. But I was more used to the demonic lord mojo now. At least that's what I told myself. It was also possible that he hadn't turned the full force of his aura onto me.

"I don't know who you are," I said, fighting to maintain something akin to dignity, "but you seem to have a great deal of interest in me, since you've been trying to summon me for quite some time now."

"I've been interested in you for far longer than that," he said. He crouched just beyond the circle, idly peering at the designs carved into the floor. "You are likely thinking that, if you can find a way to die in this realm, you will return to your own world." He lifted those silver-grey eyes to mine. "Such transfers grow progressively difficult. There is less chance you will make it through the void a second time." He said it conversationally, as if he was telling me I should bring an umbrella in case it rained.

My stomach tightened. There went my one plan for escape. My gaze dropped to an object in his hand. It looked like an intricate and lovely choker-style necklace.

Made out of a familiar pinkish-coppery metal.

I dragged my eyes away from it, casting my attention elsewhere, anywhere but that thing. And for the first time I got a good look at the room we were in. Dark grey marble walls. Enough to make the room almost circular. I looked down, half-expecting to see the shattered remains of a statue here in the circle with me, though I knew there was nothing there.

"What is this place?" I managed to say, fighting back the fear that threatened to drop me to my knees.

He moved into the circle. "Don't you recognize it?" he said, lifting the necklace.

I didn't move, or resist as he placed the thing around my neck. It wouldn't have done any good anyway. I answered him with a slight shake of my head.

A vulpine smile curved his mouth. "It's your old summoning chamber," he said.

And then he snapped the collar closed.

# Diana Rowland

## *My Life as a White Trash Zombie*
978-0-7564-0675-2

"Rowland's delightful novel jumps genre lines with a little something for everyone—mystery, horror, humor, and even a smattering of romance. Not to be missed—all that's required is a high tolerance for gray matter. For true zombiephiles, of course, that's a no brainer."

—*Library Journal*

"An intriguing mystery and a hilarious mix of the horrific and mundane aspects of zombie life open a promising new series...Humor and gore are balanced by surprisingly touching moments as Angel tries to turn her (un)life around."

—*Publishers Weekly*

And don't miss:
## *Even White Trash Zombies Get the Blues*
(July 2012)        978-0-7564-0750-6

To Order Call: 1-800-788-6262
www.dawbooks.com